Tregear was listening to the song intently,

and his face revealed a depth of emotion Jane doubted he even realized. She understood two things about him immediately. That he hadn't come to this country willingly and that he wanted nothing more than to return home again.

When he took his seat near Jane, it was all she could do to keep her resolve never to even attempt to thank him again.

Jane exhaled sharply and fidgeted in her chair.

"What is it?" Tregear quietly asked.

"Nothing," she answered.

But she lost the battle to remain indifferent to his second good deed involving her family.

"You would not let me voice my gratitude before. And now—my sister—"

"There is no need for gratitude. However, I have something I want to say to you," Tregear interrupted.

Jane made no attempt to acknowledge the remark. Tregear simply waited until her curiosity got the better, and she dared to look in his direction.

"Milla Dunwiddie's child is not mine."

**Acclaim for RITA® Award-winning author
Cheryl Reavis's books**

The Older Woman
"Compelling. Riveting. Romantic."
—The Romance Reader

The Captive Heart
"A sensual, emotionally involving romance."
—*Library Journal*

Harrigan's Bride
"…another Reavis title to add to your keeper shelf."
—The Booknook

The Prisoner
"…a Civil War novel that manages to fill the reader
with warmth and hope."
—*Romantic Times*

CHERYL REAVIS

THE FORBIDDEN BRIDE

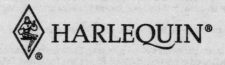

HARLEQUIN®

TORONTO • NEW YORK • LONDON
AMSTERDAM • PARIS • SYDNEY • HAMBURG
STOCKHOLM • ATHENS • TOKYO • MILAN • MADRID
PRAGUE • WARSAW • BUDAPEST • AUCKLAND

ISBN 0-373-29240-6

THE FORBIDDEN BRIDE

Copyright © 2003 by Cheryl Reavis

All rights reserved. Except for use in any review, the reproduction or utilization of this work in whole or in part in any form by any electronic, mechanical or other means, now known or hereafter invented, including xerography, photocopying and recording, or in any information storage or retrieval system, is forbidden without the written permission of the publisher, Harlequin Enterprises Limited, 225 Duncan Mill Road, Don Mills, Ontario, Canada M3B 3K9.

All characters in this book have no existence outside the imagination of the author and have no relation whatsoever to anyone bearing the same name or names. They are not even distantly inspired by any individual known or unknown to the author, and all incidents are pure invention.

This edition published by arrangement with Harlequin Books S.A.

® and TM are trademarks of the publisher. Trademarks indicated with ® are registered in the United States Patent and Trademark Office, the Canadian Trade Marks Office and in other countries.

Visit us at www.eHarlequin.com

Printed in U.S.A.

Please address questions and book requests to:
Harlequin Reader Service
U.S.: 3010 Walden Ave., P.O. Box 1325, Buffalo, NY 14269
Canadian: P.O. Box 609, Fort Erie, Ont. L2A 5X3

Chapter One

Gold Hill, North Carolina, 1845

The sudden downpour from the summer storm and the urgent pounding on the front door came almost simultaneously. Jane Ennis put aside her pen and took up the pewter candlestick, hastily making her way toward the front of the house.

Her intent should have been to stop the racket before her mother was disturbed, but the truth was that she was more concerned about the noise waking her father's cousin. The woman was only a few years Jane's senior, but she felt her authority acutely when he was away, and she would have little regard for whatever poor soul might have need of a doctor's skill this rainy night.

Indeed, Miss Chappell—as she insisted on being called—had little charity for anyone, not even Jane's frail mother, whose illness was supposedly the reason for the woman having left her home in London and come here in the first place. It still surprised Jane that her father had sent for this obscure relation of his to act as a nurse and companion. It surprised her even more that the woman had actually come. She clearly had no desire to be in this lonely place. Living in what was essentially a wilderness at the edge of a rough North Carolina mining village in no way compared to the delights she had perpetually encountered in London society—or so she often said.

There was no escaping Miss Chappell's relentless dissatisfaction, and in the ten long months since her arrival, Jane had grown more than a little weary of the added discord the woman's presence in the household caused. Nothing was the same anymore. Jane's brother, Sion, in a fit of temper, had suddenly broken faith with their father and gone who knew where—after which their mother stopped making any attempt to be up and about. Even Jane's younger sister, Eugenie, the decidedly cheerful member of the Ennis family, had grown subdued and nervous since Miss Chappell had come among them.

Jane glanced up the narrow stairway to the second floor as she passed, thankful to see it empty. She managed to get the door open ahead of the next barrage of pounding, and she held the flickering candle high so that she could see the man who stood on the porch more clearly.

She recognized him immediately. His name was Tregear. He was one of the Cornish miners who had come from England to work the gold mines. He had arrived on the same stage that had brought Miss Chappell, and Jane suspected that they both were now popular topics in what passed for polite dinner conversation in Gold Hill—Tregear, for his penchant for brawling in the taverns, and Miss Chappell for her total disdain of everyone and everything indigenous to the countryside.

Jane's gregarious and ever inquisitive brother had made Tregear's acquaintance almost immediately. Sion had been very impressed by the man's more noteworthy talents. Tregear was supposed to be able to blast new tunnels in the mines—without killing anyone—and to read the results of his handiwork with great accuracy. Those skills fed the mine owner's hopes of finding copper and tin among the gold veins—her father's hopes as well, because he owned a significant number of shares in that particular mine.

Jane had seen Tregear several times since his arrival, once when she and her father had been riding through Gold Hill on their way to the new county seat of Albemarle to fetch the medical supplies waiting at the Smith's store post office. Tregear had been carrying not one but two giggling women across the muddy street, two flamboyantly painted barmaids from the closest tavern, whose actual purpose Jane wasn't supposed to know anything about—but did.

At one point she had looked directly into Tregear's eyes, and he had looked boldly back—instead of showing at least some chagrin at being caught thus by a decent woman. The look had held for an uncomfortable moment, and Jane had seen there what she could only describe as something akin to pity. His brazen behavior with the two women had disturbed her a great deal that day—but not as much as the impertinence of his staring at her as if he had some reason to feel sorry for her. She simply couldn't fathom his impudence. Compared to the rest of the people here, she lacked for nothing.

Nothing.

The most relevant fact about the man, however, was that he should not be here now on her father's doorstep. All the mine owners in the area employed their own doctors, who were supposed to be handy at all times. Mining was not a desirable occupation for the men here, in spite of the steady pay. Most of them had been farmers, used to the out-of-doors, and the profitability of digging gold ore depended a great deal on keeping those who were willing to go underground healthy. She could count on one hand the number of times her father had ever been asked to attend any of them and then it had only been to give a second opinion.

"My father is not here," Jane said anyway. A sudden gust of wind from the open door blew out the candle, leaving them standing in darkness. Thunder rolled overhead, and the rain blew onto the porch. She couldn't see his face, and she stepped back, as if the flickering light from the candle had been some kind of physical barrier between them, and, now that it was gone, he might not stay below the salt where he belonged.

"It's you I've come for, miss," he said.

"Me? Why?" she asked, taken aback.

"One of the women sent me to fetch you. She asks if you will come, miss." His voice was deep and rough sounding, both in quality and in accent. But his version of the English language was not so difficult to follow as some of the other Cornish miners she'd heard. He actually said "you" instead of the Cornish "ee."

Jane didn't ask which woman. The fact that she had been summoned instead of her father narrowed down the possibilities considerably. Tregear might carry harlots from one side of a muddy street to the other—among other things—but of late it was Miss Jane Ennis who, quite innocently, had found herself tending their physical ailments. And all because she happened to be present when one of them came to Mrs. Oliver, the Methodist minister's wife, with a badly scalded hand, an injury that had been forced upon her by one of her drunken patrons.

Jane had been at the Oliver house delivering some medicine her father had made up for the reverend's gout. She had seen the injured hand, she had known perfectly well what to do—and she did it. Word of the success of the treatment had spread quickly and had led to more requests for medical help, all of them clandestine. While her father might treat the women and their illegitimate children if called upon, he did so reluctantly and with overt disapproval. Everyone knew it would be better for all concerned if he didn't learn that his older daughter drew no such lines.

Jane suspected that her real appeal, however, was that she accepted no pay for her work other than to request that some small sum be donated to the Methodist church. She was decidedly of the wrong gender, and she would never have attended a medical school, even if women had been allowed. She had no right to be paid, regardless of the fact that she knew a great deal of the healing art.

When it became apparent that Sion had neither the desire nor the stomach to follow in his sire's footsteps, it had fallen to Jane to accompany their father on his many rounds, to dress the wounds, to help hold a man or a woman or a child down for some required surgery or tooth extraction, to read her father's directions and make up the medicines. She had taken full advantage of the situation, and, in the last year, she'd made a point to learn as much as she possibly could at her father's elbow. It had become a personal challenge to know what he knew, and there was little she could not do and do well—except lie—which was a skill she would likely need at some point, because by no stretch of the imagination, had she her father's permission to treat anyone for anything, much less to go into the hovels in the middle of the night where these women plied their trade.

"She has need of you, miss," he said impatiently. "I would not have come otherwise."

Jane didn't say anything, and Tregear took her silence for refusal.

"I'll trouble you no longer, then," he said, turning to go. But he stopped before he reached the edge of the porch. "In future, miss, you must find yourself a harder heart.

Handing out good deeds always brings consequences. People get to expecting you to be kind all the time. You must beware showing charity to them that sorely need it—especially if you're only playing at it." He stepped off the porch.

Playing?

Jane wanted to deny it, but it was closer to the truth than she cared to admit. She had made no conscious decision to help anyone, nor to face the consequences, be it a burgeoning medical practice or her father's wrath.

"Wait," she called when he was about to disappear into the rainy darkness. Her father would find out about her doings sooner or later. She might as well be hanged for a sheep as a lamb. "Are you sober, sir?" she asked.

He came back a few steps. She could feel more than see him smile.

"I am, miss."

"Wait here on the porch, then," she said. "I will have to get some things—and a lantern."

The lantern was in the kitchen, but she felt her way upstairs instead, treading carefully past Miss Chappell's door to the room she shared with Eugenie.

"Eugenie," she whispered, shaking her sister awake. "Eugenie!"

"What is it?" her little sister said too loudly.

"Shhh. You'll wake *her*. I have to go to the village—someone is sick and asking for me. I'll be back as soon as I can."

"But it's raining," Eugenie said, because she was beautiful and of an age where ruined ringlets were a primary concern.

"I can't help that. Don't say where I am unless someone specifically asks—"

"But how are you going to get there?"

"One of the miners has come for me—Tregear."

"Jane! You can't leave the house with him! It's not proper."

"Shhh! You need not worry. He is not a stranger to me," Jane said not quite truthfully. It occurred to her that, while she might find it difficult to tell an outright lie, she had no problem dancing around the edges of one. She gave Eugenie a small hug. "Go back to sleep, little one."

"I'm taller than you," Eugenie murmured sleepily.

"Taller—but not older."

Jane moved to the pegs by the door to search for her cloak. "What?" she whispered, because she didn't hear what Eugenie said next.

"I said he's handsome at least. And such sad eyes. Why do you suppose that is?"

"He's a miner. They all have sad eyes," Jane said, flinging on her cloak.

"Yes—but they're not all handsome."

"And just where have *you* seen Tregear?"

"In front of…the church," Eugenie whispered around a yawn. "He can sing shape notes, but he won't. The reverend tried to make him come in and join us at the choir practice one evening. He wouldn't come even to the door. The reverend said…it's because he…is an angry… man…."

Jane frowned in the darkness. "Angry at whom?"

"God, the reverend…said…."

God? What kind of man—particularly one who risked his life every day underground—dared to be at odds with the Deity?

"I like his…pagan…tattoo…." Eugenie murmured.

"Tattoo? Eugenie?" Jane whispered after a moment, but her little sister had dropped off to sleep.

Jane slipped out the door and down the stairs again. Tregear stood waiting where she'd left him.

"Hurry, miss," he said, but she still didn't have the lantern. She felt her way to the kitchen and lit it, then hurried back again.

"I need to get some things from my father's surgery. It's—"

"I know where it is," he said.

"Can you tell me the woman's symptoms?" Jane asked.

He took the lantern from her without answering her question and led the way outside to the small house facing the road where her father saw his patients and made up his prescriptions. It was still raining hard, and she had to run to keep up with Tregear's long strides.

"Do you have any idea what ails the woman?" Jane asked again once they were inside the surgery.

"Childbirth, miss," he said.

"Child—" Jane stared at him. Midwifery was the one thing she had *not* learned well. On the few occasions when her father had taken her along to attend a woman in labor, she had been banished to another room or outside the house altogether. She had seen cats and dogs deliver their young. And cows and horses. She knew the gist of it—and she knew nothing.

"I can't," she said, shaking her head. "I—I won't know what to do."

"So I told her. But it's *you* she wants—not what you know or don't know about getting a baby born. It will come into this world—or not—regardless of what you do."

Jane stood there, still panicked.

"If you will not come, miss, is there something, some…potion you can send back with me—something that will give her hope?"

"Hope?"

"That's all she's wanting, miss. A little hope. And for some reason, she is looking to you for it."

Jane stared at him. It was a sentiment he clearly didn't share. And why that bothered her, she couldn't begin to say. He had no right to sit in judgment of her. None. The only thing about which she was certain was that his low opinion of her was unwarranted—and the injustice of it was insult enough to make her not want to confirm it.

"I'll go," she said after a moment. "If she truly wants it."

"I did not come all this way to tell a falsehood, miss."

"If you say so, sir."

She took the lantern out of his hand and went to her father's desk, looking until she found a book of treatments—not her father's but the one written about a man named Thomson, who apparently believed that most doctors were little more than skilled murderers and didn't mind saying so. Her father had decried the man's notions of medical treatment—and yet Jane had seen them creeping into his practice, and, more often than not, with success.

"There is no time for reading," Tregear said.

"I understand that. I mean to take it with me. Just in case."

But her mind wouldn't let her entertain what "just in case" might entail. She picked up a basket and put in a bottle of sweet oil and some of the herbs she knew her father used for women in labor—raspberry leaf, valerian, cayenne—and some honey. She could feel Tregear watching her as she worked.

"We'll have to walk," he said.

"I have a horse and buggy."

"Which everyone hereabouts knows on sight. It's best if it's not seen where we are going."

Jane looked at him, then nodded. As an afterthought she

took up a piece of waxed cloth and wrapped the book in it to keep it dry and put it in the hidden, underside pocket of her cloak.

"I mean to move quick," he said.

"I'll keep up."

And she tried, but more than once she lost sight of him and the bobbing lantern going down the narrow muddy road in front of her—a situation she thought he deliberately precipitated. But if he expected her to be afraid of the dark or the storm, he would be disappointed. She still smarted from his remark about her "playing" at helping people, and she moved doggedly on.

"This way, miss," he said at one point, leading her off the road and onto a narrow winding path she hadn't known existed. "It's quicker this way."

Quicker for him, perhaps, but more difficult for her to navigate in long skirts. She kept getting caught on briars and stumbling over fallen limbs and logs. The raindrops pattered loudly on the thick canopy of leaves overhead, so loudly that she couldn't hear where he was. The wind picked up and made the great trees around her creak and sway. The smell of wet rotted wood and leaves rose from the ground. She didn't dare let herself think about becoming lost in the dark or what wild creatures she might encounter.

Or her father.

She kept falling farther and farther behind—until he came back for her and unceremoniously took her by the hand. She was startled at first, but she didn't try to jerk free. She let him pull her along, his rough, callused fingers firm and warm around hers.

In a very little time she could see the lighted window of a dwelling up ahead and then the village beyond. Tregear immediately let go of her hand.

"It's yonder, miss," he said pointing the way to a small log house.

"Aren't you coming?" she asked, showing more alarm than she would have wished.

"I have no business there. My part was only to fetch you. And that I have done."

"But how will I find my way back?"

"Follow the path, miss. You can do that easy enough in the light of day."

"Wait," she said, when he turned to go. "The lantern. It is mine."

She took it away from him and plunged on toward the small cabin without a backward glance.

"Tregear! You sorry bastard! Where have you been!"

Tregear ignored the coarse inquiry and made his way across the dirt floor to the waist-high, pine slab bar. He didn't see the proprietor, and he stood waiting impatiently to be served.

The place was empty except for a table in the dark corner from which the call to him had come. The men seated around it clearly had a good start on their night of drinking and whoring. There were two curtained cubicles to Tregear's left—both of them in use from the sound of it. His mind went immediately to Jane Ennis.

Are you sober, sir?

How prettily she had asked. The question had taken him completely by surprise—and shouldn't have. Jane Ennis was a staunch Methodist—or at least he had seen her hanging around the church often enough. What else about him but that would she care to know? He had been sober when the question was asked—but he didn't intend to stay that way. He was soaked to the skin and cold. He needed a drink of something with authority, and he needed it now.

"Tregear!" the man at the table called again.

"Whiskey," he said to the tavern owner who finally appeared, and he still ignored the man in the corner who hailed him.

"I'll see your money first," the tavern owner said, regardless of the many times Tregear had frequented the place since he'd come to work in the mines.

"Don't worry. I have it—and the price is far too dear for the swill you're selling."

He dropped a coin on the bar, and the man, unoffended, snatched it up, bit it and dropped it into his purse before he poured.

Tregear drank the whiskey in one swift motion, ignoring the burning as it went down. The whiskey here was potent enough, he supposed, but it was not "home." He would have preferred gin. Even the poorest quality of the drink in Cornwall had been better than this.

He turned around to face the men at the table in the corner—all of them fellow miners and all of them looking for another brawl. For once, he didn't feel like obliging them.

"What do you want?" he asked anyway, but he didn't wait for the answer. The woman sitting on the lap of one of them caught his eye.

"What are *you* doing here?" he demanded.

"Well, listen to you," she said, smiling nervously and looking around the table for some evidence of support. "Who died and made you the emperor?"

"Did you leave that girl by herself?"

"Well, what if I did? Getting her brat born ain't no worry of mine."

"Is there no one there to help then?"

"How should I know? I got other business—don't I, Zachy?" she asked the man next to her, leaning over and giving him a drunken kiss. The man upon whose lap she sat immediately took exception, and the table had the fight they had been seeking after all.

Tregear dodged a flying chair and stepped back outside into the rain. He stood for a moment, then began walking in the direction of the three-story wooden hotel where his bed awaited. Getting a whore's brat born was none of his worry, either.

Except that this girl wasn't a whore—or not until lately, anyway—a fact that made her exceptionally popular among the miners. She had been a kitchen maid first—or so he'd heard. A servant in the Ennis house, until someone had gotten her with child and Dr. Ennis had sent her packing.

Who? Tregear wondered. The son? The doctor himself?

Tregear had deliberately not told Jane Ennis who was asking for her—because he thought she might not come. For all he knew, the entire family had conspired to get rid of the girl and her inconvenient baggage. In which case, Jane Ennis wouldn't stay with her, either. She might not stay in any event, and the girl would be left to have her child on her own.

He kept walking, past the blacksmith shop and the carriage maker, past the boot maker and Methodist church.

There was no escaping the Methodists. *They* were the reason he had ended up here in Gold Hill, and they were the reason his conscience weighed so heavy on him now. Forgiveness and social responsibility and brotherly love—and sobriety—sentiments he'd found essentially useless in the everyday world.

He abruptly stopped and stood with the rain beating down on him. He had said this very night that kindness had consequences—but he hadn't expected the veracity of his bold statement to be born out so quickly.

He swore under his breath and turned and began walking

the distance back to the hovel where he'd left Jane Ennis, his resentment rising in him with every step. Still, he kept going—a victory for the Wesleyans, he supposed. And who would have thought there was any remnant of *that* left in him? *He* certainly would not, and he doubted that Reverend Branwell, the man responsible for his meager religious training, would have, either.

Reverend Branwell.

As a boy, Tregear had thought the quiet and kindly man very nearly God incarnate. He had never met anyone like him before or since, and he had certainly never known what had possessed Branwell to take him in. Christian charity, Tregear supposed—the Reverend Branwell practicing what he preached.

Tregear had arrived at the Branwell house on a night like this one, newly orphaned, stunned into a dry-eyed silence by the death of his father in the copper mine. He hadn't believed the mine captain when he came to tell him the bad news. Nothing and no one ever got the better of Martin Tregear. Never sick. Never tired. Never quite drunk. Never quite sober.

And never dead.

Tregear's life with his father had been as dark and joyless as the mines themselves, and coming to live with the Branwells had been like coming out of the ground and into the sunlight. He had never even guessed that there were places where people always treated each other with respect and consideration, places where there was always warmth and food and caring. And Branwell hadn't made a "charity child" of him, one of those miserable creatures whose care and education was taken over by some well-meaning philanthropist who wanted full credit for the gesture, to the point of making the child wear a kind of badge so that all would know of he was a token object of social reform and persecute him accordingly. Branwell hadn't needed or wanted to trumpet his good deeds. Tregear had actually lived in the household as one of the family.

Ultimately, the Reverend Branwell had made it possible for Tregear to come to America—the result of a carefully crafted letter to a fellow minister, which somehow traveled preacher to preacher until it reached the one here. That had led to a quiet word with a mine owner and a subsequent offer of work. Tregear had been only too happy to accept it. There was no work in Cornwall—not for the likes of him. He had forgotten his place and he had to suffer for it. Even he could see that the sooner he left to make his fortune, the sooner he could return. And he would return, in spite of his humiliation. He would return and he would claim what was rightfully his.

And how much easier that might be if he had the kind of faith Branwell had. What a believer the old man was. Branwell had never doubted for a moment that some opportunity for his disgraced foster son would present itself. His faith in the promise of God's tender mercies was relentless, and it was the reason Tregear had left the one letter that had arrived for him at Smith's store unread. Tregear had no such faith and never would, regardless of the reverend's elegant persuasions. The knowledge that he was the Reverend Branwell's one true and very public failure weighed heavily upon him, but he could not allow himself to be dissuaded from his plan. He could not forgive. He could not turn the other cheek. And he hadn't even tried to explain to the old man. He couldn't explain, except to say that he'd loved an untrustworthy woman beyond all reason, and as a result the old, idealistic Tregear was long gone.

He gave a quiet sigh. Even so, something of Branwell's teachings must remain—or else Tregear would not be doing *this*.

He abruptly pushed the memories aside. He could see the cabin now, but the place was completely dark. He didn't bother to knock on the door. He pushed it open wide, and the rank smell of sweat and urine and rotting scraps of food rose in his nostrils.

"Miss?" he said quietly.

If she answered him, he didn't hear it. A sound came from the far corner of the room, one that began as a low moan and escalated to a piercing scream. Even having heard women in labor before, it made the hairs on the back of his neck stand up.

"The lantern—went out," Jane said when the scream subsided. "I need more light."

There was a slight tremor in her voice.

He began to feel his way around the room, finding two candles in a box on the eating table. He lit one from an ember still glowing on the hearth, then held it under the other to make the tallow soft so he could stick in on the tabletop. When the tallow had hardened, he lit the other candle, then found the lantern and lit it as well.

Jane was kneeling on the dirt floor by the narrow cot where the girl lay. She looked around at him with neither alarm nor surprise, and he thought that she had been weeping.

He brought a candle to her. She couldn't take it, because the girl had her firmly gripped by one hand. Jane's other hand held the book she'd brought—but couldn't see to read.

"Milla," she said softly. "Turn me loose now—just for a minute."

"Don't go—Miss Jane! Please!"

"No, I won't. I just need to see to some things. I'm right here."

She pulled her hand free and wriggled her fingers before

she took the candle Tregear held, sitting down on the floor and turning away a bit, lest the girl take hold of her again.

She began to turn pages, finally finding what she needed and poring over it. After a moment, she looked up at him.

"What is it?" Tregear asked her.

"I need wood for the fire. She's exhausted. I need hot water so I can make her something to drink. And then I—" Her voice broke, and she abruptly stopped.

"First things first, then," he said quickly, because if she was going to cry again, he didn't want to see it.

"Tregear!" the girl suddenly said.

"I'm here," he said, going closer to the cot.

"Thank you—thank you for bringing Miss Jane—I didn't think she'd come, did I? *You* said she'd come."

"I said she'd come one way or the other," he said, glancing at Jane. If the girl didn't understand the ominous undertones of his earlier statement, it was clear to him that Jane Ennis did. But Miss Ennis didn't know how very close she'd come to being carried here bodily. He had managed to restrain himself, and perhaps he had the Reverend Branwell to thank for that as well.

"Tregear…" Milla said, his name sliding into a moan as the pain returned.

"Be strong, lass," he said. "People like you and me have to be strong—or our betters will trample us."

He escaped the cabin to search for wood, finding a few cut logs stacked under the shelter of the eaves. Jane was still reading when he came back with them, and she had taken the girl's hand again. She didn't look up from the book.

He built up the fire, took the bucket to the well out back and filled it, marveling all the while that he was actually doing this—playing midwife's helper instead of sleeping peacefully in his own bed.

He carried the water inside and filled the iron kettle and set it on a trivet in the hot embers. Then, he cleared away the rotted food scraps and carried out the chamber pot, all the while mentally braced for another scream from the girl on the cot.

He found the axe and split more wood for the fire, taking his time about it. The girl seemed quieter when he came into the cabin again—actually sleeping. He found a blanket and some clean rags and put them within reach.

"What does the book say?" he asked when Jane looked up at him.

"It says there is nothing to do but supervise," she whispered.

"Well, you're doing that well enough," he said, because he suddenly couldn't resist the impulse to annoy her.

"We could always change places," she said, still whispering.

"No, I'll leave the hand-holding to you. What comes after the supervising?"

"Things I don't know how to do," she said obscurely.

"The baby will come anyway," he said.

She looked into his eyes. "Will it?"

"It will—or she will die," he said bluntly.

Jane gave a wavering sigh. "Is the water hot?"

"Hot enough, I reckon."

She slipped her hand free of the girl's grasp again and got up from the dirt floor, brushing off her skirts as she did so.

She began to search the room for a bowl, then she went into the basket she'd brought and took out a small twisted packet. The packet had gotten wet in the rain, and she had to scrape some of the contents into the bowl. She used her skirt to pad the handle of the kettle so she could pick it up. He could see petticoat and white stocking and laced-up boot. It didn't surprise him that he had suddenly become invisible to her. There was not that much difference in the gentry here and in England, regardless of the absence of a titled class.

He watched as she poured the hot water into the bowl and put the kettle back onto the hearth. She prepared the concoction carefully and sweetened it with honey, but she didn't wake the girl to give it to her.

"I think it best Milla sleep while she can," she said, as if he'd made some objection to her leaving the girl be.

She glanced at him, and she continued to stand.

"I should be doing something," she said, more to herself than to him.

She took up the book again and began to turn pages quickly, purposefully, until she abruptly stopped, as if she'd suddenly realized the futility of it.

"Sir," she said, looking up at him. "I...need your help."

Chapter Two

It was for Milla and Milla alone that Jane asked, and she was prepared to explain that if he required it. She would explain—but she wouldn't beg, no matter how afraid she was of being left alone here again.

She fully expected Tregear to take his leave. She realized that this situation had grown far more complicated than he would have liked, that he had intended only to fetch her on Milla's behalf and be done with it. She stood waiting for him to make his excuses and go, but he didn't, in spite of how much she sensed he wanted to be away. He stared back at her, saying nothing.

"I need your help with this birth, sir," Jane said pointedly, in case he had some doubt about what she was asking.

This time he almost smiled. "Any port in a storm, is it, miss?"

"Yes," she said evenly. "And more's the pity. Milla deserves better than the two of us."

"That she does," he agreed. "What is it you want me to do?"

"Help me arrange the bed—when Milla awakes again," she said without hesitation. She didn't think it would do for her not to have some plan in mind. "The book gives instructions,'' she added, lest he think she was exercising some whim. ''And later...''

It was here that her plan left her. She knew nothing about ''later.'' Logic told her that she must do her best to see that the child was not injured aborning, but that was all.

''Aye,'' Tregear said. ''Later will be as it must. I'll wait—for a while.''

Jane nodded, daring to breathe a sigh of relief when she thought he couldn't see.

Milla slept on. Jane sat near her in the stuffy confines of the small cabin. She no longer tried to read, snuffing out one of the candles to save it for later when she would need more light. And she made no effort to engage Tregear in conversation, for all the inclination she had to think that he could hold his own. At one point, Tregear threw open the door to let in some fresh air in spite of the rain. He stood in the open doorway, his back to the room, and Jane suddenly remembered Eugenie's remark about his ''pagan tattoo.'' How her little sister had acquired knowledge of it she couldn't begin to guess.

Tregear was a powerfully built man—from his years of digging, she supposed. She knew how physically strong he was. She'd seen him carrying not one but two harlots to keep them out of the mud. But perhaps it took a different kind of strength to be here under these circumstances. Perhaps he wouldn't be able to stand it. She wasn't entirely sure she could herself, and she would not have been the least surprised if he had suddenly bolted.

The downpour waxed and waned, but the storm showed no sign of abating. After a time, Tregear came away from the door. And Milla—poor Milla—was on the verge of being caught again in a storm of her own. She was beginning to stir, moving her head restlessly from side to side in a feeble effort to escape the pain that was about to overtake her.

"Will you lift her up, sir?" Jane asked.

"The name is Tregear, miss."

"I—" Jane fully intended to say that she knew his name—an entirely improper response—and then to say that they had never been introduced and therefore she couldn't speak to him so familiarly—a response that was entirely ridiculous, given the circumstances.

"Tregear," he said again as if she might not have understood him.

"Mr. Tregear," Jane said finally.

"Just Tregear, miss. I require nothing else."

Somehow the remark sounded like a reproach of some kind. He was close enough so that Jane could see his eyes—but she couldn't read his expression.

What a careful man he is, she thought. He wanted no one privy to his thoughts.

"Come on, lass," he said to Milla, bending over the bed. "Put your arms around my neck."

"Tregear? What—where are we going?"

"Not far," he said. "We're just making way for Miss Ennis."

He gently picked Milla up and held her while Jane rolled the feather bed toward the headboard in the manner according to Thomson's book. Jane wondered how it was that Milla managed to have such a luxury as a feather bed, but she didn't dwell on it. She had but one intent now—to put what little specific information the book held to good and proper use.

Jane spread the blanket Tregear had found on the under bed, and together they placed Milla onto it, turning her on her left side near the edge. After some searching, Jane found another blanket and rolled it tightly and placed it between Milla's knees, making certain that the girl's feet were braced against the short, rough footboard in preparation for the next siege of pain.

"Is that any better?" Jane asked.

"Much...better, Miss Jane," Milla whispered, and Jane only wished she could believe it.

"Don't go, Miss Jane," Milla cried when Jane attempted to step away from the bed, grabbing on to her skirts to keep her there. "Please! I won't be so afraid...if you're...here."

"I won't go far, Milla. I just want to bring you something to drink."

"I need nothing, Miss Jane. Truly. Just to know you are here is enough."

Jane stood there, wondering what she had ever done beyond simple courtesy to make this girl rely on her so. Tregear had told the truth. It was Jane Ennis that Milla wanted, not what she knew or didn't know about childbirth.

"The drink will help you, Milla. It's the same as my father uses for the women he attends."

Milla gave a quiet sigh, but she still held on. "You promise you will not leave?"

"I promise."

"Tregear—Tregear, don't let her go."

"She'll not go, lass," Tregear said, looking into Jane's eyes as if to verify the truth of what he said. "Rest easy."

Milla took a long, wavering breath, apparently satisfied now, and released her grip on Jane's dress. As Jane moved away, Milla whispered something to Tregear that she could not hear. He was worried that she had, however. Jane could tell that from the sudden, sharp look he gave her. It was only when he was satisfied she hadn't that he gave Milla a quiet reply.

"No one," he said.

No one.

Jane moved to the small eating table. She had no notion of what he meant, and she had other, more pressing matters to occupy her mind. The book said that "the parts" must be relaxed if the birth was to take place smoothly.

The parts.

Her best guess as to what they might be left her mortified. Thankfully, there was at least some suggestion as to how this was to be accomplished—herbal drinks and "warm baths."

She had already made up the recommended raspberry leaf, valerian and cayenne concoction for Milla to drink. On that, at least, her father and Thomson agreed. How and where and when she should be applying the "warm baths" was much more mystifying. At the very least it would require more hot water than she had if it was to be done efficiently. There were no instructions—not even a suggestion—regarding how to proceed. Or how to escape the embarrassment Tregear's presence during such an endeavor would cause. And there was no one Jane could rely on for answers but herself—and perhaps him. That she might have to ask him about it was entirely out of the question. She would simply have to figure out some way to manage the particulars alone.

She could feel Tregear watching her—no, judging her, collecting tidbits of information about her, arranging them in his mind and arriving at some less than favorable opinion she didn't deserve. She had never claimed to know anything about childbirth, and clearly he had no expectations that she would be of much use.

She fought down another urge to sigh and began to look for a second pot to fill with water and place on the hearth. Tregear didn't question her actions. He made no comment at all. Perhaps he even knew that there were no other cooking utensils, and it amused him to see her search in vain.

When she glanced around at him, she found that he had taken up her book and was quietly turning the pages.

"You can read?" she asked, realizing too late that, whether he could or couldn't, the tone of her question was insulting.

"No," he said. "I was only looking."

He was not telling the truth. He hadn't been staring at the pages with the idle curiosity of a person who had no idea what the words meant. His manner had been far too fixed and intense.

Why on earth didn't he want anyone to know he could read? Or was it only *her* he preferred to keep in the dark? She immediately concluded that it must be the latter—that, for some reason, he wished to share nothing of himself with the likes of Jane Ennis.

She gave Milla the herbal drink she had made earlier, coaxing her sip by sip until she had given her the amount the book recommended. Based on her meager experience, the drink wasn't so much for "relaxing" as it was for causing a woman's labor to return. There was nothing to do but wait and see, and perhaps doze as Tregear was dozing in the only other chair. She watched him for a time—until she realized that he was not asleep and perfectly aware of where her attention lay.

She looked away, her mind immediately going to the possible—probable—repercussions of this situation. Her reputation was nothing if not compromised, as was her trustworthiness. Who among the people who knew her would have even considered that she would leave the house in the middle of the night to follow a man like Tregear— regardless of the reason.

Even so, she didn't regret it—yet—and wouldn't until her father found out. She still couldn't quite get her mind around the fact that Milla Dunwiddie had come to this.

Milla with whom she had nothing in common, but who had always been more friend than servant. Jane had had no idea that Milla was living in the mining village or that she had become—what she'd obviously become. Jane had returned from the monthly trip to the county seat in Salisbury with her father and Eugenie to find Milla already packed up and gone and only the vaguest of explanations from her invalid mother as to where and why. Jane had supposed that Milla's leaving the Ennis household had to do with some family crisis—someone falling ill, or being injured perhaps, that required Milla's return to her father's farm along the river some fifty miles away. That Milla could actually be living so near without Jane's knowing it was incredible to her. Someone must have seen her about the village—Mrs. Oliver, her father, irrepressible Eugenie.

Yet another unanswered question to add to the night's growing pile.

"It's a waste of time," Tregear said suddenly.

"Sir?" Jane said, thinking he meant to leave after all.

"To be afraid when you have no reason." He stared at her across the room.

She glanced to where Milla lay. "No reason? I have reason enough, sir."

"No, miss, you have not. Not yet. You are wasting time being afraid of what your mind tells you *might* happen."

"You must be very familiar with that, sir—to think you can identify it so easily in others."

"Aye, miss. I am. It's easy to let your fears get away from you in the mines."

"And, pray tell, what is the remedy for it?" She could hear her own annoyance in the query, but she wouldn't apologize for it. He could talk of not being afraid. Nothing would be required of him this night save perhaps the brute strength it took to fetch and carry.

"You do the best you can—whatever comes. You cannot change nor delay whatever is going to befall, miss."

"Is that so? Why, then, do you feed the Knockers?" she asked, because she suddenly remembered one of the miner's peculiar superstitions.

"Now who would have told you about them, miss?" he asked, clearly surprised.

"My brother, Sion. He said the Cornwall men leave bits of their food for the tiny manlike creatures they think live in the mine—for good luck, I assume. The Knockers, he called them. A fatalist would not do such a thing, I think."

"Ah, well. There's always that small possibility that they exist. A man underground would be foolish to ignore it—just in case."

"I see. How would they have come here, do you think? From the mines in faraway Cornwall to the mines here?" She was neither challenging him nor mocking him—but almost.

"Miners are simple men, miss," he said quietly. "That detail we don't worry about. If the Knockers be here as well, then they're fed. If not—no harm done. And it's better if you don't scorn what you don't understand, miss. It's a hard life for a miner. Them that will survive need all the help they can get, even if they must imagine it and the wee creatures who might give it."

"It hurts!" Milla suddenly whispered. "Oh…Miss Jane!" She made a soft mewing sound and groped wildly for something to hold on to, crying out loudly as the pain washed over her.

After a moment, the worst of it seemed to have subsided, but the respite was brief. Another contraction came almost immediately, leaving Jane no time to see about the warm water for the baths she supposedly needed to be giving. Milla clung to Jane's arms, her dress, whatever she could reach. The right sleeve of Jane's dress gave way at the shoulder seam.

"Milla—I need to get—"

"No—no! I'll—be quiet. I promise. I won't be any trouble—" But the pain was too much for her, and a loud wail rose up in her and spilled into the room.

"I'm sorry—I'm—sorry," Milla whispered when the contraction began to fade.

"You make as much noise as you like," Jane said, kneeling by her, frantically trying to remember what else Thomson's book had said. Nothing came to mind except perhaps the most ridiculous instruction of all.

Be cheerful.

It was too late for "cheerful." Neither she nor Tregear was going to be able to manage that. She doubted that *he* had ever been cheerful in his entire life.

No. That wasn't true. She had seen him laughing once— the day he'd carried those two women across the street. He had certainly been cheerful enough then.

She realized suddenly that Tregear was standing at her elbow—with a washbowl of water and a rag. He sat them down on the dirt floor, and Jane wet the cloth with one hand and wiped at Milla's sweaty face. She wouldn't worry about Thomson's special "baths" for now.

Another pain began; Milla clung to her until it ended.

Is it supposed to be like this?

Jane was mortally afraid that she had made the herbal drink too strong. She simply didn't know enough to be here! She should be home in her bed, worried about nothing any worse than Miss Chappell. She tried to wipe Milla's face again, but another pain followed closely on the heels of that one, and then another. And then…nothing, until Jane had all but given up expecting it.

The siege of suffering began anew, each pain seeming

to be worse than the one before. Milla's mouth began to bleed; she needed something to bite on, and Jane had nothing that would serve the purpose.

"Is there a wooden spoon?" she asked Tregear. "Anything she could bite down on?"

"No," he said after a moment of looking.

Jane had never in her life felt so useless. From time to time, Tregear brought more water. Then he left the cabin altogether. He returned in a short time with more wood for the fire and a leather strap.

"Give her this to bite on," Tregear said, handing it to Jane.

"Tregear—!" Milla cried when she heard his voice. "You will keep—your word—"

"Aye," he said. "That I will."

"You—swear it? The place where I—said?"

"I swear it."

"What does she mean?" Jane asked when he turned away.

He looked at her a moment before he answered.

"She wants me to bury her, miss," he said.

"What!"

"She expects to die from this—can you not see that?"

"Why would she trust *you* with such a thing?"

"That you'll have to ask her, miss. I don't know the reason—any more than I know the reason she thinks she needs *you* here."

Jane stared back at him. She could not have said why the idea of Milla Dunwiddie entrusting him with something so meaningful should upset her, but it did.

"Miss—Jane!" Milla cried.

"I'm here," Jane said.

"I want—Mrs. Oliver—to take my—baby. No one—else but—Mrs. Oliver. You'll tell—her that?"

"Milla, there's no need—"

"Mrs. Oliver—it has to be her! She'll be kind to it. My mam has too many babies still at home. Please! Tell her—Mrs. Oliver—what I said! She'll believe you and—she'll do it."

"I'll tell her. Don't cry," Jane said, beginning to understand now why Milla had wanted her here. It was all part of getting her house in order. Milla had made her plans, and there was no point in trying to talk her out of the notion that she would not survive this.

"I'm so—tired, Miss Jane," Milla whispered.

"I know," Jane said, wiping her face with the wet rag again.

"I'll be glad to rest…so…glad."

But Milla's opportunity for rest would come no time soon. Another pain began, and another and another, until there was no respite between them. It went on and on. Jane had no idea how late the hour was. She would have until just before dawn until she was missed. Perhaps longer, if Miss Chappell had no reason to go looking for her, no chore she wanted done.

How long would Milla's ordeal last? How long would Milla be able to bear the terrible pain? Jane had no frame of reference, not even hearsay. She knew that women talked about such things, but she was never allowed to hear. They whispered quietly among themselves at church or at whatever rare social gathering might take place and always broke off when she or any of the other single girls came within earshot. In hindsight, the times when she had accompanied her father to deliver a child, the labor had been well advanced by the time they arrived—as if the people there somehow knew that one did not dare inconvenience Dr. Ennis with false alarms.

She recognized the sounds of childbirth, however. Milla

and the women her father had attended all responded to their ordeal in the same way—by trying to scream the pain away.

But, however long Jane might have guessed Milla's labor would continue, it came nowhere near the reality. Jane could do nothing to give Milla ease, save forcing her to take a teaspoon of honey from time to time to give her strength. Tregear did the fetching and carrying as she had hoped. He brought fresh water, found a mottled mirror to reflect the candlelight and more rags to put under Milla's hips. And whatever embarrassment Jane might have felt on her own or Milla's behalf was soon lost in the gravity of the situation. The baby was making no progress coming, and there was nothing Jane could do to help it along, no matter how much she now believed—as Milla apparently did—that Milla might truly die from the birth.

She realized suddenly Tregear had disappeared altogether. He was no longer in the cabin, and she couldn't hear him anywhere outside. The question that buzzed around the back of her mind came to the forefront. She would feel no surprise if he had abandoned them. Her curiosity concerned why he had stayed at all. She could see no good reason for it.

Unless—

The baby is his, Jane suddenly thought. It must be. Somehow he'd managed to make Milla's acquaintance—perhaps on the many trips to the boot maker's to get Eugenie's new shoes—and he had taken advantage of her. He'd been here as long as Miss Chappell had—long enough to make a child. Why else would he—a man—subject himself to this? The birth of a baby was a violent process. What else would make him stay but his guilt at having been the cause of it?

"Miss?" Tregear said behind her, making her jump. He held a small bowl carefully in his hands.

Milla moved listlessly on the bed, but she was no longer clinging to Jane's hands and clothes. Jane reached up for the bowl, thinking he'd brought water again for Milla to drink.

"No, miss," he said when she would have offered it to the girl. "It's for you. You drink it."

"No, I—"

"Drink it," he said. "I had to crack a few heads to get it. I wouldn't want all that effort to go to waste."

Jane looked at him and then at the bowl, and because she was thirsty, she accepted it. It smelled…green. Like pine needles or perhaps clover. She took a small sip and realized too late that it contained some kind of spirits, strong spirits that made her cough and burned all the way down.

"Again," he said.

"No," she protested, trying to give him the bowl. "I don't—"

"Once more," he insisted. "You need it, miss. The worst is yet to come. Who knows how much longer her labor will last?"

Who indeed? Jane thought.

She gave a small sigh and took another swallow from the bowl—and another, tolerating it better this time.

The worst is yet to come.

How can it be worse?

Milla suddenly began to thrash about on the bed, the animallike sounds she made escaping from deep in her throat.

"Sooner than I thought," Tregear said. "The child is coming now." He moved quickly away, returning with more rags, the washbowl and the kettle of hot water.

Milla let loose another cry, louder this time, clutching both bent knees until her torso rose off the bed. And then she collapsed and was suddenly still. Jane worked to uncover her, dragging the girl's ragged sleeping dress and the thin coverlet out of the way. The baby lay limp and bloody amid the bedclothes. Jane picked it up and held it head down, praying that she remembered correctly what her father had said, that the lungs must be allowed to drain and the baby stimulated to cry. She frantically tried to manage to keep the child in that position and still rub its skin briskly wherever she could reach. The baby, a girl child and still attached to its mother by the cord, stirred in her hands and made a feeble sound that could mean nothing but distress.

"Please, little girl," she whispered to Milla's daughter. "You can do it—breathe!"

The child stayed silent, limp again in her hands. "I don't know what to do!" she said to Tregear, but at that moment, the baby jerked as if in spasm and began to tremble in her grasp. Its chest heaved and it began to cry, the cry gaining in strength, resounding in the cabin. Milla tried to raise her head to see.

"It's a little girl," Jane said, swaddling it in a piece of warm cloth Tregear handed her. He had to have had the cloth heating by the fire—anticipating that the baby should be kept warm—when she had never once thought of it.

"Do you know what to do about the cord?" he asked her.

"The book says—"

But he didn't wait for her to tell him about Thomson's instructions. He tied the cord tightly in two places with narrow strips of cloth he'd appropriated from somewhere. Then he deftly cut the cord with the small sharp knife he carried in an engraved silver case in his pocket. The fancy knife seemed so incongruous in his rough hand. It was the kind of thing a gentleman might own, not a miner.

Perhaps he'd stolen it she thought, and immediately pushed the thought aside.

Milla was beginning to labor again, and with another loud cry, she followed the description in Thomson's book and expelled what he called the "afterbirth." Jane handed Tregear the baby, praying all the while that this, too, was as it should be. It took her a moment to gather her fortitude, then she began cleaning up, glancing to where Tregear stood with the child from time to time. He held it carefully, but he didn't look down at it. Indeed, he seemed oblivious to it and to Jane's activity in the room.

Jane worked quickly. She was no longer afraid—as long as Milla breathed and the child fretted. But Milla was completely exhausted. Jane bathed her as best she could and carried the soiled rags and blankets and nightdress outside. They would have to be burned; there was nothing left to salvage.

She stood for a moment, looking up at the night sky before she went back into the cabin. Daylight would come soon. Daylight—and consequences.

She could find nothing to put on Milla but a man's white lawn shirt she found hanging on a peg just inside the front door. She didn't dwell on who it might belong to except to note that it was too fine to belong to a miner.

The baby still whimpered from time to time. Jane took a quiet breath then came and lifted it from Tregear's arms, careful to avoid his eyes. His warm hands brushed hers as he gave up the child. They were rough and dirt-stained, the kind of grime that would never wash off, but she didn't mind them, not now or when he'd pulled her after him through the rain and the darkness to get to Milla's cabin.

She carried the infant to the small table and began washing it in the last of the warm water. At one point, its tiny fist gripped her finger, and she stood there, loath to remove it, trying to fight down the sudden urge to weep. There was no reason for her to feel so undone. *She* was not the one completely helpless and at the mercy of strangers.

Poor little thing.

When she finished, she wrapped it snugly in the last clean piece of muslin. It cried lustily during the bath, but Milla never once stirred in response to her infant's distress. It was clear that Milla couldn't be left alone.

And Jane couldn't stay much longer.

She tried to concentrate, to devise some plan for what she should do now, but she was so tired suddenly.

The sun would soon be up, and Tregear had disappeared again. Jane stepped outside to look for him, still carrying the baby girl. She was greatly relieved to find him standing under the eaves with a small jug in his hand—an empty jug, she immediately decided.

But she had no time to worry about his degree of sobriety. He was still standing, and that would have to suffice.

"Mr. Tregear, I need a wagon," she said with a good deal more authority than she felt. "I am taking Milla and the baby to my father's surgery."

He stood staring at her, saying nothing.

"Can you oblige me or not, sir?" she asked, fighting hard not to be intimidated by the looming presence of the man. She had had a good deal of practice at standing firm with her father—in their intellectual discussions, at least. He had encouraged—demanded—it, because he needed someone with which to spar and she was the only one handy. He had no educated equal in these parts. Eugenie was too young and her mother too frail. Jane would rely on whatever experience she had gained from it now.

"I can," he said after a moment.

"Good. As soon as possible. I need to be home before Miss—before daybreak."

The baby began to fret, and Jane turned to go back into the cabin.

"She won't thank you for it, miss," he said.

Jane looked at him, cradling the baby close. "Perhaps not. But if Milla Dunwiddie is willing to die from this, she will have to fight me for the privilege."

Chapter Three

The sun was nearly up. Jane waited anxiously for Tregear's return with the wagon, pacing back and forth with the increasingly fretful baby. She thought it a good sign that the child cried with vigor now, but at the same time she didn't want it to be in such obvious distress. It needed to be suckled, but Milla lay limp and senseless and showed no signs of waking. Jane had no idea whether or not it was safe to put the baby to breast anyway. A mother's distress was supposed to taint her milk. She didn't know what happened when the mother perhaps wanted to die.

Her temporary solution was to search the cabin until she found some hard chips of brown sugar. A gift? she wondered. Payment for services rendered? It was a luxury by any standards. Perhaps Milla hadn't gone out of the Ennis house completely empty-handed.

A thousand questions crowded Jane's mind about Milla's sudden departure. It occurred to her that her mother must have known about Milla's condition, and that her father had deliberately taken Jane and Eugenie with him into town, so that they wouldn't be on hand for Milla's dismissal. Knowing Milla's circumstances now, it seemed hardly a coincidence that she would have gone so abruptly in their absence.

Jane didn't wonder about Tregear, however. She had no expectations where he was concerned. Sometimes the Reverend Oliver would prevail upon a reluctant miner to marry a woman who was carrying a misbegotten baby, but she didn't think he would have much success with Tregear. Tregear might have helped getting the child born, but Jane couldn't see him making Milla's daughter legitimate. A son perhaps, but not a bastard girl child.

The baby cried louder, and Jane tried to soothe it—before she joined in and wailed, too. The worst was yet to come; she had no doubt about that. She had to deal with Miss Chappell—and her father. And somehow she had to take care of Milla and this unhappy infant.

Jane abruptly took out the handkerchief she always carried in her waist, wet the corner and tied a piece of the precious sugar into it. After a few false starts, the baby sucked greedily on the ''sugar tit.''

Jane gave a sigh of relief and stood looking around. The morning was cool, washed fresh by the nighttime storm. Raindrops still dripped from the eaves of the cabin and the leafy canopy overhead, but it was going to be a beautiful day.

For some.

Jane looked around sharply at the sound of a creaking wagon, horse and tack. Tregear was coming. She hadn't really believed that he would return, much less bring the transportation she wanted. She had no idea where he would have gotten the wagon—and she didn't ask. Her only hope was that they could move Milla to the surgery before he was arrested and thrown into the jailhouse for stealing it.

''Has she stirred?'' he asked, nodding toward the cabin door.

"No," Jane said. "She will have to be carried out."

He didn't say anything more. He followed her inside, wrapping Milla in Jane's damp cloak and lifting her up. Still carrying the baby, Jane took the opportunity to grab the feather bed and drag it outside as best she could, hurrying with her one free hand to get it into the back of the wagon and spread out so that Tregear could lay Milla on it.

He put the girl down gently and took the baby from Jane and placed it at Milla's side, bolstering it with the edge of the feather bed. Then, he lifted Jane up into the wagon as well, without warning, quickly before she could protest, actually putting his hands on her and begging neither permission nor pardon.

She was both flustered and affronted; she had barely recovered from the impertinence of his having taken her by the hand last night when she couldn't keep up with him in the dark. She could still feel his rough hand surrounding hers. But she was too anxious to be home ahead of Miss Chappell's arising to waste time being insulted. She realized too, that, for whatever reason, he wanted some show of indignation on her part. She refused to give him the satisfaction. She would not be provoked by his deliberately uncouth behavior. And she firmly believed that it *was* deliberate. She had the sense that he chose to be presumptuous, and the more she was upset by it, the better.

She took her place beside Milla and the child, praying all the while that she was doing the right thing, that the rough ride to the surgery wouldn't give Milla the release from this life she perhaps hoped for and clearly expected.

And all the while, the sun rose higher and higher. The wagon rolled along slowly, bogging down from time to time in the standing water from last night's rain. Twice, she and Tregear had to get out to lighten the load.

When they reached drier ground and the wagon was finally moving again, Jane sat slumped against the side and
stared at the dappled shade passing over the baby's face,
shivering once, not from the coolness of the morning but
from dread. Her dress was torn and wet and soiled. Her
hair had come undone. In her entire life, she had never
looked more bedraggled or felt more forlorn.

From time to time, Tregear glanced back at her, allowing
himself to look directly into her eyes for the briefest of
moments. She thought he had some intent in doing so, but
she had no idea what it might be. If he expected hysterics
on her part, he was going to be sadly disappointed. She was
too exhausted for hysterics. She couldn't tell what he was
thinking. She didn't care what he was thinking—or so she
told herself.

They finally reached the Ennis house and the small cabin
her father used as his surgery amid the unsettled cries of
the small flock of geese her father insisted on keeping. It
was impossible for anyone to approach the place without
them causing a commotion—unless it was dark and raining.
She hadn't heard them last night when Tregear came to
fetch her, and she had completely forgotten to consider
them in her plan to make a quiet, unnoticed return this
morning.

She braced herself for the impending encounter with
Miss Chappell, picking up the baby and sliding to the back
of the wagon to get down before Tregear decided to hasten
her along. Any hint of familiarity, much less an actual impropriety, would be all Miss Chappell needed.

Jane didn't have to wait long; the geese had done their
job well. Miss Chappell came rushing out onto the porch
and stood waiting with her arms folded. She was a tall
woman, neither handsome nor ugly but remarkably unre-
fined, regardless of her desire not to seem so. Living in

London, supposedly mingling with the upper classes, had
done little for her demeanor. Her voice was always too loud
and too harsh to bespeak a lady, even when she wasn't
angry. She was clearly angry at the moment, however, and
she obviously expected Jane to come meekly for her cas-
tigation. When Jane didn't, Miss Chappell made an exasperated sound and stepped off the porch and marched
across the yard, oblivious to the mud she dragged her skirts
through.

"What have you done?" she demanded when she was
still a distance away, the icy fury in her voice barely re-
strained. She kept glancing at Tregear, as if she expected
him to respond in some way. He got down from the wagon
to tend to the horse and completely ignored her.

Thanks to her father's tutelage, Jane never attempted to
respond to a question she didn't fully understand and so
said nothing. Her silence only fueled the woman's ire.

"You have ruined us!" Miss Chappell cried, answering
her own query. "Look at you!"

Jane still said nothing. She held the baby close and tried
to step by the woman, catching a glimpse of Eugenie on
the front porch step, her small face worried and anxious.

"Eugenie!" Jane called, and her sister immediately ran
forward. "Wait! Go into the kitchen and see if the big
basket is still in there. If it is, put one of the blankets in it
and bring it here so we can use it for the baby. Hurry! We
need to get Milla into the surgery."

Eugenie was gone only a moment before she came running with the basket and the blanket. She carried them inside the surgery, then came to take the baby from Jane's
arms. Eugenie loved babies and, for a girl her age, she had
no hesitation when it came to handling them. She would
make the best of mothers someday.

"Jane!" Eugenie whispered, holding the infant carefully,

trying to keep Miss Chappell from hearing. "I tried not to say anything—"

"It's all right. Take the baby inside."

"How dare you do such a thing!" Miss Chappell went on undeterred. "You sneak out into the night like a shameless waterfront trollop and now you throw your affiliation with this man in our faces! And if that is not enough, you bring *her* and her bastard here! Oh, I've heard all the talk about Milla Dunwiddie. This is *supposed* to be a decent house! Doctor Ennis would not stand for it and neither will I!"

"Doctor Ennis is not here."

Jane looked around sharply at her mother's voice. It had been weeks—months—since her mother had left her room and yet here she stood in the yard, dressed and looking very much her old self.

"Mother—" Jane began, but her mother held up her hand. She went immediately to the side of the wagon, reaching over it with some difficulty to gently touch the baby and to take Milla by the hand until she was satisfied about the girl's state.

"I didn't know what else to do, Mother," Jane said. "She couldn't be left alone."

"Shameless!" Miss Chappell said in preparation for another tirade.

"Miss Chappell," Jane's mother said quietly, staring the other woman down. "It is for me to reprove my daughter— *if* I think it necessary. And in my husband's absence, it is for me to say who stays on these premises and who goes. It will be better for all concerned if you remove yourself from this situation. I'm sure you have other, more pressing duties to attend to. Some gruel for the morning meal, perhaps?"

Miss Chappell hesitated, struggling for the self-control

in which she took such pride. She didn't dare go against the doctor's wife, but she clearly wanted to. "Very well," she said finally, giving Jane's mother a conciliatory incline of the head. "If cooking is my duty, then I will see to it." She walked away, her body stiff, as if the rage she felt somehow limited her ability to move.

But Miss Chappell's ire was of no concern to Jane whatsoever.

"Mother—" she began again, but her mother had not finished.

"I don't believe I have had the honor of making this gentleman's acquaintance," she said, looking at Tregear and sounding as if they were in some fine drawing room and their host had unexpectedly absented himself in the middle of the introductions.

"Ban Tregear, at your service, ma'am," he said, surprising Jane with the refined civility of his response.

"Tregear," her mother said. "A Cornwall name, I think."

"Yes, that is so," Tregear answered, and her mother smiled.

"Someone told me once that all the Cornish names begin with 'Tre,' 'Pen' and 'Pol.' Is that true?"

"Somewhat true, ma'am. Those are three often heard thereabouts."

"Have you been here—in these parts—long?"

"Ten months, ma'am," he said with the surety of a man who knew the exact length of his suffering.

"I expect you still miss your homeland, then."

Tregear looked at her in surprise. "I...yes. I do, ma'am."

"Cornwall is a wild and beautiful place, I've heard."

"Yes. It is that."

"What is it you miss the most?" Mrs. Ennis asked, and

Jane wondered if Tregear had any idea that he was being gently disarmed by an expert. Her mother's skill was such that she could conciliate the taciturn Dr. Ennis before he even realized it. A rough and ignorant miner would be no challenge for her—if indeed that was what he was.

"I miss the pounding of the sea at Land's End, ma'am," he said without hesitation. "And the wind. The smell and feel and taste of it—" He suddenly stopped, as if he were embarrassed by speaking so freely to a stranger.

Jane stood by the wagon, amazed both by her mother's calm acceptance of the situation and by the change in Tregear's demeanor. She kept looking from one to the other, and she could see that her mother's strength was ebbing. Her mother was not accustomed to such physical and emotional exertion as this.

Jane abruptly took a step forward when her mother swayed slightly and had to reach out for the wagon to steady herself.

"I am quite fine," her mother said without looking at her or Tregear. "We must get Milla to bed in the surgery now. She needs her rest. Jane, if you will ready the side room with the cot. Milla needs quiet. I don't want her gawked at should anyone else arrive today."

"Mother, please go back into the house," Jane insisted, still concerned. "This is too much for you."

Mrs. Ennis smiled slightly and patted Jane on the cheek. "No, darling Jane," she said in a way that was so gentle and loving that Jane wanted to weep. For months—years—Jane's life had drifted along with such a comforting sameness, until suddenly, in the last year, everything had changed. She wanted so badly to be happy about her mother's emergence from her self-imposed exile from the family. Here was the mother she had missed so much, but

Jane didn't dare hope that she would not disappear again. She would go as Sion had gone. As Milla had gone.

"Do as I ask, please, Jane," her mother said. "I wish to speak to Mr. Tregear."

"Mother—"

"Please, daughter," her mother said.

Jane had no choice but to go. She walked slowly, but her mother said nothing until Jane had gone inside the surgery. Jane went immediately to the nearest open window and stood beside it.

"What are you doing?" Eugenie asked, still holding the baby.

"Shh!" Jane whispered, straining to hear what her mother said around Eugenie's question.

The baby began to fret.

"Eugenie, please—"

Eugenie gave an exasperated sigh and moved to the other side of the room. "Eavesdroppers never hear anything good about themselves. That's what Mrs. Oliver says—"

"Eugenie!"

"—impetuous of Jane to allow herself to be summoned from the house in the manner she did," Jane heard her mother say.

She kept waiting for Tregear's reply, wondering if he realized that the reproach was for him as well. When none came, she dared to peep out the window.

"Is my daughter safe from this?" her mother asked.

"You have no cause to worry on my account," Tregear said finally. "No one will hear anything about this night from me. It's known in the village that Milla's child was coming—but that's all. I don't believe your daughter was seen."

"I have your word that you will not speak of it—you will guard her reputation?"

"You would accept the word of a man like me, ma'am?"

"I accept any man's word," her mother said. "Until I have reason to do otherwise."

"I give it, then, for what it's worth."

"Thank you, Mr. Tregear. For your kindness—"

"I have neither the time nor the inclination for kindness, ma'am. I leave that to my betters."

"Even so, know that you have a mother's gratitude. I do most earnestly thank you—for my daughter and for Milla and the babe. Now. If you would take Milla inside. Jane will show you where."

Jane left the window and crossed quickly to the side room to make certain it was in order.

Tregear brought Milla into the surgery, carrying her as if she were no burden to him at all and placing her on the cot. But he didn't tarry. He turned to go immediately, leaving Jane to remove the cloak and settle Milla in. Milla roused enough to murmur something, but he didn't stop. He gave no word of farewell to either of them.

"They will be well taken care of," Jane called after him. He looked back as if he were about to say something, then changed his mind.

Jane stood for a moment, watching him go. He said something to Eugenie in passing, but Jane couldn't hear. She called to Eugenie, and they put the baby in the willow basket and made Milla as comfortable as they could. Thankfully, the girl stirred and seemed about to awaken at last.

"Milla," Jane called to her as the baby began to cry again. "Milla, wake up."

The girl opened her eyes, then immediately closed them again.

"No, don't sleep. Your little girl needs you. Milla, open your eyes!"

"Oh, Miss…Jane," Milla whispered, her eyes still closed. Tears began seep out from under her lashes and roll down her cheeks. "You should…never have brought me…here…."

"It's all right. Mother says you're to stay—don't cry."

"I shouldn't be…here…."

"Of course you should. Your little girl is hungry, Milla. Do you hear her?"

"Charia," Milla said weakly, finally looking toward where her baby lay. "He said…I should call a daughter 'Charia.'"

"Who said—?" Eugenie asked, and Jane poked her hard in the ribs with her elbow.

"It's a beautiful name," Jane said. "Isn't it, Eugenie?"

"I like it," Eugenie said. "It's pretty—just like she is."

"Is she?" Milla asked, her voice trembling. "Is she pretty?"

"Yes," Jane said. "Very pretty. But she needs to be fed now. Let me bring her to you."

Jane half expected the girl to refuse, but she didn't. She closed her eyes again and said nothing at all.

Jane led Eugenie out of the room. "Go see about Mother. I'll stay here with Milla."

"Miss Chappell is going to tell father everything, Jane," Eugenie said, whispering to keep Milla from hearing. "You know she will. He's going to be so angry. What are you going to do?"

Jane sighed instead of answering.

"I could ask her not to—"

"No," Jane said quickly. Her father's wrath was a terrible thing, but not so terrible as finding herself beholden to Miss Chappell.

"Milla needs something to eat. See if there is anything in the kitchen I can give her, will you?"

Eugenie nodded, then gave Jane a quick worried hug. "Jane…"

"There is nothing to be done, Eugenie. Go on now." But she couldn't let go of her curiosity. "Eugenie?" she said as her sister reached the door. "What did Tregear say to you just now?"

Eugenie smiled, pleased at having the upper hand when it came to secrets for once. "He said for us to be careful of Miss Chappell—she will lie when she doesn't have to."

Jane frowned. And how would *he* know that?

"What is he like?" Eugenie asked. "Tregear?"

"*Mr.* Tregear, and I don't know."

"You were with him all night—"

"I was busy getting Milla's baby here," Jane said.

"Did you see his tattoo?"

"Eugenie!"

"You did talk to him?" Eugenie asked, undeterred.

"Not much—"

"What did he say?" Eugenie interrupted, clearly eager for any kind of details.

"As little as possible. I don't think he cares much for people here."

"I think he likes *you*."

"Eugenie—"

"No, truly. He looks at you a lot—when you don't see him. I heard Mrs. Oliver say he had his heart broken and that's why he came to Gold Hill. Do you think that's true? Maybe his sweetheart married another man. Maybe she *died* and he couldn't bear to stay in England anymore. Oh! Maybe you look like her! That would be so romantic and so sad."

"Eugenie, you are letting your fanciful notions completely overtake you."

"I wish I could have an adventure like you," Eugenie said wistfully. "All I ever get to do is sew samplers."

"It wasn't an adventure. It was an ordeal."

"You get to go with father all the time."

"Well, in light of recent events, I don't expect that to continue. Now go see about Mother and bring Milla something to eat."

Eugenie smiled her beautiful smile. "I will. I'll bring you something, too."

"Scat," Jane said smiling in return regardless of how little she felt like it.

She stood for a moment, then went to pick up the baby, her mind going to Eugenie's question.

What is he like?

Jane had told Eugenie the truth. She didn't know, not really. She simply couldn't take a measure of the man. Perhaps there was an air of sadness about him. Perhaps it was true that he'd had his heart broken. If it was, Jane was of a mind to think he was more angry than desolate. He was definitely a mystery to her—but then all the men she'd ever encountered were, even her brother Sion. She had never understood the logic of his mind or that of her father's. There *was* no logic as far as she could tell. They simply went about life expecting everything and everyone to bend to their will, just because they were men. And they were seldom disappointed. As far as she could tell, Tregear was no different. The only thing she knew for certain was how unsettled she felt in his presence, even more so if what Eugenie said was true, and he watched her unawares.

"Here she is, Milla," Jane said. Milla immediately raised her head to see. After a moment of fumbling, she opened the man's shirt Jane had put on her and bared her breast. Jane gently laid the little girl in her arms. The hungry baby found the nipple almost immediately and began to suckle. Jane had heard of babies who came into the world seeming not to know how to feed—but this was not one of them.

Charia.

What a strange and beautiful name. Jane wondered if it was a common name in Cornwall, if it was the name of some mine spirit or a pagan queen.

Milla gave a wavering sigh, not one of contentment, but of disbelief perhaps. She hadn't expected this to happen; she hadn't expected to live long enough to experience meeting her child.

Jane stayed close by until she was certain that Milla could manage, then she gathered up her cloak and left the small room. The cloak and she herself would both need a thorough cleaning.

She gave a quiet exhalation of breath, fighting the fatigue that threatened to overwhelm her. She was so tired suddenly. Her eyes burned from the lack of sleep, but she was not completely undone. She had found herself in a situation she should never have been in, and she had managed the best she could. She felt a certain pride in having done so. She had no regrets, regardless of what Miss Chappell or her father might say.

She wandered out onto the porch. Tregear and the wagon were gone. How indifferent men could be, she thought.

The geese suddenly began flapping and honking loudly. Jane looked down the road toward what seemed to be the source of their alarm. Her father was coming at gallop—as he almost always did—and Miss Chappell was running headlong among the trees to intercept him.

Jane watched as he sharply reined in his horse. Miss Chappell seemed not to even realize how close she'd come to being trampled. She began to disclose her unhappy tale, delivering her message with waving hands and then pointing to where Jane stood. Her father didn't listen long. He spurred his horse on, heading straight for the surgery.

Jane knew better than to try to avoid him. He was a formidable man, not in stature but in presence. His entire attitude was nothing if not commanding. She knew of no man here who would not step aside when he encountered Dr. Ennis. It suddenly occurred to her that it was not altruism that had made him become a physician, but the challenge of triumphing over whatever power inflicted diseases upon mankind. He was at war with perhaps the only adversary he considered worthy of his efforts, and the human victims themselves were only incidental.

She remained exactly where she was. As he dismounted, his eyes flicked over her disheveled appearance, but he said nothing. He brushed past her and went straight inside, she supposed to determine how badly she'd bungled the birth of Milla's child.

It seemed a long time before he reappeared.

"She was brought here at your direction?" he asked.

"Yes, Father," Jane said.

"Then it is your responsibility to take care of her."

With that, he stepped off the porch, leaving her standing, and he made his way to the house.

After a moment, Jane quietly let out the breath she had been holding. And behind her, Milla's baby began to cry.

They will be taken care of.

It wasn't until that moment that Tregear realized that the Ennis girl thought *he* was the man who had tumbled Milla Dunwiddie.

At first, he found her less than plausible conclusion amusing, but the farther he rode away from the house, the more his amusement faded. It was his own considered opinion that she would do better to look closer to home. He had seen the expression on Mrs. Ennis's face when she reached to touch Milla's babe. There had been more than compassion for the less fortunate there. In his opinion it had been the look of a woman at war with her sense of propriety and her Christian duty to do right by a bastard grandchild. No. It was Sion Ennis these three women had to thank for their troubles—not him.

His mind immediately went to Milla Dunwiddie. The girl would likely do her best to die of the shame. Some women—men as well—could be very successful at it, if they set their minds to it. Jane Ennis would have her work cut out for her if she meant to save her.

"Miss Jane" was not what Tregear had expected. She wore the air of privilege well enough—indeed, she could have held her own with any squire's daughter. If better dressed, perhaps even with the blue-blooded aristocracy.

He smiled slightly to himself. Self-assured or not, she hadn't known what to do with the likes of him. He'd wager that no man had ever taken the liberty of tossing her into the back of wagon. She hadn't known whether to laugh or cry—or bloody his nose. He didn't doubt for an instant that she would be capable of it, given the provocation and the opportunity, and there she differed from her English counterparts. He thought that "Miss Jane" would fight her own battles and not leave the dirty work to someone else.

He had grudgingly admired her determination to do what she could for Milla—even if it meant asking him for help. The whole birth experience had clearly been harrowing for her, but she had stood fast, regardless of her ignorance and her unfamiliarity with precisely how babies arrived. He wondered idly if she was equally ignorant as to how they were made. He thought not. She clearly knew enough to blame him for Milla's downfall.

He had actually admired that she hadn't plagued the girl

with questions aimed at trying to uncover the identity of the man who had lain with her. He had assumed that it must have taken a great deal of restraint on Jane Ennis's part not to make inquiries and thereby miss such a truly golden opportunity to make moral judgments.

He understood that restraint now. Jane Ennis hadn't been curious because she had already identified the guilty party to her satisfaction—which gave rise to his annoyance all over again. He didn't like taking the blame for his own sins, much less someone else's. He tried to remember if he'd ever seen Sion Ennis and Milla together. No, he decided. He would have remembered. He knew Sion well enough.

Tregear had encountered Dr. Ennis's son shortly after he arrived in Gold Hill. He had made his way to the nearest tavern as soon as he'd disembarked from the stage—as much to give Miss Chappell good reason for the miles and miles of overt disapproval as to shake the dust off and quench his thirst. The young Ennis had been inside and well on his way to a monumental hangover—already drunk enough to stand several rounds for patrons and passersby alike. Tregear hadn't minded in the least taking advantage of the young man's whiskey-induced generosity. They had even talked for a time, that afternoon and on several occasions thereafter. Sion Ennis had seemed likeable enough—if one had no reason to distrust a rich man's son—and his interest in the mines and the kind of work Tregear had been called to do there appeared genuine.

But Tregear didn't understand all the rumors he'd heard about the Ennis family. It was said that Sion was on his father's wrong side of late, apparently a very short trip, given the doctor's less than genial personality. That was simple enough to fathom. Tregear believed the friction between fathers and sons to be completely natural, even when the fathers weren't the actual sire and their natures much more kindly than the doctor's. His less than smooth relationship with the Reverend Branwell was proof enough of that. It hadn't mattered in the least that he felt an overwhelming sense of obligation toward the man—more than he'd ever felt toward his real father. The more he grew into young manhood, the more he and the reverend butted heads.

It was the rumor about Sion Ennis's sisters that baffled Tregear. More than one miner had told him that Jane and Eugenie Ennis could not marry. Ever. His first audience with Mr. Mannion, the mine owner himself, had resulted in a direct admonition not to entertain any notions about them. They were not to be approached under any circumstances—an edict Tregear had certainly breached now, albeit on Milla's behalf.

He had asked no questions at the time; he couldn't have been any more disinterested. He had simply assumed that the news of his troubles in Cornwall had preceded him and that Mannion felt duty-bound to protect all the virgins wandering about. And, even if that weren't the case, Tregear had lived all his life amid rigid class boundaries. He had by no means been expecting anything different in this country, regardless of the fact that a man was supposed to be able to rise on his own merit rather than that of his great-great-grandfather's. He knew only too well the consequences of crossing those boundaries, particularly to chase after a woman, even if it was at her invitation. The limits of elite society were nonnegotiable, regardless of an old preacher's conviction that there was no biblical justification for it, regardless of his kindness and good intentions.

Tregear had since learned that the warning regarding the Ennis daughters wasn't limited just to him but extended to every man associated with the mine. And, now that he'd seen "Miss Jane" and her sister firsthand, he couldn't help but wonder about the situation. At first, he had assumed that there was some glaring defect in their appearance or their personalities that caused them to be unfit for matrimony and thereby would make any man's attention suspect. He had seen no evidence of either in Jane's case. She was pretty enough, pleasant enough, given the circumstances. And she'd had the good sense not to deliberately antagonize him when she knew she needed his help. Perhaps it was something else, he thought, some disease the family carried.

No, he immediately decided. Dr. Ennis was particularly well off for a backwoods physician. He had money and land—and as a result, he wanted the rabble kept in their places—carefully instructed so that there was no doubt as to his daughters' unavailability to them. In Cornwall, such things were understood without having to be said, but here, apparently, rich fathers made sure there was no chance of having their bloodlines tainted or their legacies passed on to a man of insignificant means and lowly birth.

All of which was no concern of his. He had no interest Dr. Ennis's older daughter. He had learned his lesson the hard way when it came to women, particularly the ones even he would have agreed were beyond his reach. He might take his pleasure with one, given the opportunity— even the untouchable Miss Jane—but he would never let another one of them matter to him.

He was still a bit mystified as to how he had come to agree to be the keeper of the Ennis girl's reputation. He couldn't help but smile at the irony of it. Clearly, the doctor's wife didn't know of the scandal in his own life and the reason he'd come here. If that situation were any kind of measure, he should be the last person to guard a young woman's good name.

The road began to widen and level off, and he sent the horse into an easy trot. He would arrive at the mine late and without food or sleep. That alone was enough to keep him out of sorts even without the annoyance of having Jane Ennis evaluate his morals.

The day crew had already gone down into the mine by the time he arrived at the shaft house. Fitzgerald, the crew foreman, clearly wanted to know why Tregear was late and why he was driving the company wagon, but he didn't have the authority to ask.

Tregear ignored him, signaling to one of the young boys who hung around the door in the hope of earning a coin or two for running errands or for being the first to get to the mine owner with the news of a new strike—or a cave in. Mean little bastards, all of them—no more than eleven or twelve years old and still trusted to drive the supply wagons from time to time. In that capacity, they carried loaded pistols, and there was not a miner here who didn't believe that any one of them would put a ball through his brain if even minimally provoked. Not that Tregear was surprised by their dauntlessness. Nothing braced a man's—or a boy's—resolve like desperation.

"Get me a pasty from the baker woman," he told the boy, tossing him a coin. "One with apples in the other end. And don't drop it this time."

"That weren't me, Cap," the boy said, biting the coin with the expertise of a man who'd been cheated at least once. "That was Perdy."

"Who are you, then?"

"I'm Bobby, Cap."

"Well, don't take up his bad habits."

"No, sir! Just one pasty, Cap?" the boy asked.

"Just one," Tregear assured him. "And one for you,"

he added just as the boy's face fell. "And you better be back here with it before I turn around twice."

"Yes, sir, Cap," the boy said, grinning from ear to ear. And he was off at a run toward the wooden structures a hundred yards away where the widows made their livelihoods by keeping the miners fed and their work clothes laundered—among other things. Someone in the group had learned to make a decent enough Cornish pasty, the pie that was a complete meal a miner could hold in his hand. It was a little touch of home, and one for which all the Cornwall men willingly parted with some of their pay.

Fitzgerald kept looking at him.

"Something on your mind, Irishman?" Tregear asked as he took down the dirty white duck coveralls and jacket he would wear down into the mine. He would have to pay the laundresses a visit himself soon.

"You a religious man, Cap?" he asked, and Tregear laughed.

"That's what I thought. The owner's got hisself a new bee in his bonnet."

"What is it?" Tregear asked, but he was only mildly interested. His mind was already on the blasting in the latest tunnel and whether or not the walls looked promising.

"We ain't going down the shafts on Sundays no more," the man said. "Until after church—anyways. Every man, woman and child that's got anything to do with this here operation—slave and free—will be singing along with the Methodists come Sunday morning—until further notice."

"The hell you say," Tregear said. He had no intention of being herded into church.

"It's the truth, Cap. You'll get your pay docked if you don't. Mrs. Oliver has done convinced him us miners are a bunch of heathens—especially you."

Tregear gave a rare laugh. "I doubt it took much convincing," he said, reaching for a felt miner's hat and making sure the candle stuck on it with clay was secure. If there was anything good about going down into the mines here, it was that the humidity was lower and the air better than what he was used to. In Cornwall he had worked in shafts that were so hot and so devoid of fresh air that he and the rest of the men had had to snuff their candles and work naked in the dark. He had once seen a man go mad under such conditions, and it was not an experience he cared to ever repeat.

"Where's Coley?" Tregear asked.

"Down in Number Seven—"

Tregear looked around sharply. "Get him."

"Mr. Warren wants him digging—he said it was too dangerous letting him go around with you when you're blasting—and he wasn't about to lose all that money he'd paid for him at the Fayetteville market."

"Warren may own the man, but he doesn't run this operation or me. Now get Coley up—unless you want to go in his place."

Fitzgerald stared at him. He was afraid of black powder, and Tregear knew it. More afraid than he was of the foppish Warren, who acted as a kind of token supervisor because he'd married well.

"Aye, Cap," Fitzgerald said after a moment, stepping to the doorway and whistling for the boys as if they were a pack of hounds. They came at a run, pushing and shoving each other to get ahead.

"You scared to go down in the shaft?" Fitzgerald asked the first boy to plant himself in front of him.

"No, sir!"

"Ever been down?"

"Twice, sir. I ain't scared."

"All right. Mr. Tregear wants you go down in Seven and find Coley—"

"You know who Coley is, boy?" Tregear interrupted.

"Yes, sir."

"Then find him and tell his boss Tregear sent you to get him. And be quick about it if you want your penny."

"Yes, sir!" the boy cried, shooting a look at Fitzgerald to make sure the Irishman understood that this was a task with recompense.

The boy grabbed a hat and left at a run, heading for the shaft entrance, clearly eager to ride the kibble—the copper ore bucket—down. Tregear thought the boy had told the truth on one account at least. He wasn't afraid. In Tregear's experience a man—or a boy—either was or he wasn't. A person's physical and mental response to going into the bowels of the earth wasn't something that could be decided. It was an inborn thing, the fear or the lack of it. Coley was afraid, and slave or not, it couldn't be beaten out of him. It could only be redirected. The man was a danger to himself and to the rest of the crew if he was put to digging. Panic spread like wildfire underground. It didn't matter whether or not there was an actual reason for it. Men still died.

Tregear had decided to use Coley as a hole driller and a packer when he set his black powder charges—a dangerous job by reputation and in actuality, and one no white man wanted. Coley still had to go down in the mine, but the prestige he garnered shadowing Tregear in his quest for new and richer veins somehow made it tolerable.

Or so it seemed to Tregear. The man himself never said anything and his perpetual silence suited Tregear just fine.

The boy who wasn't Perdy returned with the pasty—all in one piece and wrapped in brown paper and tied with string.

"Did you get yourself one?" Tregear asked him.

"Yes, sir, Cap."

"Where is it?"

"Gave it to my mam and my sisters, Cap," he said. "They was over scrubbing clothes at the washtubs. They ain't eat nothing lately."

Tregear looked at him, trying to decide if he was telling the truth.

Yes, he decided. The boy was already used to a man's responsibilities—as Tregear had been himself at that age.

But he wasn't thinking about the boy and his hungry female relatives suddenly. He was thinking about Jane Ennis, about the way she'd looked when she'd asked for his help getting Milla's baby born.

Trapped.

The way Coley was trapped. The way this boy was trapped. All of them caught in circumstances they couldn't avoid, as he was himself. He had crossed an ocean, but he was none the better off for it. The pain and the humiliation had come with him. It was there when he went to sleep at night and there when he woke in the morning. He was always in a relentless struggle not to remember the woman who had lied so prettily, to him and to her rich father. And worse, he was clearly still in Reverend Branwell's clutches, regardless of his determination to escape the man's godly influence.

He abruptly tossed the boy the remaining pasty. The boy caught it easily in spite of his incredulity.

"Stay handy in case I need you," Tregear said.

He would assuage his moral conscience by feeding the hungry. He might even go up against the slave owner, Warren, to keep him from abusing Coley any more than he already had.

But he had done all he would do for Jane Ennis. She

represented everything he wanted—needed—to forget. His part in her decision to come with him to Milla's cabin he refused to consider. She had known better than he what the consequences of her actions would be, even if he had shamed and insulted her into doing it. He didn't want to think about the scene with Miss Chappell, or what he imagined would be a repeat of it when the doctor returned. He had other, more pressing matters to worry about. He had to prove his worth to the mine owner if he expected to keep whatever pittance and privilege he had.

Like the boy sent to fetch Coley, Tregear would be glad to go down in the mine—well away from the Jane Ennises of this world. He'd already been warned about the doctor's daughters, and there was too much at stake. He would risk himself for one thing and one thing only, and it was not the promise of gold. He cared nothing for the metal itself. By hook or by crook, it changed hands too easily to be relied upon. He wanted only to enhance his reputation as a man who could find it, because there would always be someone who would pay for the discovery. If he was credited with locating even a moderately rich vein, he could name his price. His money would come more easily than digging for it, and when he had enough he would tend to the unfinished business that plagued his thoughts night and day.

Welcome or not, he would return to Cornwall.

Chapter Four

Jane looked up sharply from the basket of plantain and sorrel she shouldn't have been sorting. She felt more than heard the sudden rumbling deep in the earth. She glanced at Milla, but the girl sat nursing the baby in a patch of shade on the porch steps, humming softly and shooing the flies away from time to time. She seemed not to have noticed anything unusual at all, or if she did, it elicited no response in her. From the placid expression on her face, she hadn't arrived at the logical conclusion—that they were blasting in the mines on the Sabbath and that the man perpetrating such impiety was likely Tregear.

Tregear had not come back to see Milla and the baby or made any inquiries about them—at least none Jane had heard about. Eugenie was on the alert for some tidbit of gossip about him when she accompanied their father to Smith's store to pick up his twice yearly shipment of cloves and cayenne, but even her diligence had resulted in nothing. Jane had expected that Milla would be distressed by his indifference, but the girl gave no indication whatsoever that that was the case. She made no mention of him. Instead, she seemed almost content in her neglect—yet another thing about the situation Jane did not understand.

Jane had missed the last three Sunday church services. Her father had said she would be responsible for Milla Dunwiddie, and he had meant it. Jane had been staying in the surgery with her and the baby night and day. She took her meals there, slept there. Tregear had been right. Good deeds had consequences. Her father had declared her both culpable and responsible, and she didn't dare try to shirk either burden, even now that Milla had apparently decided to survive the ordeal.

But, if banishment to the surgery was supposed to be some kind of fitting punishment for Jane's sins—or at the very least a test of her moral resolve—Jane would have to say she hadn't minded. The only thing that bothered her was the precariousness of it all. She simply didn't understand her father's attitude. She remained surprised by her mother's continued interest in Milla's welfare, but she couldn't begin to appreciate her father's failure to comment. He said nothing about Jane's having played the midwife. Nothing about her bringing Milla back here. Nothing about her going off unchaperoned with the miner, Tregear. Any one of those events should have provoked his indignation, particularly the latter.

Instead, he had set himself to teaching her about Milla's confinement. He'd instructed her regarding the particulars of caring for a woman after she had given birth, the untoward symptoms to watch for and what should be done for them, all the while seeming his usual, didactic self. He had even allowed her to mix up some spiced bitters for the patients who showed up on the surgery steps every day— all of which must be proving most aggravating for Miss Chappell. The last thing the woman expected was for Jane to escape retribution.

It was the last thing Jane expected, as well. She had come to believe that Tregear spoke the truth when he said that no one in the village knew she had attended Milla. The fact that no one knew was the only reason she could think of that would explain her father's silence. Even so, she was still waiting for his judgment, and it was like being dangled from a fraying rope and never knowing when it would finally break.

Jane looked down at the basket of herbs, wondering if there were degrees of breaking the Sabbath. Was her sin of sorting plants less than Tregear's sin of blowing holes in the earth? Or did God view their sins equally? She gave a sharp sigh. She had no more of an answer to that than to the number of angels that could sit on the head of a pin.

"I'm going to church this morning, Milla," she said abruptly, setting the basket aside.

"Best hurry, Miss Jane," Milla said without looking up. "The doctor won't wait for you."

"You'll be all right alone?"

"Surely, Miss Jane. Me and Charia will fare just fine. She'll be sleeping as soon as she's done—and so will I. We'll not even know you're gone. If anybody comes looking for the doctor, I can tell them where he's gone and let them decide if they want to wait. And if anybody comes for you, too," she added.

But Jane preferred not to be reminded of her illicit medical practice. She left Milla sitting and ran to the house and up to her room to change quickly into her sprigged muslin Sunday dress. Eugenie and Miss Chappell were already in the wagonette when she came back down. Jane finished tying the bonnet ribbon under her chin and said nothing to either of them, nor did she make any attempt to locate her father to ask for permission to come.

At the risk of being put firmly in her place she climbed boldly into the back of the wagonette—just ahead of him—fully expecting that he would send her back into the surgery when he saw her. He completely ignored her, leaving Miss Chappell to content herself with Jane's having escaped retribution yet again. And there was no way for the woman to satisfy her need to see Jane punished except by giving one long and hard look before she turned in her seat and stared pointedly ahead.

Out of sight, out of mind, Jane supposed—except that she could still feel Miss Chappell's hostility. Miss Chappell had used Jane's fall from favor to appropriate her place on the driver's seat next to the doctor—a coup that must please her, Jane thought. Jane sat on the bench behind them and across from Eugenie. She gave Eugenie a little wink as the wagon lurched forward, knowing this was not the time to try her father's patience by engaging Eugenie in idle conversation.

Jane looked up at the window of her mother's room as they passed, once again marveling that her mother had not reverted to the total recluse she had been. She visited Milla and the baby every day, and she had seen about hiring a much older woman to take Milla's place with the cooking and cleaning. But she was not ready to venture out into the community.

Jane sat staring at her father's back as they rode along—in much the same way she had stared at Tregear's the morning they had brought Milla home. Sometimes it was hard for her to believe that she had actually done such a rash thing or that she had had any personal contact with Tregear. Except that she kept thinking about it, whether she wanted to or not. As often as not, she found herself either remembering the event or wondering what he was doing now. Out of sight, out of mind certainly hadn't worked in his case.

The ride was rough, and she had to cling to the edge of the bench seat to keep from being jostled off it. She wondered if this manner of travel was what Miss Chappell had anticipated when she agreed to come live in the Ennis household. What a disappointment it must have been if she had been expecting barouches on cobblestones instead of wagonettes on what were essentially pig paths. It must have disappointed her in the same way that expecting to be a genteel companion to a coddled doctor's wife instead of a maid-of-all-work to the entire household had. In which light, Miss Chappell's overt discontent would be perfectly understandable—if she were not so disagreeable.

It occurred to Jane suddenly that Miss Chappell's knowledge of Tregear must exceed her own. Hers was limited to several hours beset by the drama of a baby's birth. Miss Chappell's encompassed several days in the confines of the New Bern to Salisbury stage coach. Even if she hadn't deigned to converse with him, she would still have heard his conversation with other travelers. She would have shared meals with him and even seen him sleeping. Perhaps that was why she was so certain that Jane would have behaved inappropriately with the man. Perhaps some experience during the journey made her think that the seduction of an inexperienced maiden was an absolute where he was concerned.

Miss Chappell gave a long-suffering sigh, and Jane glanced in her direction, noticing for the first time the large food basket at her feet. No wonder the woman hadn't wanted Jane's presence. This wouldn't be a simple matter of attending the church services and immediately returning home again. There must be a dinner-on-the-ground afterward, and clearly Jane's father intended to stay.

Jane had to fight down the sudden urge to smile. She'd been cooped up too long. She needed to be out and about, even if it had to be under Miss Chappell's disapproving glare. A dinner-on-the-ground would last well into the late afternoon, and they would likely stay for all of it, unless some illness or injury called her father away.

Jane welcomed the respite from the surgery, even if it turned out to be a brief one. She needed a diversion, so much so, that she suddenly understood Eugenie's longing for an "adventure." The possibility of never being allowed to accompany her father on his rounds again took on a greater significance. She would miss it terribly, if she was no longer allowed to go. And not just for the novelty going places she'd never been, but for the possibility of learning new and sometimes disturbing things. How would she survive if she was suddenly relegated to sewing samplers?

She glanced at her sister, who was trying to tell her something. In spite of her curiosity, she looked away. The last thing she needed was to be caught participating in any of Eugenie's mischief. She stared purposefully at the passing scenery instead—woods mostly, the monotonous sameness of nothing but thick briars and underbrush and hardwood trees.

If she left this place, would she miss it, she wondered, the way Tregear missed the pounding of the sea and the winds of Cornwall?

A wind one could taste—what a peculiar idea. And yet she believed him in that regard, though she could not have said why. For a brief moment, she considered the possibility of asking him more about it sometime, but then she let go of the notion almost immediately, regardless of the fact that there were any number of inquiries she would have liked to make. She wanted to know about the mine spirits, as well. And what it was like under the ground. She wanted to know if he came from a long line of miners and if he was afraid in the mines. Most of all, she wanted to know what she could never ask. If he had a broken heart.

She echoed Miss Chappell's sigh. Clearly, having had to

rely upon him during the birth of Milla's child had fostered a most unsuitable tendency toward familiarity on her part. It would not be proper for her to approach Tregear on any account. Women, especially young unmarried ones, did not initiate any kind of contact with men who were not their blood relatives. She and Tregear were worlds apart—a fact that he seemed to want to underscore—and even if they were not, her father did not encourage interest in his oldest daughter.

It wasn't that he overtly forbade the society of young men. For the most part, there were no young men to forbid. Jane was aware of their covertly interested looks and had been since she was Eugenie's age, but none came calling and none sought her out for even the mildest of polite conversation—much less a flirtation. She was not so beautiful as Eugenie, but she could make heads turn with a certain appreciation. Even so, the visual pursuit had never translated to anything tangible. She had always attributed it to the fact that there were so few suitable men in the vicinity who might want to pursue the doctor's daughter. None of the mine owners had sons. Several young men who acted as representatives for the British investors visited the area from time to time, but she only rarely saw them.

Jane supposed that she must have encountered a number of possible suitors in the market for a sizable dowry when she accompanied her father into Salisbury, but she had no proof of it. She had assumed that both her and Eugenie's marriage settlement would be significant, but if any inquiries had been made regarding Dr. Ennis's older daughter, she had never been advised of it, regardless of the fact that it was a popular pastime among the matrons to tease the girls of marriageable age about the masculine interest they were garnering. It was in this way that a daughter often knew well ahead of her family that a young man had aspirations.

Jane wondered suddenly if the custom was the same in England—in Cornwall. If Tregear had let his interest in a young lady be known to a matchmaking matron and, in the process, had somehow gotten his heart broken.

She abruptly pushed the thought away. The man Tregear was far too often in her thoughts—when he did not matter to her beyond his connection to Milla and her child.

Eugenie was trying to get her attention again.

"What?" she mouthed when she thought Miss Chappell wouldn't see, but her father cleared his throat suddenly, and Eugenie, apparently unwilling to discount the possibility that their sire had eyes in the back of his head, lost interest in communicating. Jane was left with but two words she thought she understood.

"Maybe" and "Tregear."

It took the better part of an hour to reach the Methodist church by the wagon road. The service had already started when they arrived. Jane was surprised by the number of men who stood gathered around the front door and outside the open windows.

Miners, both free and slave, she suddenly realized. There were even a few women among them, fallen women like Milla and the one whose burned hand Jane had treated, who knew better than to actually set foot inside the church with the decent folk.

There was no way to get to the front doors without passing among them. Jane's father drove the wagon under the nearest shade tree and got down, tying up the team and then forging ahead in his usual oblivious way, leaving the rest of them to follow in his wake as best they could. He walked through the crowd, seeming not to notice the overflow of worshipers at all, much less that the women in his female retinue might be in need of escort. He made his way to the door without so much as a glance at any of the people ostensibly in his way. Had he always been like this? she wondered. She had long suspected that it was not altruism that led him to become a physician. He wasn't interested in humanity, only in their ailments. He needed their illnesses not their society. It was as if disease was the only challenge he could find worthy of his intellect and his strong will. Jane had realized long ago that he rarely, if ever, took interest in the person afflicted, not even when they died.

Jane could see Mrs. Oliver and several women putting food onto a long table under the hickory trees to her left.

"I'll take the basket," Jane said, reaching past Miss Chappell to get it.

Miss Chappell took hold of the basket handle first, and she required a moment to decide that having charge of the food was a menial duty at best and therefore completely suitable for the likes of Jane. She handed it over and got down from the wagon, but she didn't follow after the doctor. She stood waiting instead for Jane to take the basket to the food tables—as if Jane had to be watched lest she go astray in the distance it took her to travel from the wagon to the tables to the church front door.

Eugenie escaped Miss Chappell's hand on her elbow and walked along with Jane to deliver the basket.

"What were you trying to tell me?" Jane whispered to her, and she smiled.

"That Miss Chappell said Mrs. Oliver said the miners are coming to church now—and maybe Tregear will be here today."

Do you see him? Jane nearly asked.

"Reverend Oliver must be very happy," she said instead, wondering why Eugenie hadn't mentioned such a newsworthy development earlier.

"Mr. Mannion says they have to come—or pay a fine.

Miss Chappell hates it—she says they're too common to be allowed to church with decent folk. I think the miners hated it, too—at first. But now they don't.''

"Don't they?" Jane said absently, looking at the men who stood by the church steps. She couldn't see Tregear standing among them and didn't really expect to, because of the blasting in the mine this morning.

Still, she kept looking.

"How could they?" Eugenie said with a giggle. "I bet they had no idea they'd get fed sometimes."

"Hopefully they won't eat more than their share and leave nothing for the ones who actually brought food."

"No need for worry. We've made our contribution to the table, miss," someone said.

Jane looked around sharply. Tregear stood behind her, holding a large basketful of...something. He looked freshly groomed—clean—and not at all as if he'd recently been underground. She had no idea which direction he'd come from. He—and the black man and the boy who shadowed him—must have walked up from among the trees. Both the boy and the slave stopped when Tregear stopped, but they stood at a distance, each seeming to have no desire to acknowledge the other's presence.

Jane had no doubt that Tregear, at least, had heard her.

Tregear reached around her and set the basket down heavily on the rough table. His hair was still damp and fell into his eyes—which bothered Jane much more than it seemed to bother him. He smelled of soap and clean clothes. It was not...unpleasant.

"Mrs. Oliver was kind enough to instruct us as to what was customary," he said, nodding in the woman's direction. Mrs. Oliver looked up and smiled at the mention of her name.

He lifted up the white starched linen cloth covering the

contents of the basket, and Jane couldn't help but wonder where he'd gotten it. She glanced at him. He seemed to be waiting for her to do just that.

"Have you ever tried a Cornish pasty, miss? Each one is a meal in hand—meat, turnips or potatoes and onions in one end—sugared apples or berries in the other. As you can see, there are plenty. Enough for the whole crowd by my reckoning even if no one else contributed."

Jane stood there, caught in her rudeness with no way out. It wasn't like her to be so uncharitable, and she owed him an apology she couldn't quite bring herself to give.

"You must try one," he said, clearly enjoying her embarrassment.

"Is that what you feed the Knockers?" she asked, determined not to be kept at a disadvantage.

"Yes, miss—only it's Knackers. That's how we call them. It only takes a bit of crust to keep them satisfied and feeling kindly toward others. Perhaps a good Cornish pasty might work for you, as well."

Jane stared at him, still feeling the flush in her cheeks.

"I'm going to try one," Eugenie offered. "I think they look…savory," she decided.

"That they are," Tregear said, but he was looking directly into Jane's eyes, as if she were the one who had made the remark. It was all she could do to hold his gaze.

"And you think I have need for something to make me more 'kindly'?" she asked.

"I think you're not feeling kindly toward me at the moment, miss—though I have no idea why."

"Haven't you?" Jane said, fully aware that Eugenie's eyes were growing larger and Miss Chappell was a breath away from running into the church to tattle to the doctor.

"Perhaps you had better tell me. I've never been much of a hand at guessing what women really mean."

"You don't even ask about them," Jane said without hesitation. "About Milla and the baby."

Tregear looked at her calmly, clearly undisturbed by her oblique accusation of neglect *and* parenthood.

"I ask, miss," he said quietly.

"Who have you asked? I am with her night and day. I have heard of no inquiries."

"Your father, miss. I believe he sees them both, as well."

"My—"

It was the last thing Jane expected him to say. She stood there, struggling not to seem as taken aback as she was. It was absolutely incredible to her that this man—this *miner*—would have dared approached her father to ask about his illegitimate child.

"I see," she said after a moment. "What—what did he tell you?"

"Before or after I paid him for the information?" Tregear asked.

But he didn't wait for her to answer.

"Coley!" he called to the black man still standing by. "You and Bobby watch these baskets for Mrs. Oliver! Keep the flies off and keep your hands out of them. After you, miss," he said to Jane. "Reverend Oliver has already begun his fine sermon."

She didn't move. She waited until he understood that she wasn't about to allow him to escort her to the church door. He gave her and Eugenie the barest of nods and turned away.

Jane stood staring after him, feeling the insult on her father's behalf and yet knowing Tregear had likely been telling her the truth. Everyone knew her father's opinion regarding bastardy. She didn't doubt that he would have made Tregear pay for the privilege of knowing how Milla fared—to shame him if nothing else.

"Good morning, Miss Chappell," she heard him say as he neared where Miss Chappell stood. The startled woman couldn't have been more taken aback if he had spit on her shoes. She abruptly turned away and began walking briskly toward the church ahead of him, as if she feared what would happen if she remained.

The one-sided exchange did not escape the notice of the rest of the miners. Some of them nudged each other, but none attempted to follow Tregear's example when Miss Chappell passed among them. At one point she looked over her shoulder to give Jane another of her hard looks—on the outside chance that Jane might not have understood who was to blame for this debacle.

Eugenie made a small sound of dismay. "She's going to tell Father."

"There's nothing to tell," Jane said.

"It won't matter. She'll make it sound bad anyway."

Jane set the basket she'd been holding down on the table. "Do you need us to help, Mrs. Oliver?" she called to the woman, ignoring the fact that Tregear stood on the church steps. The last thing she wanted was to have to walk by him.

"No, my dears," Mrs. Oliver called back. "We are managing just fine. My husband will need you to lend your sweet voices to the hymns, though. Hurry along now."

Jane gave a quiet sigh. She linked her arm with Eugenie's and began walking toward where Tregear and his kind stood.

"Are we having an adventure, do you think?" Eugenie asked.

"Perhaps," Jane answered. The morning had certainly become aggravating enough to qualify.

"Adventures are a lot of trouble, aren't they?" Eugenie said. "I'd still like to see the tattoo, though. Where do you suppose it is?"

"Eugenie!"

Thankfully, Eugenie let go of the topic as they neared the church. The miners stepped aside to let them pass—even Tregear.

"Miss," some of them said quietly, respectfully, as Jane and Eugenie made their way to the door.

Jane kept her eyes down as was proper, her hand firmly clasping Eugenie's lest either of them initiate any more conversation with people they ought not be talking to.

"What will Father say!" Eugenie whispered as they stepped into the vestibule.

What indeed? Jane thought. More sins to add to the ever growing pile.

She could hear a ripple of laughter from the men outside. It was certain that her father would not be nearly so amused by her second encounter with Tregear as they seemed to be.

Miss Chappell stood waiting just inside the door.

"It's about time," she whispered fiercely, turning several heads on the back row. "Stay away from that man—both of you."

"We didn't—" Eugenie began.

"Why?" Jane interrupted. She hadn't done anything wrong, and she refused to behave as if she had. Miss Chappell stared at her, cheeks flushed.

"If you knew what I knew," she said, barely bothering to whisper. More and more people were trying to hear the conversation, regardless of the fact that the Reverend Oliver's sermon had begun.

Jane pulled Eugenie by the arm, leaving Miss Chappell standing. There was just enough room for both of them on

the bench next to her father. Jane could hear people somewhere behind her shuffling to let Miss Chappell get wherever she had determined to sit.

The church doors had been left open so that the ones
who remained outside could hear. It occurred to Jane that
she could likely see Tregear if she turned her head even
the slightest. The notion grew in her mind until she was
barely able to concentrate on what Reverend Oliver was
saying. She had no doubt that the sermon would be a long
one. She tried harder to pay attention, but the exchange
with Tregear kept repeating over and over in her head.
There had to have been some way to put the man in his
place—and likely she would think of it days from now.

If you knew what I knew.

How ominous that sounded, and who knew if Miss Chappell was alluding to some truth or once again attempting
some of her heavy-handed manipulation.

Jane shifted her position on the bench. It was essentially
half a log on legs, and her back was beginning to ache
from sitting up so straight. Unlike Miss Chappell, she
hadn't worn a back board through most of her girlhood so
that she would never feel the need to lean against anything.
She and Eugenie both had been spared that conditioning,
and it was beginning to show. Eugenie crowded her for
more room on the bench, and Jane poked her with her elbow, causing her to make a startled sound and their father
to glance in their direction. But the effect of both was short-
lived. There was only a brief lull in Eugenie's restiveness.
She slid forward slightly. Then back. Then forward again.

It was so hot inside the church, in spite of the slight
breeze from the open doors and windows. Jane wished desperately that she'd remembered to bring her fan. Sparrows
chirped under the church eaves. A baby cried. A little boy
began to dodge the wasp bobbing over his head.

The reverend's powerful voice rose and fell, and behind her, one of the miners began to snore. The little boy gave up his occupation with the wasp to giggle until his conscientious mother boxed his ears for it.

Reverend Oliver, suddenly mindful of wandering attention, moved from the front of the church to the back, preaching as he went. Again, Jane was tempted to turn and look over her shoulder, but she didn't. If Tregear was indeed standing somewhere at the back or in the open doorway, she didn't want him to think she was trying to locate him.

She stared out the nearest window instead. She could see a man walking—reeling—in her direction, trying hard to navigate the rough ground of the fallow field that lay between the church and the edge of the woods.

One of the miners, she decided immediately, one clearly too drunk to stay on his feet, much less go walking. Even so, he still took long pulls from the jug he carried as soon as he regained his balance enough to do it.

The man suddenly looked in her direction.

"Sion!" she whispered as she recognized the drunken man. She attempted to stand up at the precise moment her father's hand clamped on to her arm. She still tried to get to her feet, but he would not release her. He didn't even look at her. He stared straight ahead. He was done with Sion Ennis and he meant for her to be, as well.

She looked out the window again. Sion was closer now. At one point he fell down, and he didn't get up again.

"Father, please…" she whispered, trying to get free again.

"He has made his bed," her father answered.

"Father, let me—"

"No!"

More and more heads were turning to look out the window. Jane kept struggling against her father's hold, but it was useless. Dr. Ennis had spoken. There would be no amendment.

She glanced at Eugenie. Eugenie's bottom lip was trembling, and she suddenly clung to Jane's other arm, as helpless as Jane herself was. They both stared out the window at their brother lying facedown on the ground.

The Reverend Oliver's voice droned on and on.

Sion didn't stir, even when the young boy she had seen following Tregear came running up and turned him over. Jane watched as Tregear strode to where her brother lay. He squatted down beside him, and, after a moment, said something to the boy and to the black man who waited nearby. He helped the two pick Sion up and bear him away.

Regardless of her father's hand on her arm, Jane stared after them until they were out of sight. If her father had observed Sion's undignified removal, he gave no indication. He was more concerned with keeping her in check than acknowledging her brother. It occurred to her that he wouldn't thank Tregear for his intervention. If anything, he would resent it, just as he likely resented Tregear's inquiries about Milla.

But she would thank Tregear, in spite of her father's wishes. She put her free arm around Eugenie and took a quiet breath of relief that Sion hadn't been left where he'd fallen. When she thought it safe to do so, she glanced over her shoulder toward the back of the church. Tregear stood in the middle of the doorway as if nothing had happened. After a moment, he gave her the barest of nods.

Tregear continued to stare at Jane Ennis long after she'd turned back around. She didn't try to get up again, and he was thankful for that. The scene with her father had given him far more insight into the workings of the Ennis family

than he cared to have. Whatever had caused the breach
between the doctor and his son, it was serious, and in spite
of Tregear's determination not to take interest in these people, he hadn't liked seeing her struggle to get free of her
father's grasp. It had bothered him enough to risk annoying
Dr. Ennis one more time.

Tregear had already put himself in the man's sights by
playing fast and loose with his daughter's reputation, albeit
on Milla's behalf. And he had dared to put himself there
again by making inquiries about Milla and the baby. The
doctor's numerous shares in the mine gave him consider-
able sway in how the mine was operated and by whom.
There was no way he would welcome Tregear's interfer-
ence in whatever was happening between him and his son
as well.

But Tregear had interfered anyway—regardless of the
consequences. For the girl, not for her drunken brother. He
knew firsthand the humiliation of having inebriated family
on display in a public place. He had put himself out again,
when he had been certain that if he happened upon her
anywhere, he would ignore her. And he had convinced himself that it would be no hardship to do so. Even when he
realized she was carrying her food basket in the same direction as he, he had meant to ignore her.

But he hadn't been able to ignore her insinuation that he
and his kind were too uncouth to know how to behave
among civilized folk. The remark—true or not—had deserved a rejoinder of some kind, and he had been only too
happy to give it.

Regardless of that, he was fully aware that his curiosity
had also gotten the better of him. He suddenly found himself wanting to see firsthand how things were with her since
her unauthorized participation in the birth of Milla's child.

There was no one he could ask without compromising her reputation—which he'd given his word he would not do.

He especially wanted to know about her after his encounter with her high-handed father. His approaching the man in the mine owner's house had been a matter of curiosity, as well. He had wanted to see the Ennis sire up close. He wanted to study, albeit briefly, the man who had produced a strong-willed daughter like Jane.

Tregear had been called to Mannion's house to give the latest progress report on the new shaft. When he ran head-on into the learned doctor in the wide front hallway, he hadn't let the opportunity pass him by. He understood only too well that inferiors were essentially invisible to men like Dr. Ennis—even the ones who could possibly make him rich. But he had stepped up to him anyway—as if they were equals.

The doctor hadn't answered his question about the state of Milla's health. He made a point of demanding his money for the delivery of Milla's baby instead. And he asked for a fee for no other reason than to put Tregear in his place for having the effrontery to approach him. The last thing he expected was for Tregear to pay it. It wasn't his debt to pay, and Tregear thought they both knew it. But he paid it anyway. He handed over the coin, forgetting for that brief moment that he needed every penny he could lay his hands on to get home.

"I believe this should rightly go to your daughter," Tregear told him—just to see the look on the man's face. There were a lot of things he could have wasted his hard-earned money on, but none of them would have provided nearly the satisfaction. It was an added bonus that the unsuspecting Milla was no longer suffering the doctor's so-called charity.

Jane Ennis suddenly stirred on the bench. He thought she

was about to renew her attempts to leave, but she didn't. She moved slightly away from her father, and she and her sister both looked out the window where their brother had been.

Tregear frowned slightly. The doctor was completely out of place here, and he wondered that there was so little comment on that fact. Dr. Ennis was far too educated and too impressed with his own self-importance to be stuck in a rough mining village. His air of privilege was finely honed—in Tregear's opinion because he'd been born to it, not because he had acquired money and property only lately.

Tregear was treading on dangerous ground here. He knew perfectly well that he had to curb his preoccupation with Dr. Ennis's affairs. However bad Jane's situation might be, there was nothing he could do to rectify it. If anything, his undue interest would make everything worse—for them both.

He could just glimpse Coley standing off to his side. When he looked in the man's direction, Coley nodded slightly to let him know that Sion Ennis had been delivered safely to the place where he would be out of sight until the effects of the strong spirits he'd downed wore off. The boy, Bobby, stood nearby as well, shifting from foot to foot and grinning from ear to ear, clearly still enjoying his latest assignment, regardless of whether or not it earned him a penny.

The reverend Oliver walked to the open doorway, thundering the final points of his message then abruptly ending his sermon and calling upon the congregation to stand for the final hymn. Tregear thought that Jane might look over her shoulder at him again when she stood to sing, but she didn't.

There was no point in his staying any longer. He had

had enough of religion and good deeds for one day, and he immediately moved away from the door to make his escape.

"We going, Cap?" Bobby asked at his elbow, trotting to keep up.

"Yes," Tregear answered. The boy's face immediately fell, but he still trotted along.

"Do you play cards, boy?" Tregear asked.

"No, sir. My mam—she don't allow it."

"Well, don't ever start. You haven't got the guile for it. You stay and eat. And make sure Coley gets fed. You get him whatever he wants and plenty of it, you hear?"

"Yes, sir!"

Tregear kept going, heading into the grove of oak trees on the far side of the now heavy-laden tables of food. He would cut through the woods and go back to the mine. Better that than returning to his rooms, which were now occupied by a snoring drunk.

"Tregear!"

He recognized the voice immediately, but he didn't stop.

"Tregear!" she called again, closer this time. Several of the closest women turned to look as Jane Ennis chased him across the churchyard.

He stopped and waited. So much for his having given his word to Jane's mother. The damage was done now.

She was out of breath from running. Tregear could see Miss Chappell standing in on the church steps, staring in their direction.

"I want to thank you—" Jane began.

"Don't," Tregear interrupted. He attempted to move on, suddenly taken by the memory of another girl in a bonnet lined with rose satin who dogged his heels and begged him to stay.

She reached out to put her hand on his arm to detain him. He took a step back to keep her from doing it.

"Where is my brother?" she asked, staring into his eyes. "Where did they take him."

"He'll be all right. He just has to sleep it off."

"Will you tell him—"

"No," Tregear interrupted again. "I won't."

And he left her—and their rapt audience—standing.

Coley fell into step a few paces behind him. Tregear glanced at him, realizing as he did so that the man was perfectly aware of Tregear's struggle to stay out of Jane Ennis's way. It occurred to him that the watchful man might even understand more about the situation than Tregear himself did. Perhaps he even knew that Tregear had watched for Jane Ennis's arrival every Sunday he'd been forced to attend church services. Perhaps he even understood that Tregear had held back delivering the basket of pasties until he saw which way she was heading.

It didn't matter that Coley was as silent and inscrutable as ever. Coley saw everything, and it was for that reason and that reason alone that Tregear didn't turn back now and engage Jane Ennis in conversation after all. In spite of the warning he had given to Eugenie, he still had the notion that Jane wouldn't understand the situation with the Chappell woman.

Miss Chappell had overstepped her authority and had been set down hard for it. She wasn't about to forget it or that Tregear had been a witness to it. She would need to prove herself in the right, the virtuous woman who suffered for her convictions at the hands of the wicked one. He understood Chappell, for all her airs. He knew the social ambitions of her kind. *He* was her kind. She wouldn't rest until she had been vindicated, and she wouldn't particularly care how she managed it.

Coley was closing the distance between them. Tregear glanced at him, recognizing immediately that he had been caught again.

Coley knows.

"You talk too damn much," he said to the silent man. And, for the first time in all the months they'd been in each other's company, Coley smiled.

Chapter Five

"**I** want you to teach me," Sion Ennis said, accepting the drop of whiskey Tregear offered him with trembling hands and no word of thanks. As indebted as Ennis should have been to Tregear for keeping him from making a spectacle of himself and his family, he still had the audacity to ask—order—yet another favor.

"You've no need of my teaching, lad. You're a master at drinking and carousing in your own right."

"No—you know what I mean," Ennis said after he'd downed the drink in one swift gulp. Clearly, he had both the taste and the tolerance for it—up to a point.

"I fear I don't. What could I possibly teach the likes of you?"

"I want you to teach me how to handle black powder. Coley says you could blow the eyelashes off a butterfly and leave the wings intact—"

"Coley? Coley talks to you?"

"Yes, of course."

"Maybe I should have you teach me how to get a word out of the man."

Sion Ennis made an impatient gesture. "I've known him ever since we came to live here, when he still belonged to the Yardley plantation down on the Pee Dee. He taught me how to fish the river, how to read where the catfish pools were.''

''In that case, you need never fear going hungry.''

The young man looked up at him, his eyes bleary from yesterday's binge. ''I need a better skill, Tregear. A real one.''

''I'm thinking you've a better opportunity than most to learn one. Your sire is a physician.''

''I want to learn yours.''

''Why?''

''Because there's honor in it.''

Tregear laughed out loud. ''I think you rattled that brain of yours when you went face first into the dirt, lad.''

''Respect, then,'' Ennis said to qualify his assessment. ''The men respect you—all of them—from Mannion on down. Coley tells me your way of working is careful and strict. You measure everything—the expanse of the wall you want cleared, how deep the powder is to be set into the surface. Even the size of the cylinders to hold the powder is calculated. He says you take no chances. You must use mathematics. I'm good at mathematics. I could learn this—''

''You could kill yourself, as well,'' Tregear said, pouring his drink from the bottle. ''When it comes to mining, you belong in the drawing room toasting the profits with the rest of the adventurers, not down in the shafts. Your father is a shareholder. He wouldn't stand for you turning miner. Besides that, there's more to blasting than setting charges.''

''I'm certain there is. Which is why I'm willing for you to teach me.''

''Are you now?'' Tregear said. He had to admire the boy's audacity if nothing else.

''I am,'' Ennis assured him.

"Well, I'm not. I can think of no reason why you need to learn—beyond a rich boy's whim."

"I am not a boy. I'm of legal age."

"You might be of legal age, but you're still a boy. The lad who helped drag you here—Bobby—he's barely seen twelve summers, but he's older than you'll ever be."

"I would pay."

"With what? I don't see that father of yours keeping you solvent."

"I have my own money—for a time anyway. One has to spend money to make money, you know. I'm willing to spend what I have left to learn something I can use later. I will pay you to teach me and I will pay for the powder. That's the best I can do. Take it or leave it."

"In that case I'll leave it."

"Tregear, I need to do this!"

"The only thing you *need* to do is figure out how to get back at your old man without making the women in your family suffer, as well."

"I would never hurt them—"

"I take it having both your sisters see you lying face-down in the dirt yesterday was entirely for their pleasure, then."

"They saw me?"

"They, and most of the congregation. And your father, of course. And Miss Chappell."

Ennis swore under his breath. "Did Jane...say anything?"

"She was scared for you. She's a strong-willed lass. She would have come and picked you off the ground herself, but your father wouldn't let go of her so she could. That job fell to me—and I can't tell you how much I'm beginning to regret it."

"You think my sister is strong-willed?"

"I guessed as much—from the struggle she put up trying to get off the church bench."

Ennis looked at him for a moment, then suddenly smiled. "It appears our Jane has garnered herself yet another secret admirer. Poor old Tregear."

The smile suddenly faded.

"I have to have a way to make money, Tregear."

"You'd do better turning highwayman on the Salisbury road."

"I'm serious!"

"Then more's the pity. You're no miner, lad. You have to be born to that kind of suffering."

"There are worse ways to suffer than going underground."

"None you'll ever meet. I'll not risk my job and your life—*my* life, as well, come to think of it, not to mention Coley's—just to keep you entertained. Or is it some girl you want to impress?"

Ennis looked away and said nothing.

"Take yourself out of here," Tregear said after a moment. "Go get some calluses on your hands and then see how bad you want to be a miner."

Ennis got slowly to his feet. "The offer still stands," he said.

When he reached the door, he stopped and looked back. "The damage is already done, you know."

"What damage?"

"The damage you did when you didn't let my public humiliation run its course. My father isn't going to thank you for it and he's got a long memory. You might as well take me on. You're already on his wrong—" He suddenly smiled. "Oh, I see! It's her, isn't it? You put yourself out for me because of Jane. Poor old Tregear!" he said for the second time and making no attempt to hide his amusement.

"Out!" Tregear said, his annoyance rising.

"I'm going—but one last thing. If you did do it for her, don't ever let my father know it."

Jane looked up from the book she was only pretending to read, thinking that her father had come in search of her. She breathed a quiet sigh of relief when his footsteps continued past her door and down the stairs.

Since the incident with Sion at the church, she had taken to hiding herself away in the room she shared with Eugenie whenever possible, in spite of the fact that she wasn't precisely at liberty to do so. Even when the surgery was empty of patients and there were no medicines to mix, her father expected her to be close at hand. It was as if he thought she might slip off on another errand of mercy—this time on behalf of her prodigal brother.

But it wasn't because she was angry with her father that she wanted to be alone. It was because of Tregear. She wanted—needed—to think about him. Nearly a week had passed since she had approached him at the church, and she was still bewildered. He had personally seen to it that no greater harm had come to Sion. It was a kindness she couldn't possibly ignore, regardless of her father's wishes, regardless of who might be looking on. She had simply wanted to *tell* him how grateful she was. He had to have realized the gesture she was making, and yet he had thrown her gratitude back in her face.

She didn't understand. Nothing she knew of getting along with people seemed to apply to him, and the confusing array of emotions his behavior caused in her left her exhausted. And angry.

And hurt.

She still didn't know where her brother had been taken after the spectacle he'd made of himself, and she didn't know where he was now. The only thing she knew with certainty was that her father remained unmoved. Sion's name was not to be mentioned in the household, and it was breaking her heart.

She gave a heavy sigh and moved to look out the window. An unusual number of patients had come to see her father today, and she could see Milla diligently sweeping away the mud that had accumulated on the surgery porch, her baby lying in a cradle out of the way. There was at least some good in Tregear—Jane had seen it with her own eyes—but he still hadn't come for them.

I don't understand.

"Jane, darling," her mother said in the doorway, making her jump. "Are you not feeling well?"

"I feel quite well, Mother," Jane said, thinking how frail her mother looked this afternoon. And how unhappy.

"Are you sure? I hear from Mrs. Oliver there is fever about."

"Quite sure."

"Good, then. Your father requires your company."

"Now?"

"At Mr. Mannion's house this evening. It's time for the quarterly report to the shareholders. The ladies have been invited to the dinner afterward. I don't feel well enough to attempt it. He says you and Eugenie are to go."

"I don't want to go," Jane said, and her mother sighed.

"Please, Jane. Let us have no more strife in the household than we already do. It is his wish—you know how he likes to show the two of you off—and Eugenie is quite over the moon at being allowed to attend. This will be her first social outing since she left the schoolroom. She needs practice at behaving like a young lady."

Jane gave a resigned sigh and made no comment.

"You may wear my pearl-and-cameo brooch. It will go

very nicely with the green taffeta. And I will help you and Eugenie both with your hair—how is that?''

"Mother, I don't wish to go," Jane said in spite of Eugenie's need for social exercise or of the tempting bribe of jewelry her mother offered. The cameo was beautiful; Jane had loved it since she was a little girl. It could be pinned or worn on a black velvet ribbon and would indeed add something special to her dark-green taffeta dress.

"Miss Chappell has been invited, as well," her mother said quietly. "You will need to be there."

Her mother stared at her gravely. There was nothing to say beyond that. That bit of news settled the argument. Jane had no intention leaving Miss Chappell free to say whatever she pleased in what passed for society here. She was not surprised that Miss Chappell had been included. Miss Chappell was still a novelty hereabouts, much as Tregear was.

But Eugenie by herself likely wouldn't be much of a deterrent if Miss Chappell felt the need to moralize about Dr. Ennis's shameless older daughter. If the woman revealed anything about Jane's having gone off with Tregear in the dead of night, she wanted to be on hand to hear it, in spite of the fact that she couldn't really defend herself. When all was said and done, she *had* gone off alone with Tregear. There was no defense against the truth except to do as Sion did—shamelessly behave as if one were not guilty.

It suddenly occurred to her that if her father ever chose to accept Miss Chappell's assessment of her behavior, she could be as ostracized from the family as Sion was.

She abruptly put her book aside and went to kiss her mother gently on the cheek, thinking as she did so how removed from fact they both were. Sion was lost to them and yet they behaved as if nothing was the matter—because Dr. Ennis wished it.

Perhaps her father would be in a better, more forgiving mood if the mine profits were significant, Jane thought suddenly. And they must be if wives and daughters and so-called companions were invited. Heretofore, father had always attended the dinners alone, and he had been unexpectedly impressed by Mr. Mannion's extravagance. It looked as if Eugenie might have her adventure at last.

There was not much time to get ready for such an important occasion, but Jane did the best she could. Mostly, she stayed out of Eugenie's path to the mirror. Their mother hadn't exaggerated when she described Eugenie's degree of excitement as "over the moon." And her enthusiasm was nothing if not contagious. Neither of them had extensive wardrobes, but Jane helped Eugenie try on every dress she had until she finally settled on one made from the pale-blue moire silk their mother's relatives had sent all the way from France. The cloth had languished in the cedar chest for months until a competent enough seamstress could be found to be trusted with it.

"Do you think anyone my age will be there?" Eugenie asked, twirling slowly in front of the mirror to try to catch a glimpse of herself on all sides.

"I have no idea. I expect this will be a very dull affair," Jane added just to tease.

"Surely not! Oh, I don't care who is there. I just want to *see*. Everything! Mr. Mannion's house and his china and his silverware and his candelabras. I hear they're *gold*."

"Silver, if anything," Jane said absently. "Or likely brass."

"Will there be music, do you think?"

"No."

"What will they feed us, I wonder?"

"I have—"

"No idea," Eugenie finished for her. "It's going to be wonderful, though. I just know it will. I shall have something exciting to put in my journal at last."

"Not too exciting, I hope," Jane said, thinking of Sion and their last venture into the community.

"You look very nice," Eugenie offered without looking and still twirling.

"If you say so—I don't seem to be able to approach the mirror to decide for myself."

Eugenie laughed—but she didn't move out of the way. "Miss Chappell looks nice, too. I saw her when I passed her door. She's wearing something striped. Brown and yellow. I'll bet she's not a bit nervous. She's used to this kind of thing—oh, no, what if I faint!"

"You've never fainted in your life."

"And I don't want to start now. What if I do, Jane?"

"Then we shall step over your fallen body and go on about our business."

"If ever I fainted—and Tregear saw me—do you suppose he might carry me to a couch—the way he carried Milla?"

"No," Jane assured her.

"I think he would carry *you*, if *you* fainted. Look how he's protecting your reputation. He told mother he wouldn't speak of the night you went with him—and he hasn't. No one knows about that—except Miss Chappell, of course."

"Eugenie, enough. Go show Mother how you look so I can see to tie my brooch. Honestly!"

Her little sister grinned and took one last look before she danced away. Jane stood before the mirror, studying her reflection. The dark-green color of the taffeta dress was becoming, she thought in a brief moment of vanity. The long tight sleeves were confining, though, as was the bodice and the petticoats. A woman's lot. To be confined.

I think he would carry you....

Jane pushed Eugenie's notion aside. She couldn't elicit even the most basic courtesy from the man—and she wouldn't make the mistake of ever trying again.

She tied the velvet ribbon carefully so that the brooch rested on her bosom just above the narrow expanse of green material showing under the cream lace fichu. She didn't have Eugenie's enthusiasm for seeing inside the Mannion house. The house was not far from the mine or the Methodist church. She didn't care for it much, she thought because it had the same stacked stone wall around the yard as the village cemetery—and perhaps appropriately so. The cemetery was full of the graves of men who had died making the Mannion family rich. The notion left her feeling troubled and uneasy.

She had no expectations that this trip would be any less strained than the last time the four representatives of Ennis family had ventured forth, and it wasn't—except that there was a storm coming and arrangements had to suddenly be made to transport their finery in a trunk instead of on their backs. Eugenie's distress over the prospect of rain was short-lived as soon as she realized the situation might lead to her having access to even more of the Mannion house. Mrs. Mannion would surely admit them to a bedchamber so that they could change into their dinner dresses after they arrived.

Miss Chappell said nothing along the way. No one did, and it was a great hardship for Eugenie to keep her excitement contained. Jane amused herself watching for the path through the woods she'd taken with Tregear. That route would have greatly lessened the time required to reach the Mannion house, even if she'd been on foot. She wondered idly if her father knew the shortcut existed. Probably not, she decided. It wasn't suitable for horse or wagon. As she recalled it was barely passable walking, especially in the dark.

They arrived at the Mannion house rain spotted and damp and just ahead of a heavy downpour. A manservant opened the grand front doors before they even reached the porch. He turned all his attention to the prominent Dr. Ennis, seeming not to notice the females trailing him or that they were all inappropriately turned out for any kind of occasion in this house.

With great efficiency he showed Jane's father into the drawing room where the shareholders' meeting was about to begin, giving orders to a second servant to bring the trunk inside and another to show the ladies to the "yellow room" upstairs.

The yellow room turned out to be a small bedchamber at the back of the house, so named apparently because of the warm golden color of the stenciled pattern at the top of the walls and the yellow quilted counterpane. The room smelled of dresser drawers filled with rose petal sachets and windows hung with hidden camphor balls to keep the mosquitos away.

Eugenie was eager to get into her finery, but Miss Chappell wasn't about to participate in such intimacy with the two of them. She immediately removed herself from the room and stood outside in the hallway while the young maid helped Eugenie and Jane put on their frocks and then tried to salvage at least something of their dampened coiffures. The end result wasn't quite as polished as if their mother had seen to the final touches, but it was acceptable. In Eugenie's case, at any rate.

"There you are, miss," the maid told her. "You'll be

just like one of them pretty blue cornflowers in the bean patch, that's for sure."

Jane smiled at her sister, taking in the heightened color in her cheeks and the sparkle in her eyes. Clearly, Eugenie was very suited to adventures—of this sort.

A muted gong sounded somewhere in the house.

"Oh, it's time for me to be helping them downstairs," the maid said reaching for the door. "Can you do the rest yourselves?"

"Yes, of course," Jane said, wondering if the girl actually thought she and Eugenie were that dependent. "Thank you for your help."

"Oh, it's my job to do it, miss—help the ladies what come to the house and the mistress. I use to stand on the rockers at the mine—washing the gold out of the crushed rock. This here is a lot cleaner and everything. My feet ain't wet all the time, neither," she added with a certain satisfaction. "Just you wait around here, then. One of us will come for you directly and take you to the little parlor. Should I tell the other lady to come in now?"

"I wouldn't," Jane said, and the girl tried not to smile.

"Yes, miss. I'll leave that to you, then."

The maid slipped out into the hallway, and Jane let Eugenie primp a few moments longer.

"I'm letting Miss Chappell in now," Jane warned her, and Eugenie grinned. Nothing, not even Miss Chappell was going to detract from this evening.

"Do you need any help, Miss Chappell?" Eugenie asked as the woman entered, because she was better at practicing the courtesy their mother had taught them than Jane was and because it was her nature to be kind. Miss Chappell immediately took offense.

"I do not," the woman said shortly. "Other than closing

the door firmly on your way out and having the common decency not to open it again without my leave.''

"Yes, Miss Chappell," Eugenie said, giving Jane a resigned look. Miss Chappell was Miss Chappell, and there was no remedy for it.

"Wait for me in the hall," Miss Chappell said as Jane was pulling the door to.

Jane intended to do that, but her intention was based on the maid's remark that someone would come for them, not on Miss Chappell's edict. She didn't acknowledge the "request" and closed the door firmly on any subsequent orders.

The storm was at its height now. Jane could hear the rain beating down on the roof. She walked to the end of the hallway to look out, careful of the starched lace curtains covering the two-over-two windows. The house was very grand, but not the view. The mine shafts and the surrounding buildings were clearly visible, as were the piles of earth brought up to the surface. The huge trees in the yard swayed in the wind. She could see several women running with pots and trays from the summer kitchen to the back of the house.

A loud crack of thunder sounded overhead.

"Oh, no," Eugenie said. "The rain is going to keep the other guests away."

"I don't think so," Jane said. "Who would miss an opportunity like this?"

"Well, I wouldn't," Eugenie said. "Unless Father said so—oh, I hear someone coming in the front door." She immediately ran to the head of the stairs and leaned over the banister in a most unladylike manner.

"Eugenie!" Jane said as loudly as she dared.

Eugenie ignored her, giving a little gasp before she came rushing back.

"I think it's Tregear!" she whispered. "I think Tregear is here! He's all dressed up!"

Jane said nothing, fighting down the urge to go see for herself. She could understand his being present for the quarterly report—who would know the status of the new shafts better than he? But "all dressed up"? She couldn't in her wildest imaginings think that he would be invited to sit down at the Mannion dinner table—not with her father present.

Tregear wouldn't mind in the least, she suddenly thought. She did understand that much of the man, that he seemed to want to unsettle people.

Some people.

He had been kind to her mother in promising that he would guard Jane's reputation. And he was kind to Milla— up to a point.

She glanced at Eugenie. Her little sister was positively aglow at the possibility of seeing Tregear here.

"If it is Tregear, he's here for the meeting," Jane said to rein Eugenie in.

"No, this man was dressed for a dinner. Black frock coat, dark-blue weskit, white shirt and a black cravat. He wouldn't wear *that* just for a meeting."

"Eugenie, don't—"

"What have you done now?" Miss Chappell interrupted from behind them, causing them both to jump.

Jane closed her eyes in exasperation. Miss Chappell needed to be belled like a troublesome cat. Neither she nor Eugenie dignified the question with the denial the woman surely expected. Jane was far too busy struggling with the notion that Tregear might be downstairs.

She could see another maid coming up the staircase.

"This way please," the girl said when she reached the

top step—as if she'd rehearsed the phrase many times, but she didn't quite understand its meaning.

Jane hung back, letting Miss Chappell take the lead, so that she could keep watch for some sign of Tregear without the woman seeing her. Miss Chappell had already warned her more or less of his supposedly unsavory reputation, and she didn't want her all incensed again. If Tregear *was* here, Jane had no intention of trying to thank him again—but she did want to press him for whatever news he had of her brother. The question was how?

The door to the room her father had entered earlier was closed when she reached the foyer. She could hear men's voices on the other side of it, but not precisely what they said. She lingered as much as she dared, then finally followed Eugenie into the "little parlor."

While the yellow room was definitely yellow, the little parlor was by no means "little." It ran the full depth of the house, and Jane realized after a moment that there were two sets of folding doors that could be extended across it to break up the room into three smaller compartments, if desired. Regardless of their small number, the mine owner's wife hadn't implemented them on this occasion, apparently preferring her guests to rattle around in a very large space.

Mrs. Mannion sat on one of a pair of red velvet couches at the far end of the room, conversing with Mrs. Oliver. Jane noted immediately that, had the nearest set of doors been used, the space would have indeed been a "little parlor."

She wondered idly if Mrs. Oliver's presence was a matter of business or if it was due to some spiritual obligation on the Mannions' behalf. Or perhaps the reverend was the only man here the rest of the shareholders trusted to be the purser. Whether Mrs. Oliver's husband had been invited as a pastor or as one of the adventurers, Jane knew the little woman would not let this golden opportunity pass her by. She would leave with some much needed donation or favor for the church or for miners' widows and orphans—or else.

"Jane, dear, is it cold in here, do you think?" Mrs. Oliver asked ahead of Mrs. Mannion's greeting. "Or is it me?"

"I'm quite comfortable, Mrs. Oliver," Jane said. "Perhaps you're in a draft."

"Then I have been in a draft all day," she said with a laugh. "Maybe I should trouble your father for some elixir to take. Or perhaps *you*, miss. I think *your* healing skills are growing by leaps and bounds."

Jane smiled slightly and made no reply, trying not to look as nonplused as she felt.

"Ah, but I've lost my manners, haven't I?" Mrs. Oliver said suddenly, as if she were the hostess, or at the very least, the liaison between the social strata. "Mrs. Mannion—you know the Misses Ennis, of course. And this is their relative, Miss Chappell—all the way from…London, I believe?"

"Indeed, yes," Miss Chappell said, immediately assuming her role as civilized person among the savages. Jane stopped paying attention. She stared through the open doorway. She could see into the hallway, but not the entrance to the room where Tregear might be.

She could hear loud laughter coming from across the hall suddenly, and try as she might, she couldn't imagine him contributing anything to the mirthful sound. She drew a quiet breath, trying to decide if she really did want to encounter him this evening. The answer to that question was all too apparent.

Yes.

She wanted to see him. She wanted to speak to him, and not necessarily on Sion's behalf. She wanted to study and observe him and try to puzzle through the enigma of his personality.

Tregear.

She abruptly shifted in her seat. She was getting to be as bad as Eugenie.

"Jane?" Mrs. Mannion said.

"Yes?" Jane said, startled. She looked toward her hostess, admiring the woman's choice of dress and jewelry as she always did. This evening Mrs. Mannion was also wearing taffeta, hers a soft, shimmering gray set off by an intricate mother-of-pearl and black diamond necklace and earrings. The neckline was low enough to allow several shorter strands of the necklace to lie perfectly on her alabaster skin. The sleeves of the dress, in keeping with the accepted fashion trend, were puffed slightly at the shoulders, then tightly fitted all the way to the wrists. She wore diamond rings on both hands, and, in spite of her age, a pink rose in her hair.

"I asked if you had been to the capitol lately?" Mrs. Mannion said, smiling.

"No, not lately, Mrs. Mannion. Eugenie and I were there when my father had some legal business to attend to last winter."

"Ah, yes. I remember. Something to do with that large tract of land he bought, as I recall. My husband tells me the acreage is quite secluded."

Jane made no reply. She had no idea of the reason for her father's trip and no inkling whatsoever that he had purchased any land, secluded or otherwise.

"Such an inopportune time to visit," Mrs. Mannion went on. "You and your sister should summer there, especially if your father decides to remove to his new lands. Young girls need society and entertainment and there is precious little of it hereabouts. You must have a number of school friends in Raleigh—from when you attended the young ladies' academy, yes?"

"Yes," Jane said. She and Eugenie both had made friendships which could have translated into summer-long house visits—if their father had allowed it. It suddenly occurred to her that he would be perfectly happy to live away from the rest of the people here and that perhaps her mother's taking to her room coincided with the purchase of the land as well as Sion's departure.

"There are such elegant balls and parties to attend during the season," Mrs. Mannion said. "You both would be wonderful additions to any guest list, so lovely and accomplished as you are."

"You are very kind," Jane said, feeling a pang at the hopeful anticipation she saw in Eugenie's face that such a thing might actually happen, that they might be allowed to spend the summer in the state capitol and participate in the social life.

The door across the hall opened, and Jane could see her father briefly before it closed again. She made a concentrated effort to pay closer attention to the ebb and flow of the conversation around her, to Miss Chappell's description of the kind of "season" she had witnessed in London and the long litany of attenders—important people all.

The men seemed to be in no hurry to join them. The manservant passed down the hallway once, and occasionally one of the maids.

The conversation in the "little" parlor continued, with Mrs. Mannion very much in control of it. She even summoned a passing maid to move the chairs around and bring them more into a circle, Jane suspected because her own inattention had been duly noted. Thus rearranged, with all the guests' backs to the hallway, Mrs. Mannion handled her now captive audience with great skill, including one guest and then another, drawing out answers and becoming either delighted or amused or thoughtful as good manners dictated. It occurred to Jane that Eugenie wasn't the only one who was "practicing" here. She felt suddenly that Mrs. Mannion was, in actuality, using this hodgepodge of guests to keep her own social skills polished and ready—for the really important social gatherings somewhere down the road.

"Ah!" Mrs. Mannion said suddenly. "Do come and join us."

As much as she wanted to, Jane didn't turn to see who had just entered. She didn't have to, if Miss Chappell's and Eugenie's faces were any indication.

"Thank you, ma'am," Tregear said from just behind Jane's chair—and in the same cultivated tone as when he had spoken to Jane's mother.

"Is my husband soon to follow?"

"He and the shareholders are naming officers, I believe, ma'am. I think most are of a mind to retain their same position, so it shouldn't take long."

"Excellent," Mrs. Mannion said, smiling. "Will you take a seat, please, Mr. Tregear? I was just about to show the ladies the new piano in the hopes that there is someone among us who can play."

"A very fine piano it is, ma'am," he said, still standing.

"You are a judge of musical instruments, then, Mr. Tregear?" Miss Chappell said. "If so, perhaps *you* could play it for us," she added with an amused slyness clearly calculated to embarrass him.

He moved to where Jane could see him out of the corner of her eye and sat down in an empty chair. Even without looking directly at him, she could see how presentable he looked in spite of the storm or his profession.

"Only the left-hand parts," he said easily, holding up

his other hand. "I fear I injured my right hand unloading powder kegs this afternoon."

"I wonder you do such…menial work yourself," Miss Chappell said.

"My life depends on the powder being carefully kept. I trust no one to see to the storing—except Coley, of course."

"That slave of Mr. Warren's?" Miss Chappell said incredulously.

"The very same," Tregear said.

"Well, really," she said, finally finding something of which to disapprove. "Surely, Mr. Mannion wouldn't permit that—if he knew."

"The powder belongs to me, Miss Chappell, as does every piece of equipment I use in the mine. Mr. Mannion kindly lets me attend to my property however I think necessary."

"And with very good results, I'm told," Mrs. Mannion said, smiling brightly.

"I believe he is pleased," Tregear said. "Perhaps you could play in my stead, Miss Chappell."

"I have no ear for piano music," Miss Chappell said as if he should have been perfectly aware of that fact and therefore not have troubled her with such a remark. "I suppose you would have us think you actually can play."

"Well, I know for a fact he can sing," Mrs. Oliver said. "That I've heard with my own ears. I've tried in vain to lure him to the church choir, haven't I?"

"You have, ma'am," he said, smiling.

"I should prevail upon him to sing now," she said, "but I fear his songs are bit too…"

"Common?" Miss Chappell interrupted without even a suggestion of civility in the remark.

"No. Sad," Mrs. Oliver answered easily. "Very sad."

She suddenly shivered and seemed to look around for the shawl she obviously didn't have with her. After a moment, she looked at Tregear again. "*Can* you play as well as sing, Tregear?"

"It's a matter of opinion, I suspect, but yes. I can play a bit, Mrs. Oliver, though I've not done so in a long time. My adopted mother insisted that I learn something of music—if it killed us both. I must confess we were at death's door on many more than one occasion."

Mrs. Mannion laughed—genuinely for the first time this evening, Jane thought. Eugenie beamed her approval of Tregear's self-deprecating wit in his direction—whether she should have or not. Mrs. Oliver chuckled into her hand, and Miss Chappell—

Miss Chappell seemed to be on the verge of another one of her gifted tirades. Jane suspected that it was only Mrs. Mannion's presence that held her in restraint. None of the rest of them were high enough on the social or the moral ladder to reel her in.

"Mr. Tregear, have you made the acquaintance of Misses Jane and Eugenie Ennis?" Mrs. Mannion asked to direct the conversation into more neutral territory—she thought.

"Miss Ennis," he said to Eugenie, without acknowledging whether he had or hadn't. "And Miss Ennis," he added, turning his attention to Jane.

"And this is Miss Chappell."

"I had the unique pleasure of traveling here from New Bern in Miss Chappell's company," he said, still looking at Jane. She looked back, refusing to be unsettled.

Or rather to *look* unsettled.

Miss Chappell gave a sniff, which seemed not to affect him in the least.

He's amused, Jane thought incredulously. And why not?

His reputation wouldn't suffer whatever information about his having passed the night unchaperoned with the doctor's daughter might come to light. No matter how innocent or justified circumstances might have been, the incident would become more and more embellished with every telling—and he would escape unscathed.

"I believe the storm is passing," he said, only to have the west windows suddenly lashed with heavy rain.

"Perhaps spending a great deal of time underground doesn't lend itself well to reading the elements," Jane said.

"Perhaps not," he agreed. "Though I am out in the rain from time to time," he added.

Jane understood perfectly which time he meant, but she was saved from having to respond to the remark by the maid who had helped her and Eugenie with their dresses. The maid walked to Mrs. Mannion's side as quickly as she dared, apparently to consult with her privately about some distressing household matter.

Jane saw her opportunity and took it.

"I want to know about my brother," she whispered, staring straight ahead so as not to attract Miss Chappell's attention. She half expected Tregear to get up and walk away again, as he had at the church.

"I have not seen him," he said.

Jane looked at him. "Truly?"

"I have not seen him," he said again, and she gave a quiet sigh.

"We didn't part on good terms," he said after a moment.

Jane forced herself to look away from him. "Why on earth not? He should be indebted to you for your help."

"Because he wants to be a miner—"

"A miner!" Jane whispered.

"So he says."

"Was he sober?"

"Painfully sober."

"He can't want that. Our father would never have it."

"I believe he's gone far beyond being directed by your father's wishes."

"Will you excuse me for a moment?" Mrs. Mannion asked suddenly. "It seems there is a question regarding our dinner. I simply must see to it."

"Of course," Miss Chappell said for all of them. She waited until Mrs. Mannion had left the room, then turned her attention immediately to Tregear.

But she said nothing, and the silence in the room grew more and more awkward. Jane looked to Mrs. Oliver for help, but she kept rubbing her arms as if the cold she'd experienced earlier had grown worse or had changed from sensation to pain.

"Miss Eugenie Ennis," Tregear said to Jane's clearly startled sister. "Do you play the piano?"

"I have had music lessons, sir," Eugenie said, blushing.

"Ah, good. I see there is plenty of sheet music. I'm certain Mrs. Mannion wouldn't mind if you tried your hand."

"I…" Eugenie began. She gave Jane a bewildered look, and Jane nodded. Eugenie was much more accomplished than Jane would ever be, and she needed something important for her journal.

"Perhaps Miss Chappell will turn the pages for you," Mrs. Oliver suddenly suggested.

"Well, I—" Miss Chappell began.

"So kind, Miss Chappell," Mrs. Oliver said ahead of her refusal. "Eugenie, my dear, Miss Chappell will turn for you. I'm sure she can help you find something wonderful to play. She will know what will be an appropriate piece for us to hear."

Miss Chappell got to her feet, apparently won over by

being given charge of the selection. But she still intended to chaperon. She chose her place by the piano carefully—so she could still see Tregear, even while she picked out a sheet of music and handed it to Eugenie.

"This is very hard, Miss Chappell—" Eugenie said, looking at the music Miss Chappell had shoved at her.

"Nonsense," Miss Chappell said. "Either you can play or you can't. If you cannot, then you shouldn't have put yourself forward."

Eugenie took a deep breath and placed the music carefully on the piano. After a moment, she began to play. Very badly. She struggled on for a few more bars, then stopped and bowed her head.

"Miss Eugenie," Tregear said, getting up from his chair. "May I make a selection? There is a favorite of mine—I believe Mrs. Mannion has it here." He crossed to the piano and began to look through the sheets of music. "Ah. Here it is. Would you kindly oblige me by playing this?"

Eugenie hesitated, then took a deep breath and looked at the sheet of music he handed her. "I think I can do this," she said, smiling up at him and then at Jane. "Shall I sing as well?"

"Please," Tregear told her.

"Well, I leave it to the two of you, then," Miss Chappell said, returning to her chair, her annoyance on display for anyone who cared to look.

Eugenie began to play, hesitantly at first. Jane recognized the song immediately. It was one of the Lady John Scott's, and it was, as Mrs. Oliver had predicted, sad.

Eugenie's pure soprano voice was perfect for the melody. Jane glanced in Tregear's direction. He was listening intently, and his face revealed a depth of emotion Jane doubted he even realized. She understood two things about him immediately: that he hadn't come to this country willingly and that he wanted nothing more than to return home again.

Tregear found two more pieces for Eugenie to play. When the final song ended and both Mrs. Oliver and Jane applauded appreciatively, he fetched the beaming Eugenie and escorted her back to her chair.

When he took his own seat near Jane, it was all she could do to keep her resolve never to even attempt to thank him again. She sat there, determined, staring straight ahead, watching Miss Chappell jump up and huffily restack the sheet music he had disarrayed in his search for songs Eugenie could play, listening as Mrs. Oliver enthusiastically reassured Eugenie that her renditions had been superb.

The rain still beat upon the windowpanes. Miss Chappell still shuffled the sheet music according to her own private plan.

Jane exhaled sharply and fidgeted in her chair.

"What is it?" Tregear quietly asked.

"Nothing," she answered, turning her head farther away from where he sat.

But she lost the battle to remain indifferent to his second good deed involving her family.

"You would not let me voice my gratitude for what you did for Sion. And now—my sister—"

"Your sister was in an awkward situation," he said. "It was my doing. So it was my duty to try to help her extract herself. There is no need for gratitude."

"Perhaps not—where you come from. But here—"

"I have something I want to say to you," Tregear interrupted.

Jane made no attempt to acknowledge the remark, but her feigned lack of interest made no impression on him at all. He simply waited until her curiosity got the better of her, and she dared to look in his direction.

"Milla Dunwiddie's child is not mine," he said.

Chapter Six

The rain stopped—abruptly—leaving the room strangely quiet.

There was no sign of Mrs. Mannion or of the shareholders still meeting in the room across the hall. Mrs. Oliver and Eugenie were no longer talking. Jane could feel Miss Chappell watching her, trying to decide if something had passed between her and Tregear.

"And you, my dear boy," Mrs. Oliver suddenly said to him. "What do you hear from the Reverend Branwell?"

"Nothing," Tregear said.

"Nothing? But I had thought you only just received several letters. Mr. Oliver picked them up at Smith's store when he retrieved our mail packet. Did he not give them to you?"

"I have not read them," he said with neither apology nor regret.

Mrs. Oliver looked at him, clearly perplexed by the statement. "Sometimes letters from home can be—unsettling," she said after a moment. "Ignorance *is* bliss, by some accounts. Do you find that to be true, Jane?"

"I—yes," Jane managed to say, not really knowing which part of the question she was answering—whether letters could be unsettling or whether ignorance was bliss. In the case of Milla's child, she would have been hard-pressed to say which was preferred—knowing that Tregear was its father or knowing that he wasn't.

She was trying not to look at him—when she wanted so much to do exactly that. She wanted to see into his eyes, because if she did, she thought she would know if he had been telling her the truth.

Why he would be telling her—truthfully or otherwise—was another matter. As startled as she was by his revelation, she had been careful to give no indication that she was troubled by it. Or so she hoped. In all honesty, she had been mortified that he had actually made such a remark. She was *still* mortified, regardless of the fact that from the very first she had thought him responsible.

No.

She had been absolutely certain that he was. Now she wanted to believe him. There was no accounting for the relief she felt that he may not have sired Milla's little girl.

"The miners are famous for their singing, did you know that?" Mrs. Oliver said to the room at large.

"I didn't," Eugenie offered. Miss Chappell merely looked pained.

And Jane said nothing.

"I saw and heard them when I was in Cornwall—visiting the Methodist churches," Mrs. Oliver continued. "It was just after Mr. Oliver and I were wed, before we were sent here to America. It was a beautiful thing to behold—all of them marching into the mines—men and boys alike singing in perfect harmony as if they were going off to some glorious battle."

"I'm not certain about the 'glorious' part, but it is a battle, Mrs. Oliver," Tregear said. "The battle is to come marching out again."

"Yes," she said. "As it is here. Now where do you suppose our hostess is?" she asked, abruptly changing the subject. "I confess I'm beginning to wonder."

There was no answer for that, and she suddenly drew a deep breath. "Is no one here cold?"

"I am not," Miss Chappell said. "But then I always choose not to be discommoded by such things."

"Perhaps if I stir around a bit," Mrs. Oliver said, ignoring Miss Chappell's heavy-handed reproach for her lack of fortitude. "Your hand, please, Jane."

Jane welcomed the opportunity to escape the room and went to assist Mrs. Oliver to her feet—something she had never known the little woman to require before. But the reverend's wife leaned heavily on her now, unsteady at first until she got her balance.

"Let us step out onto the porch—and promenade a bit," she said, letting go of Jane's hand. "I really feel the need for some air. Tregear? Do come with us. You can explain what I see of the mine from out there. Miss Chappell? Will you and Eugenie join us?"

"No, thank you," Miss Chappell said. "The eaves are dripping and Mrs. Mannion shouldn't return and find *all* her guests dispersed. I shall wait here. Eugenie can keep me company."

Eugenie's face fell, but Jane didn't intervene. If Mrs. Mannion returned, she wanted to know what Miss Chappell said to her. Given the golden opportunity of having them all out of the room, Miss Chappell would surely take it.

Jane dared to glance in Tregear's direction. He was going to oblige Mrs. Oliver and accompany them, and there was no help for it.

"I fear I'm—" Mrs. Oliver said as they stepped out the side door onto the wide porch, but she didn't continue. She took a deep breath. "What would that be yonder, Tregear?'' she asked, again leaving the ''Mr.'' off his name as he must have asked her to.

''The winding shaft, ma'am,'' he said. ''It's where they bring the ore to grass.''

''Grass?''

''To the surface. The kibbles—the big ore buckets—are let down. The miners fill them up, and whoever is minding the mules at the top cranks them back up again. Sometimes it's the miners themselves who ride the kibbles up and down. Or the boys who run errands for the shift captains. They are particularly fond of standing on the rims for the trip. It's much more of a lark than using the ladders or the tunnel.''

''Boys. What makes boys so fearless, do you think?'' Mrs. Oliver asked.

''I have no idea, ma'am.''

''*You* were a fearless lad, I'll wager.''

''So I was, ma'am. Until I got a little sense knocked into me.''

He glanced at Jane. She immediately looked away, pretending to be interested in the architecture of the Mannion house.

There was a second-story porch above them, and the house was impressive to say the least. There was no other structure in the vicinity to match it. Oddly, Mr. Mannion had had a four-sided cupola constructed on the roof, a kind of ''widow's watch,'' with top-to-bottom windows all the way around. The view from there must be spectacular—if one were content with the debris and gouged-out earth of a mining camp.

Jane looked around to find that she had Mrs. Oliver's full attention.

''Now,'' the woman said. ''I intend to walk very slowly all the way to the end of the porch. I shall stand still for a moment, then return. I do not require either of you for the trip.''

She smiled at them both, and Jane realized suddenly that Mrs. Oliver had been perfectly aware of the surreptitious conversation she had had with Tregear and had mistakenly concluded that she wanted to finish it.

''Mrs. Oliver—'' Jane began.

''You heard me,'' Mrs. Oliver said. And she walked away, slowly, as promised.

Jane stood there, not knowing whether to follow Mrs. Oliver or to go back inside. In the end, she did neither. She moved away from the nearest window and hopefully out of Miss Chappell's line of vision.

Tregear immediately understood the maneuver. ''She can't see you,'' he said.

''Sometimes I think Miss Chappell can see through walls,'' Jane answered.

''You don't understand the Miss Chappells of this world.''

''Meaning?''

''Meaning, unlikable or not, she has good reason for being the way she is.''

''Is that why you thought you needed to warn Eugenie about her?''

He took a moment to answer. ''I didn't think the two of you would understand her kind of determination.''

''Why not?''

''Because you are too privileged,'' he said bluntly, and when Jane would have objected to the remark, he held up his hand.

''Miss Chappell has to be on her guard all the time, because she's trying to hang on to her notion of who she is. Demanding to be called 'Miss Chappell' and allowing no familiarity of any kind isn't just her getting above herself—though that's a big part of it. The other part is that it's different in England. If she'd stayed there, she would likely have had to go into service to earn her living, regardless of what she wants people here to think. And if she was lucky enough to have the aristocracy employ her, she would probably lose who she is. Those people can't be inconvenienced on any account, so they give you the same name as the servant you're replacing—or a name that suits *them*—just to keep things simple. It matters not in the least that it *isn't* your real name or that you might not like it— no more than if you were a animal. You see?''

Jane did see. And she wasn't at all certain she wanted to understand Miss Chappell or her motives. She was more concerned about *his*.

''Why did you feel the need to tell me about Milla's baby?'' she asked abruptly.

''I thought you might want to know—''

''I assure you I do not—''

''—because you have a certain regard for Milla,'' he continued as if she had not interrupted. ''—and I wouldn't want her and her babe to suffer the disrepute of supposedly having been involved with the likes of me.''

''I had the impression you enjoyed your bad reputation.''

''I enjoy it. I feel no need to inflict it on others.'' He stared into her eyes, and Jane had to force herself to look away.

''There is another reason I want you to know.''

''What is it?''

''I was wrong,'' he said simply.

Jane looked at him. ''About what?''

''I thought your low opinion of me didn't matter to me in the least. I've decided it does.'' He stopped, as if he expected her to make some comment.

''I wanted you to know the truth,'' he continued when

she didn't. "At least about that particular sin. I have plenty of sins, of course—but Milla Dunwiddie was never one of them."

Jane looked away, then back at him, still not knowing what to say. She thought for a moment he was actually going to smile.

"Never fear, Miss Ennis. The information requires no action on your part. It is only…information."

Mrs. Oliver walked toward them, holding carefully to the porch banister.

Jane abruptly turned her attention toward the mining camp. She realized after a moment that she could hear music—not singing, but a lively fiddle tune.

"Ah," Mrs. Oliver said. "Listen. Are the miners celebrating the new profits, as well?"

"Yes," Tregear said, and something in his voice made Jane turn to look at him again. He was staring at the sky, at the break in the clouds and the setting sun, and clearly he was seeing something she did not.

He suddenly seemed to realize that both she and Mrs. Oliver were looking at him.

"I'm reminded," he said.

"Of what, my dear?" Mrs. Oliver asked.

"Of—"

He didn't continue, and Mrs. Oliver looked toward the horizon.

"It reminds me of looking out on a vast sea," she said after a moment. "The way the clouds lie, like small islands—there and there. Now when I was a little girl, my dear mother—God rest her—would have said we were looking on the Borders of Heaven. Is that what you were told as well, Tregear?"

"No," he said. "I knew no one quite so…fanciful."

"Ah. Then it must remind you of home. I rather think it looks a bit like Land's End?"

"Yes," he said.

"Will you go home again, Tregear?" she asked gently.

"Sometimes I think so."

"And other times?"

"Other times I know better."

"God puts us…where he…where he…"

"Are you all right, ma'am?" he asked, taking a step in her direction.

"Oh, yes," Mrs. Oliver said, but she swayed on her feet, and would have toppled if Jane had not grabbed her.

"I think I had better go sit," she said, trying to smile. She reached out to take Tregear's arm, as well. Together they moved her along the porch toward the side door.

As the entered the house, Mrs. Oliver stumbled and nearly fell. "Oh, dear. Miss Chappell isn't going to like *this*," she whispered.

"*Now* what's the matter?" Miss Chappell said as they walked Mrs. Oliver into the room, and all three of them had to suppress a laugh.

"Well, really!" Miss Chappell said. "Are you indisposed Mrs. Oliver, or not?"

"I've…felt better," Mrs. Oliver decided. "I think perhaps I should collect the dear reverend and be away."

"My father should look at you," Jane said, helping Mrs. Oliver sit down on a velvet couch.

"No, I think, I've just overdone it. I'm not as young as I used to be." She smiled and gestured toward Eugenie. "Can you believe I was once as lively as this one?"

But her smile abruptly faded. "Oh, dear," she said, pressing both hands to her cheeks.

"Eugenie, go get Father," Jane said, alarmed now. This was more than simple overdoing.

"All the men went down to the miners' party," Eugenie said. "They have to make a speech and hand out gifts and tell them they did well for the company."

"I'll find him," Tregear said, briefly looking into Jane's eyes before he turned to go.

Mrs. Oliver began to shiver and suddenly lay back in the corner of the couch, one foot still on the floor. Jane placed her wrist against Mrs. Oliver's forehead, watching her closely. She didn't look or feel as if she had a fever. She was very pale, her skin cool and clammy feeling. Her pulse seemed strong enough—not the weak and thready beat of someone with a bad heart and not the heavy bounding pulse of someone with the ague or any of the many other fevers no one knew how to cure.

It's the cold phase, Jane suddenly thought in dismay. Chills and shaking often were often the first sign of the most serious illnesses. A high fever and pain and delirium would come next. Then the crisis, when the person would sweat profusely until the body cooled—and then the whole process would start all over again. If it happened enough times, even a strong heart wouldn't be able to stand the strain, and the patient would die.

Jane glanced at the window. The sky was growing dark again. Another storm was coming. Miss Chappell removed herself to the far side of the room. For once she had no desire to put herself in charge.

"Nothing to worry...about...I'm sure," Mrs. Oliver said, more to herself than to Jane. The shivering continued.

"Where did Mrs. Mannion go?" Jane asked Eugenie because she had been sitting close enough to hear whatever the maid had told her earlier.

"Two of the servants are sick," Eugenie said. "She had to—"

"Here I am," Mrs. Mannion said in the doorway. And

she was by no means the same serene woman Jane had seen earlier. She came into the room, but she didn't go to Mrs. Oliver. She stood staring at her instead.

"Is it the typhoid?" she asked finally, looking at Jane.

"I don't—"

"I lost two children in the last epidemic," Mrs. Mannion said abruptly. Two—" She looked out the window. "Another storm," she said absently. "I should—"

"Could I trouble you for a quilt to cover Mrs. Oliver?" Jane asked.

"Oh—yes. I'll send Midge to fetch one—no, I can't send her. She's ill, too. I can go myself—"

"I'll go, Mrs. Mannion," Eugenie said. "There are some on the cedar chest in the yellow room. Would one of those be all right?"

Mrs. Mannion looked at Eugenie as if she didn't quite remember who she was or how she happened to be here.

"Yes. Yes," she said. "The yellow room. Bring all the quilts. Mrs. Oliver must be kept warm. And she should be put to bed here. It's better if they're all kept together, you know," she said, looking at Jane. "It was so hard for the ones who weren't sick to see to everyone. We shall put them in here, I think, so there is no going up and down stairs. I must see to it." She hurried away.

"Run get the quilts," Jane said to Eugenie, because Mrs. Oliver's teeth were beginning to chatter, and Eugenie rushed away.

"Mrs. Oliver?" Jane said. "Eugenie has gone to fetch you some cover. We'll get you warm soon."

The woman nodded her head but did not reply.

Jane moved away. She stood for a moment, then looked down at her dress. Green taffeta was totally unsuitable for the turn this evening had taken.

Milla Dunwiddie's child is not mine.

The memory suddenly surfaced without her bidding. Milla had never once *said* that Tregear was the father of her baby. Jane had just assumed it—because he was the wild Cornishman who brawled in the taverns and carried immoral women across muddy streets, and because she couldn't account for his consideration for Milla in any other way.

She looked around at the sound of footsteps in the hallway, but it wasn't Tregear or her father. The manservant and several other men came into the room to begin readying it for the sick. Two of them took down the heavy draperies at the windows and two others collected the figurines and vases, wrapping them each carefully in linen cloths and placing them in a basket to be stored away. When they were done and apparently at Mrs. Mannion's instruction, they shoved the piano and all the tables into the far corners out of the way.

Miss Chappell abruptly crossed the room to Jane's side, looking absolutely panicked.

"We have to go," she said, plucking at Jane's sleeve. "We can't stay here."

"I'm sure Father will send Eugenie back to the house. You can both go then."

"Well, when will that be?" she asked, her voice rising. One of the men still clearing the room looked in their direction.

"I don't know. Father will be here soon. He'll tell you what is to be done."

"I don't want to be told. I want to get away!"

"Are you ill?" Jane asked suddenly because of the high color in her cheeks. She looked at Miss Chappell closely and impulsively reached out to press her wrist against her face. Miss Chappell slapped it away.

"You have no fever," Jane said. "Please. Go sit down.
Father will be here directly."

"No—" Miss Chappell said, backing away. "I
don't—"

"Sit down," Jane insisted.

Miss Chappell stared at her, her bottom lip trembling.
"My head hurts," she whispered. "It's hurt all day. I didn't
say anything—it's not my way to complain—"

Jane took her by the arm. "Sit down, Miss Chappell,"
she said again, more kindly this time and all because Tregear had explained the unexplainable to her. "Over there
by the window. You're upset. Father will be here soon. He
can give you something for the headache."

Miss Chappell let herself be led to the nearest chair. She
sat down heavily, her head bowed.

Jane took a quiet breath and went to Mrs. Oliver again.
The woman lay with her eyes closed, and she was still
shivering.

Jane looked around as Eugenie hurried in, her arms full
of quilts. She put all but one down on the nearest chair,
and together she and Jane covered Mrs. Oliver. Jane put a
second one folded double over her feet.

"I wish Father was here," Eugenie said, whispering so
Mrs. Oliver wouldn't hear her. "Is it the typhoid, do you
think?"

"I don't know. It might be. Or it might be ague."

"A lot of people died the last time it happened, didn't
they?"

"Yes," Jane said, moving the remaining quilts to another chair for no reason than that it was closer to the door.
She kept glancing out into the hall. Hoping.

For what? she thought.

No. For whom.

"I think Father won't come if Tregear fetches him," Eugenie said. "He doesn't like Tregear."

Jane made no comment. The maid who had helped her and Eugenie dress stood motioning for her to come to the doorway. Jane crossed quickly to her. The girl had brought a folded piece of brown paper, the kind Smith's store used to wrap purchases.

"What is this?" Jane asked, taking it.

"The doctor sent it, miss," the girl said.

Jane moved into the light where she could see better. She recognized flourishes of her father's hand immediately. She was to return home with Eugenie and Miss Chappell. Now. He would send someone to escort all of them into Salisbury and relative safety from the disease as soon as it could be arranged—except for Jane. Jane was to return to the Mannion house with the herbs and the ingredients necessary to make the pills and elixirs for the sick.

And not once did he say what those might be. She understood immediately that he was leaving it to her, that it was yet another trial, one that could result in no words of praise whatsoever if she chose correctly or in complete humiliation if she didn't. She still had to pay for presuming to assist a woman in childbirth.

"I must go home," Jane said to the girl. "Can someone bring our wagon around?"

"Your father took the wagon, miss."

"Where?"

"He didn't say, miss. He just come back from the mine and got it and he went. I think there's a bunch of people falling sick hereabouts."

"Is there another one I can have?"

"Wagons and buggies, yes—but there ain't no horse able enough to pull them. Two is lame and one's sick from getting into the back meadow. And Mr. Mannion gave the good ones over to some of the men what was at the meeting—so they could get away from here before the sickness got to them. They'll be leaving them horses at Smith's store until somebody as can fetches them back here. Ain't nothing left but the mules they use at the mine and you'd never handle them, miss.''

Jane gave a sharp sigh. There was only one thing to be done. She looked at Eugenie.

"Go change your dress," she said. "You, too, Miss Chappell. Father is sending us home. We're going to have to walk."

"I can't walk all that way!" Miss Chappell cried.

"There's a shortcut," Jane said. "Through the woods—"

"There's more rain coming—it's getting dark!"

Jane ignored Miss Chappell's perfectly legitimate concerns. "Can you find me a lantern?" she asked the maid.

"Yes, miss. That I can do—but you aren't really going to walk it, are you. I'd be scared to death to be out tonight after all the celebrating going on. Miners is bad enough as it is. A bunch of whiskey and fiddle music ain't going to quiet them down none.''

"I've done it before," Jane said. "The lantern, please?"

"Yes, miss."

The girl hurried away, and Miss Chappell sat back down on her chair again. "I will not stumble around in the dark in this wild place," she said.

"As you wish," Jane answered. "You can stay by Mrs. Oliver, in case she needs anything."

"I know nothing of sick people."

"You don't have to know anything. Just stay with her."

Miss Chappell looked sharply away, but she didn't offer any further argument. Jane went to Mrs. Oliver to tell her that she was leaving and that she would be back soon with medicine. But if Mrs. Oliver heard her, Jane couldn't tell it.

She glanced at Eugenie, who was wringing her hands and close to tears.

"Eugenie, what is it?"

"I—I want to stay here, Jane. With Miss Chappell and Miss Oliver. I can be a help. Truly. Don't make me go. I'll tell Father I wanted to stay. Please—"

"All right!" Jane said in exasperation, more with her sire than with her sister. Their father *would* write out his commands with no thought whatsoever as to whether or not they could be carried out.

She left the room and hurried up the stairs to change into the still damp muslin dress she'd arrived in. When she came back down, Eugenie stood in the hallway holding a lighted lantern.

"Jane, you're not angry, are you?" she began.

"No. *I'm* not. I can't say how Father will be."

"I'm afraid, Jane! I'd rather be here—where Father will be."

"I know. It'll be all right."

"Can't you stay, too? Can't you send somebody else?"

"They wouldn't know what to bring back."

"I'm afraid you'll get lost."

"I know the way," Jane said, in spite of the fact that it was more lie than truth. "Help Mrs. Oliver, if you can. And when Mrs. Mannion comes back, tell her where I've gone. And try to stay out of Miss Chappell's way."

"I think she's sick already," Eugenie whispered. "She's been trying not to shiver like Mrs. Oliver."

"*You're* all right, aren't you?"

"I'm fine—except I'm so hungry. And I don't think anybody's going to be setting out a spread tonight."

Jane smiled and kissed her cheek. "Maybe someone will

give you a crust of bread. I'll be back as quickly as I can. Tell Father that, if he returns before I do.''

Jane took the lantern and the small corked bottle stuffed with lucifer matches Eugenie handed her. She made sure the list her father had written out was safe in her pocket before she slipped out the door.

''Jane!'' Eugenie called after her as she stepped off the porch. ''You were right!''

''About what?''

''About adventures. They are an awful lot of trouble.''

Jane smiled, in spite of the gravity of the situation, and hurried away. There was still enough light to see, but she let the lantern burn. If she put it out and the rain came harder, she'd never get it lit again.

She walked as quickly as she could, purposefully and with her head down in case she encountered anyone. She would find the cabin where Milla had lived, and then she would know which way the path through the woods to the wagon road lay.

The wind was blowing, but the rain was minimal—as if the village was only on the edge of this particular storm. But for the trees rustling and creaking in the wind, it was very quiet. There was no music now. She saw no one around the cabins she passed.

She kept up her brisk pace, knowing she needed to get as far as she could along the path before it got completely dark and she could no longer see any landmarks. And she kept thinking about the fearless way Tregear had navigated the woods, dragging her along behind him. She could do it, too.

She hoped.

She found Milla's cabin easily enough—no one seemed to be about here, either. She stood for a moment, listening, but there was no sound but the crickets and tree frogs and the spattering of raindrops on the leaves overhead. The path was clearly visible, and she waited until she was well down it before she let her mind go where it wanted to go.

Tregear.

Her opinion of him mattered to him. Or so he said.

Why would he tell her such a thing? Did she dare believe it? And if she did believe it—what if it was true? Then what?

She kept thinking about the way he looked tonight—as much a gentleman as anyone she'd ever seen here—or any-where, for that matter. He could have held his own in any Salisbury drawing room she'd ever visited—or even in the capitol itself.

And he didn't just *look* the part. He had at least some refinement. He seemed perfectly at ease in the Mannion house as if he'd been there many times or had been to houses so much finer that he wasn't intimidated by it.

His adoptive mother had taught him music.

Jane smiled in the darkness, thinking about what a trial *that* must have been.

But she was no closer to understanding the man than she'd been when he'd first pounded on their door. It seemed the more tidbits of information she gleaned, the less she knew. He had been kind to Milla. And to Sion and Eugenie and even to Miss Chappell, though Miss Chappell would never know it and certainly wouldn't appreciate it even if she did.

Jane suddenly stopped in her tracks and listened hard. She was certain she heard something.

No. Someone.

Voices.

She looked wildly around her, but she couldn't tell where they were coming from. She began to walk faster. She could no longer hear them talking, but it seemed the sound of footsteps was growing nearer.

Someone laughed. It wasn't a pleasant sound.

She closed the window on the lantern and put it and herself behind the nearest big tree, pressing herself against it in an effort not to be noticed. She couldn't see the path at all, but she could hear that whoever followed her was getting closer.

"Now where the hell did she get to?" a man's voice said.

"I told you there weren't no woman wandering out here in the woods—at least not no obliging one."

"Ain't no other kind going to be out by herself in the dark," the first one said. "Anyways, I like a good chase—"

"Reckon how much she'll charge us."

"Who's paying?" he said, and they both laughed.

One of them abruptly stopped just ahead of where Jane was hiding.

"I smell a lantern," he said, coming closer. "Smell that?"

"I don't smell nothing—"

"I'm telling you it's over this way."

A branch snapped close to the tree, and Jane didn't wait. She lunged forward and fled in the direction she'd come, realizing too late that there were more than two of them. Another one stepped into her path, and she veered sharply away into the underbrush. One of the men behind her headed her off. He grabbed her by the shoulders and dragged her around to face him.

"Now what you going to do, sweetheart?" he said, leering in her face—and he would have kissed her if she hadn't shoved him hard. He recovered easily and spun her around, clamping his arms around her and holding her fast, his whiskey breath hot against her cheek.

"Look what I got!" he yelled, his hand clamping down hard over Jane's mouth when she would have screamed.

The other one came running. Together they began to drag Jane away.

"Stand!" a different voice yelled, but they didn't stop. Jane struggled hard to get free, but she couldn't get her arms up, couldn't get any leverage on the ground.

"I got a pistol and I know where to aim!" the new voice said, and they abruptly stopped.

"Aw, Bobby, you ain't going to use that thing," the man holding Jane said. "Get on back home where you belong—"

"I'm on the job here, boys. I got the authority and I got the will. Turn her loose."

"Now, Bobby, you ain't going to shoot me. We both know that," the man said.

"No, I ain't," the boy said, leveling the pistol at the other man. "I'm going to shoot *him*. Mikey, if he's going to hide behind a woman, looks like the honor goes to you. When you see your dead mama, you tell her Bobby Reid sends her his regards."

There was the ominous sound of the pistol being cocked.

"Now, wait now," the man who had been designated the target said, holding up both hands. "Wait! This here weren't my idea. I ain't in this. You let her go like he says, Maurice."

"I ain't a-scared of some runt boy—"

"He'll gut-shoot me for sure, damn it! I seen him do it before! He killed a man for putting his hand on the supply wagon mule—and Mannion gave him a damn bonus for it! Let her go!"

"Count of three, boys," Bobby said. "I'll go real slow so you can keep up. One...two..."

"Maurice! Don't you let him shoot me!"

The man holding Jane swore and shoved her forward. She fell to her knees as both of the men fled into the darkness. She stayed where she was, trembling and not at all sure if she was safe. The boy came closer. She knew who he was now. He was the one who helped carry Sion away from the church.

"They gone?" he asked, and Jane looked around to see Coley standing nearby.

"Long gone," Coley said.

"You hurt, miss?" the boy asked her.

"No," she said, but her voice trembled.

"Reckon you can get up now?" He made no attempt to help her. He was still watching for the two men to return.

"I—yes."

"You was heading home, is that right?"

"Yes," Jane said.

"Let's get going, then," he said. "Afore them two get sober enough to come back."

"Did—did Tregear send you?"

"No, miss. He didn't send us. We got to get some medicine from your daddy. Tregear's done fell sick, too."

Chapter Seven

Jane had no idea what time it was. She put off asking the one thing she wanted to know until after she'd clandestinely gathered up all the medical supplies her father needed, and she had nearly completed the return trip to the Mannion house. Only Milla knew that she had returned to the surgery and in whose company. She didn't dare wake her mother and tell her that there was fever in the village or that she'd left Eugenie in the middle of it, no matter how much she needed her comfort.

"Tregear," she asked Bobby Reid abruptly as the lighted windows of the house came into view. "How bad is he?"

Bobby was looking at the house, and for a moment she thought he wasn't going to answer her.

"Don't know for sure," he said finally. "Me and Coley was going to see to him when he toppled, but Mr. Sion said he owed Tregear a good picking up from the dirt on account of the other Sunday—so he sent us off to get the medicine from your daddy. He said he'd tote Tregear. Tregear, he said he could walk—but he couldn't. So then Mr. Sion said for us to go on—he'd get him off the street one way or t'other. Tregear told Mr. Sion to go to hell and Mr. Sion said, 'When you're there to open the gates for me, you sorry son of a you-know-what.' And that made Tregear laugh, but then the laugh, it kind of went out of him and he didn't put up no more fuss. Coley, he says the fever just about always comes on you like a crack of thunder, and I reckon it does. Tregear, he weren't cussing no more, anyways—how did you say to make this?'' he abruptly asked, holding up the folded piece of paper holding the carefully measured dried herbs she'd given him.

"Put the herbs in a pint of hot water—everything in that paper all at one time—don't try to save part of it for later. And let it steep until the water gets cool," Jane said, starting from the beginning. "The dose is a half cupful every three hours—do you know where he is?"

"Mr. Sion?"

"No—yes."

"Don't know, miss. He didn't say where him and Tregear was heading—but I reckon we can find him."

"My brother is well?" she asked belatedly.

"Was when I left him, miss."

"If—when—you see him, will you tell him I asked after him—tell him his sister Jane asked."

"I'll do that, miss."

"And thank you. You and Coley both, for your help…earlier."

"Weren't nothing, miss. The men, they get big notions when they've been drinking—and that's most of the time. A lot of them can't go down in the mine without a little whiskey courage. They ain't like Tregear. Being down there don't bother him a lick. Anyways, I'm kind of used to scaring off them hardheaded rascals with a pistol."

"It meant a lot to me. I won't forget." She turned and stepped through the gate to the house.

"Miss?" Bobby said, and she looked at him.

"Miss Eugenie—is she in there—in Mr. Mannion's house?"

"As far as I know."

"Would you tell her I'm hoping she stays well? Tell her Bobby Reid said that. I heard her sing at the church on Easter Sunday morning. She sure can sing pretty. You can tell her that, too."

"I will," Jane said, trying not to smile.

He nodded solemnly then looked at Coley. "Let's go," he said. "Tregear's going to need this here medicine."

He trotted away with Coley close behind him.

Jane had no opportunity to pass along Bobby's message. When she opened the front door, her father was standing in the downstairs hallway.

She waited for him to say something. He took the saddlebag full of herbs from her hands instead and immediately began to evaluate what she had brought, dumping out the contents on the large mahogany table in the Mannion foyer and opening each packet by the light of the oil lamp as if he didn't trust the labeling she'd done.

"You brought opium?"

"Yes, Father."

She had also included two nervines—lady's slipper and skullcap—which he didn't fail to note.

"Why did you bring these?" he asked.

"For Miss Chappell," she said. "And Mrs. Mannion. They are both...disquieted."

"And you are not, I take it?"

"I haven't had the time, Father," she said. But she had certainly had the incentive, given her encounter with the men in the woods and the news about Tregear.

She wanted to know where Tregear was—especially if he was in Sion's unpredictable care. But however irresponsible her brother might be, it was a good thing for her that he had sent Bobby and Coley for medicine. She shivered suddenly, remembering the rank whiskey smell of the men who had grabbed her.

She realized suddenly that her father was looking at her.

"You should have taken Eugenie home with you," her father said.

"Yes, Father." She had no argument for that. She *should* have taken her, and would have if she'd had the means and Eugenie's cooperation.

"I'm sure your mother was distraught. You advised her of the situation here?"

"No. I didn't awaken her. I spoke to Milla. She will tell her in the morning."

"Am I to have no explanation for Eugenie's having remained here when you were instructed to take her home?"

"No, Father."

He stared at her, waiting for her to make some excuse— something she would never do, primarily because he wouldn't have permitted it. She had learned very early on that if she was in the wrong, then she was in the wrong. She had to take the responsibility for her own choices— what few she'd ever been allowed to have.

"What is this disease, Father?" she asked instead.

"What is *your* diagnosis?" he countered.

"I have none," she said. "Mrs. Mannion thinks it is typhoid," she added.

"Perhaps Mrs. Mannion is a better diagnostician than you are."

"And perhaps she's had the benefit of having seen the disease before," Jane said.

"Perhaps," he said after a moment. "Since you've asked, I, too, believe it to be the typhoid. We will discuss the signs to look for which will either prove or disprove my opinion later."

Jane stood there, surprised that he was still willing to teach her.

"It is wise never to guess at what ails a patient when the symptoms presented are beyond one's experience. Remember that, Daughter."

"Yes, Father," she said. "Is Eugenie sleeping?"

"Eugenie has been sent home. I had to see to the completion of that task and your sister's safety myself."

"*You* have the power to do so, Father," Jane said, refusing to feel guilty because there were no horses available and because Eugenie needed to be where *he* was.

"Precisely," her father answered.

"And Miss Chappell?"

"Miss Chappell has the disease. Mrs. Mannion has been gracious enough to allow her to remain here. Now. Do you know the dosage of the infusion to be given?"

"Yes, Father," she said again.

"Then instruct these women on how it is to be prepared and administered. And make sure that they understand what to do during the delirium."

Jane nodded, and when no further instructions were forthcoming, she dared another question, hoping it sounded more innocent than it was.

"Will you be treating the miners, Father?"

"The mine employs its own doctor—as you well know. I will be available for the Mannion household only."

"And the guests, as well?"

"Guests?"

"Mrs. Oliver," Jane said, hoping to lead him in the direction she wanted him to go.

"Yes. Mrs. Oliver. And her husband, too. I expect a manifestation of the disease in him very soon."

She waited for him to expand the list of guests to be treated, but he didn't. He returned all of the packets to the saddlebag, and, after a moment she turned and walked away.

"Jane," he called after her.

She stopped and waited, but she didn't look back at him.

"These are…adequate. You chose well," he said, and she closed her eyes. He had never, ever said such a thing to her before, never given her any indication that he was even content with something she had done, much less pleased.

She took a quiet breath. "Thank you, Father."

There was a commotion at the front door—Mr. Mannion returning from somewhere and eager to speak to her father.

Jane walked on toward the parlor. As singular and as prized as it was, she had no real desire to bask in her father's praise. She had but one thing in her mind.

Tregear.

If her father knew anything of him, he wasn't saying so. And if Sion didn't stay sober, who knew what kind of care he would get? She trusted that Bobby would get the herbs to him—up to a point, but it wouldn't help if he didn't stay close by and Tregear was too ill to use them.

She sighed and slipped quietly into the room. Everything in the parlor shone golden with candlelight, looking as it would have for some festive gathering—a party or a ball. But there were no softly illuminated women in silk and satins here. No music, no laugher. The only guests were the ones lying on their sick beds and the few servants still well enough to care for them.

The folding doors had been put into use since Jane had left, dividing the large room into three separate ones. Mrs. Oliver and Miss Chappell lay on makeshift cots at the far end. And the little maid who had come upstairs to show the way to Mrs. Mannion's company. No wonder the girl had seemed so vacant, Jane thought. She must have been fighting the illness even then.

Three other women lay across from them. More Mannion servants, Jane assumed. The maid who had helped Jane to dress was still on her feet and working to sponge off Mrs. Oliver with cider vinegar. The pungent smell of it rose from the bowl she had sitting on the floor beside her.

The reverend sat on the other side of the cot, clasping his wife's hand, completely unaware of Dr. Ennis's expectation that he would soon become ill himself, his head bowed in prayer. His frock coat lay spread over his wife's body to help keep her warm, likely the only gesture he could make to try to lessen her suffering. Jane tried to picture her father doing such a thing for her mother—and couldn't.

She went quietly to Miss Chappell's side. The woman was awake and miserable. She kept tossing her head from side to side. Her red hair was coming undone from the pins and falling into her face. Once she attempted to sit up and put her feet on the floor.

"Rest, Miss Chappell," Jane said, forcing her to lie back down again.

Jane reached to gather the loose pins from her hair and raked through the tangles with her fingers. Surprisingly, Miss Chappell allowed her to do it.

"I cannot rest here," she said. "*He* made me stay here. I begged him to let me go with Eugenie—I told him he could not forbid my going. He said forbidding only makes the fruit more desirable. He said he would never forbid me anything, but neither would he accommodate me. He just walked away—I deserve better!"

"You have the disease, Miss Chappell. You don't want to take it to Mother and Milla and the baby."

"What do I care about them? I should not be in a common room like this! I want my privacy—my own bed!"

"No one will be at the house, Miss Chappell. Father will likely send everyone to Salisbury until this is over—"

"I saw you," she said suddenly. "You and Tregear. You think I don't know what's happening—"

"Nothing is happening, Miss Chappell. I will bring you something to help you rest. You'll feel better if you can sleep."

"I've warned your father. Don't think I have not—my pins!" she cried, snatching them out of Jane's hand.

One fell to the floor. Jane reached to pick it up and hand it to Miss Chappell, more than aware that the maid was listening—and perhaps Reverend Oliver as well.

In spite of that, Jane moved to Mrs. Oliver's bedside to speak to the maid.

"I have brought some herbs—I'm sorry. I don't know your name," she said to the girl.

"Midge," she said.

"I thought Midge had fallen sick."

"That Midge has," she said, wringing the vinegar out of the cloth she was using.

"How many Midges are there?"

"However many girls are working in the house," she said, and Jane suddenly understood that Mrs. Mannion had taken up the English custom of renaming one's servants— only she had apparently expanded it to the point of having only one name for all her female help, so that she could say it anywhere and anytime and always get a response.

The height of organization.

"What is your real name?"

The girl looked at her. "It don't matter," she said. "I'm used to the other one."

"In that case, perhaps I should be called 'Midge,' as well."

The girl smiled. "Now wouldn't that be a funny thing— the Mistress yelling for one of the Midges and getting *you*. All of us are glad—" She stopped and went back to sponging Mrs. Oliver, as the reverend abruptly stood. He placed his wife's hand gently on the cot.

"I must speak to your father," he said to Jane.

Jane waited until he had gone.

"What were you saying? All of you are glad about what?"

"We're glad you're here, miss, on account of the way you came and helped Milla."

"How did you know about that? Tregear told you?"

"No, miss. It weren't Tregear. He don't tell nobody nothing. Ever. None of them Cornwall men do. And I reckon if they did, you couldn't half understand it. I can't tell when they're talking like us from when they're using their own talk. Anyway, all anybody can know about Tregear is just what they can see right in front of them. It was Milla that said it—when she came into the village to get some mended harness for Dr. Ennis. She says you went against what people would say if they found out—all on her account—and you was as good a doctor as ever was."

"No, I'm not," Jane said. "I just—"

"Well, you're better than nothing," she assured her, and Jane smiled. She earnestly hoped that she would always be that at least—better than nothing.

"My name is Lolly," the girl said quietly, still working to cool Mrs. Oliver's fever.

"It's a lovely name. Much better than Jane. Or Midge."

The girl smiled, and Jane took the chance.

"I'm told Tregear has the fever," she said, and the girl glanced at her.

"Then he'd be took to the hotel, miss. That's where Mr. Mannion said to put all the sick miners."

"If you hear…anything about him, will you tell me?"

"I will, miss." The girl looked past her, and Jane realized that someone had come near—Mrs. Mannion. She had changed out of her finery and seemed much more herself than she had earlier.

"Miss Ennis—Jane—your father requires you," she said. "You are to explain to me about the herbal infusion before you go and leave me enough packets for these sick people."

Jane did so—quickly—reciting the instructions to her and Lolly both and then writing them down. And she included instructions for quieting Miss Chappell, as well. Her father stood waiting for her in the hall when she'd finished, and he was not happy.

He motioned for her to pick up the lantern and follow him out. They both had to stand back and wait at the front door. Two men were carrying a third man into the house. Jane recognized him immediately. The company doctor, clearly too ill to walk under his own power.

She looked at her father, expecting that he would stop and see to the man, but he didn't. He walked out of the house, leaving her to trail along behind him with the lantern. She had no idea where he was going or why—or why he should want her along except as the go-between for whatever he wanted done.

She held the lantern higher, trying to light his way and hers, stumbling occasionally on the rough ground. As they walked along, she suddenly understood the reason for their departure. The company doctor had fallen ill with the typhoid. Mr. Mannion must have prevailed upon her father—probably for a significant sum—to take his place.

They were going to the hotel.

* * *

"Leave me."

He thought at first that he must not have spoken aloud, because they didn't stop pulling on his arms and dragging him upward. He tried to say the words again, but it hurt too much. His mouth was parched and dry. He could feel the skin split with the effort. They kept pulling and pulling on him. He didn't have the strength to resist. He didn't have the strength even to open his eyes to see his tormentors. He could only suffer.

Suffer...

Voices swirled around him. A woman's voice.

"Catryn...?"

No. Not Catryn. Never Catryn.

"Can you hear me, Tregear?" a man's voice said, and he tried to get away from the intrusion. He just wanted to be left in peace.

Rest in peace.

Die in peace.

"Catryn?"

"Who is Catherine?" a woman's voice asked, and he turned his face away.

"Don't know, miss," a third voice said. "Sweetheart, maybe—or one of the—well, you know what I mean. He's going up to the house, is he? Don't surprise me none. He's Mannion's prize, he is. If anybody can put money in a mine owner's pockets, it's Tregear. If he don't die, o' course. There's some that says he's too mean to die. It ain't meanness that would keep a man like Tregear alive, though. It's just that he don't care one way or t'other. I noticed a long time ago how that works out. A man what don't care about dying—well, he'll live forever. Same with money, miss. If he don't crave it, seems like it just falls in his lap. Best pack up his things over there, miss. If you take him away and leave all his belongings, they won't be here if he gets back.''

Tregear tried to object to the plan. He wasn't going anywhere, and he didn't want his belongings moved. He strained to raise himself up, but the effort was too much for him. He hurt so. Everywhere. All the time.

"Try to drink this," the woman said very close to his ear. "Just a little at a time. It will make you feel better."

He felt the rim of the metal cup against his lips, then the slightly warm liquid. His mouth was so dry. He swallowed some of what she offered, and the pain was excruciating.

"More," she said. "I know it hurts your throat—but you need this."

Need?

He had long since given up *needing*.

But he took another swallow. And another and another until she moved the cup away.

"Can we take him out now?" a voice said.

"Yes—take him straight to the house. Mr. Mannion's gone on ahead to show you where."

Hands rolled him roughly onto his side.

"Ain't he hot, though—that there fever's got a real hold on him, ain't it, miss?"

"Yes," the woman said.

"You reckon he's going to die?"

She didn't answer the question put to her, and somehow Tregear was in a place with different sensations. Darkness. Damp, cool air. Tree frogs. Crickets. Blowing horses.

He was being put into the back of a wagon, and he gave himself up to it, no longer struggling against the inevitable. There was no point in it.

If he had been able, he would have smiled. What a long way he must have come to arrive at that realization. Tregear, who might give out, but never gave in no matter what the odds.

Never.

A cool hand touched his forehead.

"Catryn!" He reached out blindly, trying to find her, trying to keep her from disappearing again.

"Tregear, you're hurting me," she said close to his ear.

Hurting?

"Tregear—"

He let go, let his hand fall.

"It'll be all right," she said, but he didn't believe it. He would never believe her again.

Chapter Eight

The wagon stopped. Tregear braced himself, expecting to be dragged bodily off the tailgate and carried like a sack of grain again.

Nothing happened—except conversation. He could hear men's voices somewhere nearby, but not what they said. He relaxed slightly and looked upward.

Stars. Thousands and thousands of stars. But no wind from the sea.

Where is the wind?

He couldn't feel it, couldn't hear the breakers.

He closed his eyes again and tried to force his mind into some kind of logical thought. Perhaps this was the charnel wagon. Perhaps they thought he was dead, and they were taking him to the cemetery. He felt dead—more dead than alive at any rate. Someone sat very near to him, but he didn't turn his head to see. It was far too much trouble.

The voices came closer.

"The other doctors have arrived. They can handle the situation."

"You're the best there is hereabouts—as he is. I want him alive and I trust you will see to it."

"I am not a miracle worker, sir. The disease has come

upon him with great speed. I doubt my treatment or anyone else's will help. He is already far gone.''

"Far gone or not, I don't intend to lose my investment.''

"I have my own practice to attend to,'' the other one said. "I cannot in good conscience remain here for the sake of one man.''

"Then take him with you. I don't care *where* he recovers, only that he does it under your watchful eye. It will be worth your while, I can assure you.''

Tregear made a small sound. He was cold suddenly. So cold.

"Father,'' he heard a woman say as the shaking began.

"He needs opium,'' the man said.

"There's none left—''

The wagon began to move again, and Tregear stopped listening, stopped caring. There was only the pain and the cold.

Jane woke with a start when the wagon stopped abruptly. She sat there for a moment, gripping the reins, trying to get her bearings.

She was home, she thought incredulously—or almost. The horses began to prance, and she spoke to them gently, thankful that they knew the way back without her guidance and that they had halted not far from the barn instead of wandering into the vegetable patch or upsetting the wagon in the middle of the creek bed. She looked back over her shoulder. Tregear had been quiet for a long time.

She tied the reins securely and climbed down. She was stiff and tired, but she was reassured by the fact that she was also hungry. That alone must mean that she wasn't getting sick—not yet.

It surprised her that the lamps were lit in the surgery, and she realized suddenly that there were people lying on the porch on makeshift pallets. She saw Milla come out of the surgery door, stepping carefully among them to reach the steps to the yard. She was literally wearing her sleeping baby tied up like a bundle of clothing in a shawl she'd put around her neck and over one shoulder. She held her little girl close as she ran to the wagon.

"Miss Jane, I'm so glad you're back! All these sick people are asking for somebody to take care of them—"

"Are Mother and Eugenie still here?"

"No, Miss Jane. They left hours ago. Mrs. Ennis tried to take me along, too, but there wasn't no room for me and the baby, and the doctor told the man I wasn't to go, so he wouldn't take me." She sniffed loudly. "I've been so scared, Miss Jane. All these people started coming here after they left—I didn't know what to do. I told them the doctor was in the village and I didn't know if he'd be back any time soon. They was give out by the time they got here, and I didn't have the heart to send them away. I—I—"

"Don't cry," Jane said. "We have to figure out how to get Tregear inside."

"Tregear? Is that Tregear? Lord, Miss Jane, there ain't no room in the surgery for him. There's people lying everywhere in there, too. Did you come by yourself?"

"Father's on his way. I came on with the wagon."

"Oh, Miss Jane, aren't you scared about going out in the dark like that?"

"Yes. But to tell you the truth, I'm getting kind of used to it."

Milla missed the heavy-handed irony of her remark altogether.

Jane climbed back into the driver's seat. "I'm going to move the wagon close to the house. We'll have to take him in there."

"Where are you going to put him, Miss Jane?"

"My bed," she said. Her father had already set the precedent. If she made an independent decision, then it was she who would be inconvenienced.

"We'll never get him up the stairs," Milla said.

"Go put your baby down someplace safe so you can help me. Maybe Tregear can walk a little."

"He might walk, but he ain't going to be climbing no steps. What are we going to do with all these people, Miss Jane?"

"First things first, Milla—is there anything to eat? I'm so hungry my knees are shaking."

"Corn bread left over from this morning. And maybe some dried apples. I'll get some for you. And I've been keeping a kettle on in the house in case the doctor got back and wanted to mix up medicine for these folk. I'll be back in a minute."

Jane had to use the whip to persuade the horses to move away from the barn, but eventually she managed it. Milla returned with the cradle balanced awkwardly on one hip, the corn bread and apples wrapped in a cloth and laid inside.

"Here, Miss Jane. You eat and I'll put the baby to bed on the porch."

The horses were prancing nervously again. Jane had to struggle to hold on to them. Milla put the cradle and baby and the cloth holding the corn bread down on the porch and took their heads.

"I reckon we'd better unhitch the team and take them to the barn—before they bust loose and go on their own. I fear we're going to need them before this is all over."

Jane jumped down from the wagon seat again and began unfastening the traces so that Milla could lead the team away. Then she took the corn bread, devouring the crum-

bling pieces where she stood and with none of the grace
and manners her mother and the girls' school she had attended in the capitol had taught her. The corn bread was
cold and greasy but she had no idea how it actually tasted.
She'd had no interest in savoring, only in keeping body and
soul together.

She ate a few of the dried apples, as well, and put the
rest in her pocket. Then she stood up on the hub of the
wheel to reach Tregear. She had wanted desperately to
know where he was and how he fared. The last thing she
expected was to find herself responsible for him.

He was still feverish, and he spoke a random word from
time to time. She couldn't understand any of it. She wasn't
certain if it was English or if he had lapsed into the accent
Lolly had declared just as unintelligible as the Cornish language itself. In his right mind, he might believe he would
never go home again, but in his delirium, she thought, he
must surely have done so.

"Tregear," she whispered, but he didn't respond. Anything would have been welcome, even the name he'd called
out so many times.

Catherine.

She gave a quiet sigh and pushed aside her curiosity. It
was none of her concern who the woman he called was or
that he might die with her name on his lips.

"Tregear," she said, again trying to rouse him.

Her father was right. He was too far gone. And she and
Milla would never get him into the house. She would have
to leave him here in the damp night air until someone arrived who would help move him. She sighed heavily, wondering what her father's plans for Tregear were. He hadn't
wanted to take on his care, wouldn't have if the fee Mannion offered had not been so significant.

She got down and went into the house, feeling her way

up the stairs as best she could in the dark. She made her way into her bedchamber and located a candle, but she had difficulty lighting it. It surprised her that her hands were shaking so.

When she finally got the candle to burn, she removed a quilt from the foot of her bed and lighted her way back down the stairs and outside. She let the wax from the candle drip on the edge of the wagon bed and stuck the candle into it. Tregear was shivering again, and she covered him with the quilt as best she could. He would have to be sponged with vinegar water soon to keep his fever from soaring any higher.

Milla's baby began to fret on the porch, and Jane stepped close enough to rock the cradle.

"Charia...Charia..." she crooned. "This is not the time, little girl."

But babies cared nothing for convenience, and she began to cry louder. Jane pulled the cradle closer and lifted her up and put her over her shoulder. It didn't help.

Milla came hurrying from the barn, unbuttoning her bodice as she approached. Jane handed the baby over in relief and left them both to return to Tregear. He was quieter now, but he was breathing rapidly. A lot of money had exchanged hands on his behalf this night. She wondered if he realized it.

But money or no, she couldn't do the impossible. She took the candle, and went to see about the people lying on the porch. They all seemed to be sleeping, some of them heavily. She thought at first look that they were perhaps not ill yet, but had accompanied someone who was. She moved as quietly as she could so as not to wake them. Sick or well, she had nothing to offer them.

She moved to the inside of the surgery. A woman and three small children lay on the floor just inside the door, and two men on the far side of the room. An elderly woman lay on Milla's bed in the side room, her eyes closed, her bony fingers repeatedly clutching at the top quilt. A younger woman sat upright on the floor, her head resting against the mattress—a daughter, or perhaps a granddaughter. She didn't stir when Jane walked closer.

Jane gave a quiet sigh, praying she could make enough of the infusion to go around. Her father still had the saddlebag with the packets she'd put together. Even if she could find enough of the ingredients here, it would take time to make the infusion, and there was nothing to be done for any of them until she had that ready. She gathered up what goldenseal and cayenne and bayberry she could find and took all of it back to the house, checking on Tregear once again as she passed the wagon. He was lying quietly.

She went into the kitchen and stoked up the fire, and when the kettle was bubbling again, she carefully measured out the amount of each of the herbs and put them into several bowls. Then she poured the boiling water and left the concoction to steep. The sun would be up soon, and she tried to feel encouraged. Her father would surely have returned by then.

She walked out onto the porch carrying the candle. Milla sat with her back against the wall, holding her now sated baby, nodding in sleep.

"Milla," she whispered, touching the girl on the shoulder. "Go lie down."

"I can't, Miss Jane. I don't have nowhere—"

"Go lie down on Miss Chappell's bed. She won't—" Jane stopped. She was going to say that Miss Chappell wouldn't mind, but that couldn't have been farther from the truth. Miss Chappell minded everything.

"She won't be back any time soon," Jane amended. "Go on now."

"What are you going to do, Miss Jane?" she asked sleepily.

"I'll keep watch over Tregear. You sleep. One of us has to be able to be up and around in the morning."

Milla stared at her, then nodded. She got up from the porch carefully so as not to wake the baby. When she opened the front door, she looked back.

"I'm glad you're seeing to him. Tregear, he ain't nearly as bad as people want to make out he is," she said.

"No," Jane said, thinking of the way he had coaxed Eugenie through her humiliation at the piano. She walked to the wagon and climbed over the side, taking a place at Tregear's head so that she could see him. She would just sit here by him until the infusion had cooled, then she would try to get some of it down him. She wondered idly what had become of Bobby and the packets she had given him. And Sion, for that matter. She hadn't seen either of them among the sick at the hotel.

She shivered suddenly, but it was from near exhaustion, not cold. She reached out to touch Tregear's forehead.

Cooler now, she thought. She pulled her knees up and briefly rested her head on them, but then she reached out to touch him again, this time simply because she wanted to. She gently let her fingers run over his brow, then the stubble of his beard. She could just make out the shape of his mouth and the way his eyelashes lay upon his cheek.

He gave a heavy, wavering sigh, and she jerked her hand away, but he didn't rouse.

She was so tired suddenly. She couldn't keep her eyes open any longer, and she let them go closed, resting her head on her knees again.

Don't die, Tregear, she thought. *Please.*

She lifted her head suddenly at the sound of distant thunder.

"Oh, no," she whispered.

"What's...wrong?" Tregear asked, making her jump.

She was so startled she made no attempt to answer him.

"You...touched me...." he said. "Why?"

"I—I wanted to see if you were dead."

"Am I?"

"Not yet."

"Well. That's something, I...guess."

She leaned closer to look at him. His eyes were bright with fever, but she thought he was in his right mind. For the moment.

The thunder rumbled again, closer now, and the wind was picking up.

"Where...are we?"

"Outside the surgery."

"Where are...my belongings—the hammer and tools?"

"Everything is here in the wagon."

"Are you going to leave me in the...rain?"

"I don't know. I may have to."

"Don't let the tools...get wet. Take them...someplace dry."

"All right."

"I think I can walk," he said after a moment.

"So I've heard," she said, getting to her knees and moving closer to his side.

"Your brother...didn't believe me."

"Neither do I—and I don't have Coley and Bobby Reid to fall back on. If I help you, can you make it to the porch?"

"No," he said, but he was trying to sit up, and she couldn't keep from smiling.

"If you fall, I fear you'll stay where you land," she said in warning.

"I...understand."

"Wait," she said. "Do you know who I am?"

"Miss Chappell," he said, and it took her a moment to realize that sick or not, he was actually teasing her.

"I think I have been worrying about you unnecessarily," she said. She managed to get him upright, but he began to topple immediately. She had to hold on to him to keep him from falling, his head resting heavily on her shoulder.

"Perhaps...not," he said. "Let me...I think..."

He didn't finish the sentence. He slid from her grasp and lay back on the wagon floor.

"Tregear," she said. "Tregear—"

Wherever his brief lucidity had come from, it was gone again.

She made a small sound of defeat, and she didn't realize that a man stood nearby until he spoke.

"You needing help here, miss?"

She looked around sharply at him, recognizing him as one of the people who had been asleep on the surgery porch.

"I need to get him in the house—and upstairs."

"Well, I can tote him for you. Reckon that would be worth the medicine my old lady is needing? She's sick over yonder in the doctor's little house. I ain't got no money till I sell my harvest."

"It would be worth it," Jane said.

She moved to the end of the wagon and got down. The man didn't wait for her instructions. He pulled Tregear upward and slung him over his shoulder. She grabbed up the quilt and the candle and the satchel with Tregear's belongings and led the way. The satchel held more mining equipment than anything else, and she had to struggle not to drop it. Clearly, the man was much stronger than he looked. He managed to get Tregear inside and up the stairs, dumping him unceremoniously on the bed Jane barely got turned down in time.

"Anything else you'd be needing?" he asked, looking around the room.

"No. Thank you. I'll bring the medicine for your wife as soon as it's ready."

"Much obliged," he said. Then, "Are you the doctor's girl?"

"I'm his older daughter."

The man nodded. "I heard tell of you—or my old lady has. She was saying how your daddy was taking you around with him—teaching you doctoring. Is that the truth? Is he teaching a *girl* something like that?"

"Sometimes," Jane answered.

He stared at her as if he was trying to decide whether or not he believed it. "Well, I'd best go see if *she* needs anything. She's a good woman. I'd hate to have to break in another one."

Jane had nothing to say to his bold assumption that he himself would escape the disease which just might inflict the inconvenience of having to remarry—if he'd ever bothered with the technicality of participating in an actual wedding ceremony in the first place. It was one of her father's constant criticisms of the people here—that they were so casual about having their unions sanctified by the law or by the church. He had no patience with bastardy—which caused her to still marvel that Milla had been allowed to remain as long as she had.

She needed to see to Tregear, and she barely noticed when the man left the room.

"Tregear," she said quietly, because she didn't want to wake up Milla and the baby if the commotion of getting him upstairs hadn't already done so. He was shivering again, and he didn't answer her.

She had to fetch the water and vinegar, and she took the pitcher from the wash basin and chanced leaving him long enough to go downstairs. Milla, bless her, had the water bucket full. She filled it quickly, sloshing water onto the floor in her haste. But she didn't bother about cleaning it up. She tested the infusions sitting on the worktable with a fingertip. They were all still too hot, but she picked up one of the bowls and seated it in the top of the pitcher. She put a small cup in her pocket, then took up the vinegar jug and several cloths from her mother's linen chest. She managed to get back up the stairs without dropping anything.

Tregear lay where she left him, only more restlessly so. He reached out for something—or someone—only he could see from time to time.

She shoved his satchel under the bed out of the way, and poured some water and vinegar into the washbasin. Then she wet one of the cloths and began to wipe his face and neck. His hand gripped her wrist, but not tightly enough to prevent her from doing her task. He gave a heavy sigh. She took his hand away and wiped it and the part of his arm she could reach. She needed to get his shirt off.

And his breeches.

She should have asked the man who had carried him upstairs to do it, but she'd been too embarrassed to do so. She threw back the quilt and unbuttoned the waist of his breeches and began to try to pull them off. He was no longer wearing the clothes he'd had on at the Mannion house. These were his working clothes, mended and re-mended to get as much wear out of them as possible. Tregear was dead weight and no help, which, when she thought about it, was probably for the best. The last thing she wanted was to have him know that she was stripping him naked.

She kept pulling until she had the breeches down to his

knees, and she made no pretense of trying not to look at him. She looked—marveling at the strength of his body. He was so muscular, his abdomen, his thighs.

And the male part of him.

She had seen baby boys undressed before, but never a grown man, never anyone so powerfully masculine. She was surprised by the amount of scarring he had on his belly and thighs, a legacy of his years in the mines, she supposed. Even so, he was...beautiful, and she wondered how many other women had seen him like this.

No. Not like this. This, now, when he was helpless wasn't what she was curious about. She was wondering about the women who had lain next to him, who had touched him with a lover's touch, kissed him, known every part of his man's body. She knew nothing of such things, except for what she could imagine, and she wanted desperately to know. Moreover, she wanted to know how it would be with him.

She gave a quiet sigh.

When she finally had the breeches in her hands, she realized that the waistband was weighted down with something. She ran her fingers along the underside.

Money. There were coins sewed inside all the way around for safekeeping.

She pulled the quilt up over his lower body and hid the breeches in the bottom of her cedar chest. Then she tried to remove his shirt. It was hard going, but easier than getting his breeches off had been. She gave no thought to the impropriety of what she was doing, only to the necessity. She wanted him to live.

She finally got the shirt over his head, and she immediately saw that Eugenie's rumor of a ''tattoo'' was indeed grounded in fact. It was high on the left side of his chest, a kind of circle with three swirling arms inside it, each one arising from the center point and ending in a dot. It suggested a kind of spinning motion to her—and not much else.

She began to sponge him off again, his arms and legs and finally his chest. Then she took up one of her palmetto fans and fanned him until his skin dried and grew hot again and she repeated the entire process. She continued the cycle of sponging and fanning, losing all track of time, until his body finally stayed cool.

He spoke now and then, softly mumbled words she couldn't understand. Again, she had the impression that he was not speaking English, that he was lost in another place and time.

His breath suddenly caught. "She did not lie!" he said distinctly. "No—where is she—?"

"Tregear," she whispered. "Tregear!" His eyelids fluttered, but he didn't open them.

She gave a quiet sigh and put the cloth aside. She poured some water into the cup and dipped her fingers into it, gently moistening his parched lips again and again until she thought she had given him some relief.

The infusion had cooled, and she used the cup she'd brought to dip a small amount out. If she couldn't get Tregear to drink it, she didn't want to waste any more than was necessary.

Surprisingly, he took what she offered him, swallowing painfully. Then more, until she had gotten the necessary dose into him. She waited, afraid that he wouldn't keep it down, but he did, and she sighed in relief. She wet his lips again, and the cloth for his forehead. She pulled the one chair in the room to the bedside and sat down close enough to fan him. After a time, her arm grew weary, and she propped her elbow on the edge of the bed, still trying to keep a current of air going.

She suddenly nodded off, and she stood up to fight off the sleep that threatened to overtake her. She touched Tregear's face again. He was much cooler now. And quieter.

She waited for a moment, until she was satisfied that he could be left alone, then went downstairs to see to the infusions.

She strained all the bowls into a large jug and picked up several tin dosing cups her father had had made, hooking them over her fingers. He always carried a few of the cups with him, not to leave with a patient, but to show them in their own drinking cups and dippers what the correct dosages would be.

The sun was coming up when she stepped out into the yard. She crossed quickly to the surgery. The man who had carried Tregear stood anxiously on the porch. She gave him a cup and filled it carefully.

"Get your wife to drink all of this," she said. "Slowly, so she doesn't choke or throw it back up again."

He nodded. "Much obliged."

She walked among the people on the porch and on the inside, giving out the half cupful of the concoction she prayed would help to each one who had symptoms. There were not as many people actually sick as she feared, and she had a significant amount of the infusion left.

She reassured them all that her father would be returning, then hurried back to the house. She looked in on Milla, who slept heavily on top of Miss Chappell's counterpane. The baby was awake in its cradle, but not yet fussy.

Jane walked down the hallway to Tregear. He was asleep, breathing heavily. She sat down in the chair and stared at him, and for the first time, she willingly faced the truth. She was as captivated by this wild Cornishman as Eugenie would ever be.

Chapter Nine

"**W**here is it! Where—!"

Jane stood in the doorway, not certain whether or not Tregear was actually awake. But he was suddenly trying to get out of bed, and she ran to him, placing both hands on his shoulders.

"It's all right," she said. "Lie back—"

"No," he said, fighting her off. "I want to find it. I have to see—"

"Coley—" Jane called, still struggling to keep him from falling. "Coley!"

She could hear the black man running up the stairs.

"Help me—" she said when he reached the doorway.

He came quickly to the bedside. "Easy, Cap'n," he said, holding Tregear at bay. "What is it you looking for?"

"I need to see it," Tregear said. "I can't—"

"Don't worry none, Cap. Old Coley will get it for you," the man said. "You rest now—before you go and hurt yourself. Mr. Mannion, he wouldn't be liking that, now would he? Here—you let Coley help you, you hear?"

Tregear lay back, because his strength was no match for Coley's and he couldn't do otherwise.

"You're not...Coley," Tregear said. "You...talk too...damn much."

"That's right, Cap," Coley said to placate him. "You and me, we'll be going to work soon, though. No talking then. Just finding the gold."

"I have to get back. I don't want...to die...without seeing the sea again. I have to get back!"

"You'll see it, Cap. You got the good luck mark on you—ain't you told Coley that time and time? And Miss Jane, she ain't going to let the death angel get you. She stay by you night and day keeping her away."

"Jane!" he cried. "Where—where—is it?"

She suddenly realized what he was worried about. She moved closer and whispered in his ear.

"It's safe. All of it. Don't worry."

He looked at her and tried to reach up to touch her. He couldn't get free of Coley's grasp.

"You swear?" he asked.

"I swear," she said.

Tregear sighed heavily and closed his eyes. Coley released him as soon as he was certain that he had calmed.

"I think it's all right now," Jane said. "You can go back to helping Milla with the people in the surgery." She took a deep breath. "Are there any more?" she asked, not because she wanted to know, but because she couldn't help it.

"Two come, and two more go," Coley said, and Jane nodded. She didn't have to ask how they had gone.

Two more.

The church bell sounded the death knell nearly all the time now, so much so that she hardly noticed it anymore, and she no longer tried to keep up with whether it rang for man, woman or child.

She didn't ask specifically who had died since the sun

came up. So many had arrived at the surgery in the last ten days, she no longer knew any of their names. There was so much to do and no time to eat, much less sleep. She and her father, and Milla and Coley and Bobby worked night and day to give the sick what little comfort they could. At times, her father tried to instruct her about some aspect of the illness, but she was too exhausted to learn. She had no idea how Mrs. Oliver and Miss Chappell fared; she didn't know if her mother and Eugenie had escaped the illness and were safely biding their time in Salisbury.

But, when she could, she took the time to feel grateful—that Mr. Mannion had sent Coley and Bobby to help, that she and Milla and her father remained well.

That Tregear still lived.

He had been so sick, and there were times when she did not think he would make it through the night. Most of the time he didn't know where he was, didn't recognize her or Coley. Even after so many days, she couldn't measure whether or not he was getting better. The only thing she knew was that he fought his illness as if it were a living being.

She sat down in the chair by his bed, and she reached out to touch his face as she had done so many times now. This time he stirred under her hand and reached up with his to keep it there, as if the coolness of her skin brought him some comfort. She didn't try to pull away. She closed her eyes and savored it, knowing it was Catherine he held on to, not Jane Ennis. After a moment, she leaned forward and rested her head on the edge of the bed, letting the fatigue wash over her. She had no idea how long she stayed that way. When she opened her eyes again, she was aware that the shadows had changed and that some sound had awakened her. When she looked around, her stonily silent father stood in the doorway.

He said nothing.

Forbidding only makes the fruit more desirable.

Who had told her that?

Miss Chappell. It was Miss Chappell. And how long ago that seemed.

She stood up after a moment and forced herself to walk into the hallway. She made it as far as the downstairs before a great swirling blackness seemed to encroach upon her vision. She heard Milla say her name and tried to answer, but there was nothing more.

When she opened her eyes again, she was surprised to find herself in Miss Chappell's bed. She lay very still, hoping to find oblivion again, until a desperate need to heed the call of nature drove her to get up.

It was dark outside—too dark to make the trip to the privy. The window was open. She could hear the night sounds, the murmuring voices of the people camped outside. She could smell the smoke from their campfires.

She threw her legs over the edge of the bed. Someone— Milla—had put her into her night dress, and she didn't even remember it. But she didn't feel ill, just hungry and a bit befuddled and unsteady.

She listened for the sound of anyone else moving about upstairs, then got out of bed and found the chamber pot in the dark. Her dress lay over the back of the one chair in the room, and she dressed quickly. Then, she lit a candle, catching a glimpse of herself in the small mirror. Her hair had been braided and wrapped into a coil at the nape of her neck when last she remembered. There wasn't much left of the arrangement now.

She undid the rest of it and raked her fingers through her hair, finally tying it back with a scarlet ribbon and letting it hang down her back the way she had when she was ten. She moved to the washbasin to wash the sleep from her eyes, then stepped out into the hallway and went in search of Tregear.

The house seemed very quiet. She walked to her bed-chamber door, pausing for a moment before she went inside. There was a candle lit, and Tregear seemed much as when she had left him—except that he was so still. She entered quietly and stopped by the bed, watching him closely. She looked down to uncover his arm and touch him, to take his wrist. His pulse beat slow and full under her fingertips. His skin was cool and dry.

When she looked back at his face, she was startled to find him awake and watching. She didn't say anything, because she didn't know if he was in his right mind or not.

"What…is it?" he asked.

She still hesitated, but he seemed different from when he'd been so determined to know what became of his coin.

"What is what?" she asked finally.

"The…question."

"I have no question."

"I thought you…did. I always…think you are… wondering about something."

"Only if you are in your right mind," she said, and he nearly smiled.

"I suspect…you've wondered that for some time… now."

She didn't deny it. She stood there, ill at ease under his scrutiny, knowing her father would want her at hand if he knew she was awake.

"Whose…bed have I taken?" he asked.

"Mine."

"You gave up your bed…for me?"

"You needed it more than I did."

He tried to swallow and couldn't manage it. As she had many times, she dipped her fingers in the nearby pitcher without thinking and pressed them against his lips—only it was different this time. He was aware of it, and suddenly so was she. He stared into her eyes, and she let her fingers rest against his mouth too long.

She jerked her hand away with an abruptness they both ignored.

"I...still see a...question," he said after a moment. "Now is a good time to...ask. When I know who...and where I am...and I'm still...breathing."

It wasn't like him to want to talk, even when he was well, and it occurred to her that perhaps he didn't want to be alone and he was trying to keep her there.

She sat down in the chair.

Catherine. She wanted to know about Catherine.

"The mine," she said. "I often wonder about it. I wonder what it's like so far under the ground."

He was looking directly into her eyes, and if he doubted her sincerity, she couldn't tell.

"Dark," he said simply. "With a darkness you could never...imagine. And beautiful."

"Beautiful?"

"The light...from a candle goes a long...way in that kind of...blackness. Not like...in a house. The walls sparkle in some...places. Like thousands and thousands of...tiny stars. You can't believe...what you are seeing."

"They say you're never afraid when you're down."

"Do they? I am. When I hear the Knockers."

"You've...heard them?"

"Twice. I was only a boy the first time. I was...following after the man who taught me how to...blast. The tapping...tapping and tapping...came first. And then the trapped water broke...through the wall. Men who didn't heed it...died. Drowned. They didn't make it to the ladder. A mine can kill you...quick or slow. Or not at all. Or it can leave you a crippled…beggar on the village streets."

"But you still do it."

"Yes. It's all I…know."

Jane didn't say anything to that, in spite of fact that she disagreed. He had refinements—music, manners, when he chose to use them. Mining was not all he knew. Even so, when she listened to him speak, she could hear the remnants of the Cornwall accent wander through his speech.

"What else?" he asked.

"The tattoo. I wonder what is its meaning."

She had just given him a perfect opening to be crude, to embarrass her because of the intimacy they'd shared during his illness, but he didn't take it.

"It's for…good luck. For the three omens. Do you understand?"

"No."

He closed his eyes, and for a moment, she thought he had gone to sleep.

"In Cornwall one thing alone…doesn't foretell good luck," he said, looking at her again. "One thing alone doesn't foretell bad luck. It takes…three to have…meaning."

"Like what?"

"For good luck…a red sunrise. And a ship at full sail."

"Isn't a red sunrise bad for sailing ships?"

"For the ship—not for the those waiting on the rocks in the hope of a wreck to salvage."

"Have you done that? Waited on the rocks to salvage the cargo of a wrecked ship?"

"I have. And would do it…again. You should not… condemn what you don't…understand."

"I understand," she said. And she wondered if he was

as bold retrieving the wreckage of ship as he was going underground.

"Do you?"

"You're talking about desperation. Desperation is a hard taskmaster—or so Reverend Oliver says. And the third good omen?"

"A woman with child."

They stared at each other. She should have felt even more awkward after such a remark, but she didn't. Even knowing suddenly that he wanted to touch her, she didn't.

The realization didn't frighten her as it might have with any other man. She merely marveled at it and at her response to it. She wanted to come closer. She wanted to touch him, as well.

"What else?" he asked.

"I..." she began, then faltered.

"Go on. Ask."

"I wonder at your having dark hair and eyes. The other Cornwall men do not."

"The Saracen's...youngest daughter," he said, and once again she thought that his mind was wandering. "People say it comes from the Crusades...a Cornwall man...a knight held for ransom. The Saracen who imprisoned him had a daughter. She fell in love with him and...when the ransom was paid and he came home again, to save her life he brought her and their child with him."

"And did she live happily ever after?"

"I think not. Likely...the wife he already had...poisoned her. But they do say those of us who have the look of the Saracen come from her."

"Saracens and knights. It seems a magical place—Cornwall."

"You mustn't forget King Arthur," he said.

He was looking into her eyes again.

"Have you no questions?" she abruptly asked.

"I have...two."

"Then ask them."

"Where is my...money?"

"There," she said. "In the chest. The satchel with the rest of your belongings is under the bed."

"If I die, I want the mine tools given to Bobby Reid," he said. "He's to have the pick and hammer—and the steel borer and the tapering rod. The money goes to Oliver. He knows what to do with it."

She didn't try to dissuade him of his notions. She merely nodded.

"And the second question?"

He looked at her, as if he were searching for something, some expression on her face or in her eyes that he needed to find or wanted to understand. "Are you not...sad?" he finally asked.

"Sad? Because you are planning on dying?"

"Sad that you...can't marry," he said, ignoring her flippancy.

"I don't know what you mean," she said. "What makes you think I cannot marry?"

"Your father will not give his blessing...no matter...who comes asking. He knows you...will not take a husband without...it."

Jane frowned, still not understanding. She had wanted to believe he was clearheaded, but now she wasn't at all sure if he was talking to her or reliving some incident with Catherine. He closed his eyes again, and he didn't say anything more.

"Tregear," she said, and he opened his eyes again.

"Who says my father will not give his blessing?"

He didn't answer her. He merely looked at her.

"Who?" she asked again.

He took a quiet breath. "I think...Sion wants money...for you—"

"Sion?"

"—and Eugenie."

He closed his eyes again. Jane stood—and then sat back down again, her mind in turmoil. Tregear wasn't confused—and yet he must be. The entire notion was absurd. Even if it was true, how would he know such a thing?

It isn't true. It's some wild rumor conceived by people who have no better entertainment.

Except for the one small detail that couldn't be denied. She had no suitors. Even as isolated as she and Eugenie lived, there should have been someone interested in Dr. Ennis' daughter—for her supposed dowry, if nothing else. All this time, she hadn't really concerned herself about it. She had been aware of her beauless situation, but she hadn't believed there was an actual reason for it, and certainly she had never considered that the reason might be her father. If her father had made it known that he would not give his blessing and there would be no dowry, then she couldn't help but conclude that she had lost all of her appeal.

Who here would dare go against Dr. Ennis?

Money for me and Eugenie, she suddenly thought. Did that mean both of them were to stay spinsters?

"Miss Jane," Milla said behind her, and Jane looked around.

"Your father is wanting you—he said I was to wake you. He said I was to tell you to make a decoction of bayberry bark right away."

Jane stood and looked down at Tregear. "Is Coley around?" she asked. "I'm not sure Tregear is in his right mind."

"He's been clear all day, Miss Jane—he knew me every time I seen him, anyway. I checked on him whenever I come up here to see about you. You had a nice sleep, you did. You're looking better—like our Miss Jane again."

Jane glanced at her. She was smiling, and Jane managed to return it, no matter how little she felt like smiling. She didn't want to leave Tregear. She had wanted to be in his company under any circumstances, but now she had real questions, and she wanted answers.

"Your father is in the surgery, Miss Jane. He says bring the bayberry drink there."

Jane sighed and went downstairs to see to it. But her father didn't wait until the bayberry decoction was ready. He came to the kitchen in search of her. She looked up, startled to find him in the doorway.

"It hasn't boiled long enough, Father," she said, but he didn't leave. He stood staring at her.

"Is something the matter?" she asked, afraid suddenly that he had had some word from her mother.

"You possess all the qualities a man would wish for," he said. "In his son."

Jane looked at him, unsure if the remark was meant to be a compliment or a criticism.

Neither, she immediately decided. It was more a complaint than anything, and one not aimed at her, but at whatever power had brought such irony about.

"You have the gift for healing Sion should have had," he went on. "You have both the intellect and the necessary audacity. You are even dauntless enough to steal the knowledge from me you should not have."

She would have taken exception to that, but he held up his hand for her to be silent.

"Even so, there is still a great deal for you to learn. I have decided that such potential as you possess should not be wasted. Female or not, I will have the last word here. I will teach you. I will make a doctor of you. What I know, you will know—if you agree to the terms.''

''What terms, Father?''

''I do not intend to waste my time. I will not begin this and then see my efforts frivolously tossed aside in favor of some more amusing interest. If you want to learn the craft from me, then you must give your complete dedication. I will accept no less. You must have no other purpose but to learn and ultimately to practice what I will teach you. You must reconcile yourself to the fact that there will be no room for anything else in your life, now or in the future. Do you understand?''

Jane stood looking at him, and what she understood suddenly was his duplicity. Unless she was very mistaken, Tregear had been telling the truth, and her father was asking her to voluntarily relinquish all thoughts of marriage— something he never intended for her in the first place. But he wouldn't forbid it outright. He would negotiate it. She understood, too, that everything he had ever bought for her—the education at the girls' school in Raleigh, the books, the newspapers he had sent to him all the way from Philadelphia—had been for *his* benefit, not hers. He had not been making her into a prize catch so that some impressed suitor would take her off his hands. He had been making her into something he could keep.

He had never been able to abide the company of the people here except in the most superficial way. He found them lacking in everything he required of society—and so he had set about to create someone more to his liking. Her function would be to test his intellect and keep it sharp, and Eugenie—Eugenie would provide the artistic accoutrements—the music and the singing and the poetry readings. He could move them all on to the secluded land he'd supposedly bought and never be bothered with outsiders again—unless it suited him.

"Are these the same terms you would have set for Sion?" she abruptly asked.

"There was no need. Sion is a man. I have asked you a question. Do you understand them?"

"Yes," she said, turning away to see to the decoction. "I understand."

"You will think on it, and you will give me your decision in a few days' time. Whatever you decide is binding. There will be no second thoughts either way," he said, turning to go. "Bring the decoction to the surgery when it's ready."

She stood in the middle of the kitchen after he'd gone, her mind in turmoil. It occurred to her suddenly that her mother wasn't privy to her father's plan for her and Eugenie. Her mother had given them both inlaid mahogany marriage chests, and helped her, as the older daughter, to fill it with scores of embroidered linens and choice pieces of porcelain to take with her when she wed. She remembered, too, a wedding she had attended shortly after the Olivers arrived. It had been the reverend's first marriage service. A young man who worked in the mines had married a girl from one of the German farms along Dutch Creek, and the happiness of the occasion had shown in both their faces.

"You're next," the bride had said to her—within earshot of a number of the men, most of them miners. And they had all looked at her and laughed. She had thought that she understood their crudeness at the time, but she realized now that she hadn't, not completely.

They had known she would not be allowed to marry. How many other times had she been a laughingstock and not realized it?

She gave a wavering sigh.

Are you not sad?

Yes, she was sad. Sad that she had no prerogative in matters pertaining to her own life, unless she was willing to go against her father. Sad for herself and especially for Eugenie.

But she was feeling more than that. She was angry. She hated that people knew about her father's eccentric decision almost as much as she hated the decision itself. She wanted to yell and throw things. And she wanted to weep. Sion was the beloved only son, and yet he had been all but obliterated from the family. Nothing of him remained in the house—and all because he had refused to follow the path laid out for him. She had no expectations that she would not suffer the same fate if she dared defy her father.

She could hear him returning, and she took a deep breath.

"Jane," he said from the doorway. "I have been called to the village. Leave the bayberry and attend to the next doses of the fever infusion for these people."

He didn't wait for her to acquiesce. It didn't occur to him that she would not comply. Even after her reckless decisions regarding Milla and her baby, her reputation for obedience was apparently still intact. And it didn't occur to him that she would have dispensed medicine without his directions.

She and Milla kept busy for a time after he'd gone, doling out the midafternoon doses, and when that was done, she could have sent Milla to Tregear with his, but she didn't. Instead, she set Milla to filling the bowls and cups of vegetable broth and spoon-feeding those who couldn't manage it themselves.

"Will you sing, then, Milla?" one of the old man asked as Jane was leaving.

"What is it you want to hear, Russell?" Milla said, still dipping the broth.

"The old song," the man answered—to the approval of all those well enough to voice it. "Sing me the old song, lass."

Jane slipped away, carrying the last of the medicine with her and heading back to the house. She went silently up the stairs to her bedchamber. Tregear was awake. He raised up on one elbow as she entered the room, but he didn't say anything. She wondered if he even remembered his revelation.

She took his cup and filled it from the jug she carried. Outside, Milla began to sing the "old song," the words Jane didn't understand soaring aloft on the melancholy melody and Milla's pure soprano voice.

She looked toward the window. The song was beautiful.

Still listening, Jane offered the cup to Tregear and waited for him to drink it. He took a swallow, but then his gaze met hers and stayed. The song swirled around them, but she barely heard it now. She was lost in his sorrowful eyes.

When he handed her back the cup, their fingers touched. She had touched him before, more times than she could count, but this was different somehow. This time it had nothing to do with his being ill, and she felt it deep inside her.

And so, she thought, did he.

She made no attempt to leave. She stood there, still looking at him.

"What's wrong?" he asked.

She gave a small shrug. "I didn't know," she said. "I didn't know my father would not give his blessing." She gave a wavering sigh. "I'm trapped, Tregear."

"So are we all," he said. "By something."

"You sound like Reverend Oliver."

"No, I sound like Reverend Branwell of Land's End—
something I swore...I'd never do."

"What has trapped *you*, Tregear?"

"Wrong choices," he said without hesitation.

"Was Catherine a wrong choice?" she asked, and he
looked at her sharply, the blunt question taking him—and
her—by surprise.

"Catryn—not Catherine," he said after a moment.

"You often ask for her."

He said nothing to that. He lay back on the pillow and
closed his eyes.

"It was a long time ago," he said after a moment.

"Where is she now?"

"I don't know. Cornwall—London."

He suddenly looked at her. "You are a strong woman—
but you're not strong enough for this," he said. "Not for
this."

"I don't understand."

"Nothing good is going to come of it. You know that."

"Of what?"

He reached out and grabbed her by the arm, pulling himself into a sitting position, his grip belying his illness. With
his other hand he cupped her face and made her look at
him.

"What you feel. What I feel. What we both try...to pretend isn't there," he said. "It will get trampled. Believe
me. I know. It's best to let it die. I want you to stay away
from me. Don't come back in here again—for both our
sakes."

But she stood there, even after he released her, still
caught in the abject misery in his eyes.

"Get out," he said.

She made no move to leave.

"Get out!" he shouted, causing Milla to stop abruptly stop singing.

Jane stood a moment longer, but she didn't turn and flee the way he might have expected. She stepped closer to him instead.

He tried to stop her, grabbing her by the shoulders and holding her at arm's length to prevent her from coming any nearer. "I can't help you! Do you not understand! If you're trapped, I can't save you!"

"Don't keep me away," she said. "Tregear—"

He made a small sound, one of both anger and longing, and his arms suddenly enfolded her, holding her so tightly it hurt, pulling her halfway onto the bed with him. His mouth brushed against hers, then sought it in earnest.

"Jane—"

She clung to him, her heart soaring at the sound of her name, *her* name.

She stiffened suddenly. Someone—her father—was coming up the stairs. She slipped from Tregear's grasp, pausing to give him one last look before she fled the room.

She encountered her father at the head of the stairs.

"The blacksmith is dead," he said bluntly.

"Of the fever?" she asked, trying to keep her voice from trembling.

"Of a rambunctious horse."

Her father stared at her. She knew he wanted to say more, but he didn't. She even knew why he didn't.

Forbidding makes the fruit sweeter.

Chapter Ten

*N*ew graves.

Part of the bad luck triad. He had forgotten that he would have to pass the cemetery if he and Coley came in this direction. So many mounds of raw earth and likely the bodies of people he knew. He could feel Coley glancing at him as they rode along, but he said nothing.

New graves. A slovenly woman. A dead mine.

It wasn't difficult to see a woman like that hereabouts, but the mine wasn't dead. Only the miners who worked it. He knew that by the placement of a number of the graves in the far corner near the stone wall. He was damned lucky not to have been among them—at least not yet. But he didn't necessarily credit the Almighty with that rather remarkable fact; he and the deity had parted ways long ago.

He didn't remember much about the worst of his illness—except Jane Ennis. If he had to credit anyone with the fact that he was alive, it would have to be her. Every time he opened his eyes, she seemed to be there, her fierce determination that he live like a beacon in the darkness. Somehow he had known that she wanted him to survive, and he had tried his best to oblige her—when heretofore he had believed that he had all but given up on living. Even now, he wasn't entirely sure he thanked her for it.

He had not seen her for days; her father had seen to that. The doctor brought the medicine Mannion had paid for himself—or sent Milla or Bobby with it. And Tregear found himself in the hellish place of hating what was happening with Jane and needing her so badly he ached with it. All he could do was listen for her footfall or watch for a glimpse of her at the door.

He wanted her, regardless of her father, regardless of all that had gone on before with Catryn and the consequences he knew would come from chasing after a woman who was his better. How had he ever come to this—again?

He shifted his position suddenly on the buggy seat and felt Coley's immediate attention. Coley didn't believe he was well enough to make the trip to his own rooms at the hotel. Perhaps he wasn't. Either way, there had been no choice. He had to go because his pride hadn't let him wait until the doctor ordered him to leave.

Coley slowed the horse to a walk as soon as they had passed the cemetery, and Tregear closed his eyes, savoring the sun on his face, forcing his mind to register the sounds around him.

Rooks—no, crows—in the treetops to his left and a scattering of other bird songs he still didn't recognize.

Crickets in the tall grass.

The sighing wind in the tree tops.

All of them things he might never have experienced again were it not for her.

Jane.

He tried not to remember the way she had felt in his arms. The woman smell and taste of her. The sweet torture of lying in her bed.

And the sound of her voice.

Don't keep me away—
Jane, I can't save you!

"Where did you get this buggy?" he said abruptly to Coley.

The man didn't answer him.

"You didn't, steal it, did you?"

"Don't worry, Cap'n," Coley said in his own good time. "We give it back."

"Before or after they arrest us for horse thieves?"

"Before like, I'm hoping."

Tregear looked at the man. Clearly his troubles regarding Jane Ennis could be over a lot sooner than he might have expected.

"I've survived the fever so you can get me hung for horse stealing, then."

"Could be like," Coley said.

"And here I thought this had the makings of an uneventful day."

"Jane, I am calling you!"

Jane stood in the middle of the room, staring at the empty bed, ignoring Miss Chappell's persistent summons from the wagon outside. The bed had been stripped and freshly made, and there was no sign of Tregear, who had just this morning occupied it. And Eugenie's bed had been brought back from the surgery where it had been taken for their father's use when the epidemic was at its worst. Everything looked much as it always had. It was only she who was so different.

Jane crossed the room to the cedar chest at the foot of her bed, still ignoring Miss Chappell's angry voice coming through the open window. She lifted the lid and quickly searched through the contents. Only her winter clothes were inside it.

"Milla?" Jane called out in case the girl was somewhere upstairs. No one answered.

She gave a sharp sigh. She had been gone less than a day, and she should have recognized her father's ulterior motive at the outset. He had done it before—sent her off someplace so he could rid the household of an undesirable presence. This time she'd been obliged to go to the Mannion house to bring Miss Chappell back. Jane hadn't wanted to go, and thanks to the woman's petulance at not having been consulted regarding her removal beforehand, what should have taken several hours had lasted from sunup to sundown—and had given her father plenty of time to have Tregear removed from the house. Jane supposed that someone must have been drafted to take him away, in spite of the fact that her father had been paid handsomely to see that Tregear recovered.

Everyone else seemed to be gone, as well—Milla, Jane's father. Even the patients who had been camped out on the surgery porch and in the yard. As far as Jane could tell, there was no one here except her and Miss Chappell, and she closed her eyes at the mere thought of that being the case.

She moved to the bed and sat down on the edge.

Nothing good will come of it.

She hadn't needed to be told that. She believed it—even as Tregear did—but she still wanted to be close to him, in whatever way she could. For days she had been trying to examine the import of that realization. She should be ashamed of such feelings, but she wasn't. She had kissed him and she had wanted more. He was all she could think about. Her mind, asleep and awake, was filled with what it had been like to be in his embrace.

"Jane! I'm calling you!" Miss Chappell yelled again from the wagon where Jane had left her.

Jane stayed where she was. After a moment, she stretched out on the bed, lying where he had lain.

Tregear.

Better to let it die, unnamed and unrequited, whatever it was—or so he had said. She searched for a word to describe what she felt for him. *Lust?* How could it be anything but that? They both knew their places in this world, knew what borders could and could not be crossed. Even if her father had been a reasonable man, nothing would have been possible between them.

Nothing.

Please let him be all right. Please…

"Miss Jane?" Milla said in the doorway, and Jane immediately sat up.

"Are you all right, Miss Jane?"

"I—yes." She stood and smoothed down her dress. "Where is Tregear?" she asked, trying to keep her voice neutral.

"He got Coley to take him back to the village. Coley brought a buggy from someplace—Mr. Mannion's, I guess."

"It was Tregear's idea to go?"

"Yes."

"What did he say? Did he say anything?"

"No. He wasn't talking all that much—you know Tregear."

"And my father—where is he?"

"He's gone to Salisbury to fetch Mrs. Ennis and Miss Eugenie. He left right after Tregear did. He took Bobby with him to drive the wagon. He said he'd be back tomorrow—with your mam and your sister—if all is well."

Jane stood there, wondering if Eugenie had any idea that young Bobby admired her. For a brief moment she forgot that admiring an Ennis daughter was a consummate waste of a young man's time, just as filling a mahogany marriage chest had been a waste of hers.

"He knew Tregear was going, then," Jane said, still trying not to sound as urgent as she felt.

"Oh, yes. The doctor, he was sending everybody on their way, but Tregear set out before the doctor got around to him. I reckon Tregear was of a mind not to wait to be showed the door. Miss Jane?" Milla said, and she looked as if she were about to cry.

"What is it?"

"I'm going now," Milla said, her mouth trembling. "Me and Charia."

Jane frowned. "But why?"

Milla shrugged. "I'm well now and there ain't no more sick people here."

"Miss Chappell's here—and she's a lot of work sick or well."

"Now that's heaven's own truth, Miss Jane—and I was thinking you'd have need of me for a while longer, what with your mam and Eugenie coming home. The widow woman that was coming to cook—she can't do it now because some of her people died of the fever and there's all these orphaned young-uns to look after. Lolly says the fever's been so bad around here, there ain't that many womenfolk able to come work for somebody else now—not even for Mrs. Mannion." She gave a heavy sigh and wiped at her eyes with the back of her hand. "I could stay, Miss Jane—but the doctor, he don't want us here."

"I'll speak to Mother," Jane said.

"Won't do no good."

"Then I'll speak to him myself," Jane said, knowing there was a very good chance that her effort wouldn't do any good, either.

Milla clearly knew it, as well, because she began to cry in earnest.

"I'm sorry, Miss—Jane. I just—don't know what—I'm going to do. If it was just me—"

"Don't cry, Milla. If you do, I will, too—and then where will we be?"

"We'll be a—sorry—sight," Milla said, sniffing loudly in an effort to do as Jane asked. "I got—Miss Chappell's—bed—ready. We ain't telling her I slept in it, are we? She'd probably want a fire set to it."

Miss Chappell.

Jane had all but forgotten about her, regardless of the racket she was making.

"I guess I'd better get her upstairs then," she said.

Milla nodded, wiping her eyes on her apron. "I'll help you—before I go."

Jane looked around the room one last time before she followed Milla out.

"It's about time!" Miss Chappell said as they came out onto the porch.

"Your bed's ready," Jane said.

"I can't possibly climb those stairs," Miss Chappell said.

"Well, you're going to have to. Milla and I can't carry you. It's either that or sit in the wagon until somebody stronger happens by."

"I don't see why you had to drag me back here!"

"I can assure you it wasn't my doing. And I believe it was you who complained so bitterly because Father wouldn't let you return to the house. Well, you're here now—so try to be at least a little happy about getting what you wanted in the first place."

Miss Chappell opened her mouth to say something, then closed it again. But her silence didn't last long. "What are *you* still doing here," she asked Milla. "I thought you and that misbegotten whelp of yours would be long gone."

"Milla isn't leaving," Jane said, hoping she was telling the truth.

"Isn't she?" Miss Chappell asked in mock surprise. "She has quite worn out her welcome here. Isn't that so, Milla?"

Jane glanced in Milla's direction, marveling at the ease with which the woman could find another person's vulnerable point and jab it hard. Even if Milla hadn't already been told to go, Miss Chappell's remarks would have had the girl undone.

Milla stood with her head down, trying hard not to cry.

"Some men just aren't the marrying kind, baby or no," Miss Chappell said. "If Milla *will* take up with that sort, then she must suffer the consequences. She is unwed and she has a bastard child. Respectable people will have nothing to do with her now, and I'm surprised she's been allowed to stay here this long."

Milla gave a muffled sob. Miss Chappell ignored her.

"Really, Jane. Your father needs to be more careful who he lets into this house."

"Indeed he does," Jane said, but Miss Chappell missed the significance of the remark. Clearly, her forte was taking insult when there was none—and then totally missing the real barbs.

"All men are liars," Miss Chappell went on. "I'm sure Milla's seducer spun her a pretty tale to get her on her back—"

"Miss Jane—it wasn't nothing like what *she's* saying—" Milla said.

"It's all right, Milla," Jane said, rubbing the point on her forehead that had begun to ache. "I have things to attend to. Do, please, let me know, Miss Chappell, if you decide to come inside.'' She looked up at the sky. ''It doesn't look like rain, so you needn't worry about that. You may want to open your parasol to protect your complexion from the sun, however. It wouldn't do for you to get freckled.''

''Miss Jane—'' Milla said as Jane stepped back into the house.

''I'll speak to Father, Milla,'' she said. ''Don't leave yet.''

She went into the kitchen, stood for a moment, then went out the back door and across the yard to the surgery. Miss Chappell was correct on at least one account. Respectable people wouldn't have anything to do with Milla Dunwiddie or her child. Mrs. Oliver would likely help—up to a point—but her charity was limited and completely at the mercy of people like Jane's father and the Mannions. Milla might find work at the mine—manning the rockers the way Lolly had done—but it wasn't likely. There was no chance whatsoever that Milla might become one of the Midges, and the only other avenue left to her was harlotry in the tavern, here or in one of the other towns.

Jane tried the surgery door, half expecting to find it locked. Charia was asleep inside, lying peacefully in her cradle by an open window where a soft breeze came in. Jane stood staring down at her. Some part of her still wondered if she were Tregear's child. It surprised her that it didn't really matter. She had helped bring the baby girl into the world; she wanted her to always be as content as she seemed at this very moment.

She reached down and gently caressed the baby's head, then forced herself to go to her father's big plantation desk in the corner and open it. She stood staring at the array of tin boxes on the shelves and seeing none of them. All she could see, all she could feel was Tregear.

She abruptly began to take tin boxes down one by one and checking the contents, drawing up a careful list as she went along of what was on hand and what was needed, trying to concentrate on the monotonous task so that she wouldn't think about Tregear.

The baby slept on. And Miss Chappell stayed perched on the seat of the wagon, the war of wills now full-blown. She wondered idly if Miss Chappell realized it was only herself she inconvenienced.

Jane caught a glimpse of Milla going to the well for water, and at one point she heard a horse ride into the yard.

"You see how I have been left?" she heard Miss Chappell say, but she didn't hear a reply to the querulous inquiry. She kept working.

"I shall surely become ill all over again," Miss Chappell insisted.

Someone stepped up on the porch. Jane looked up as her father strode into the surgery—alone.

"Is something the matter with Mother and Eugenie?" she asked in alarm.

"They have remained to attend a wedding—your sister has managed to get herself invited to sing at the ceremony. They will be here day after tomorrow."

"They are both well?"

"Quite well. The town has missed the epidemic entirely." He glanced at the array of tins she had spread out on the desktop, but he didn't comment.

"You've had long enough to consider my offer," he said. "It's time for you to say what you will do."

Jane looked at him. How sure he was that she would do as he wanted.

"I—" she began, then took a deep breath. "I have a question."

"Ask it then," he said, and if he expected her to make an inquiry about Tregear, she couldn't tell.

"If I am to...dedicate myself to this study and nothing else, who will help with the running of the house? Mother is not well enough. Eugenie is not skilled in household chores and Miss Chappell is at best hopeless. And there are very few women about to be hired," she added to bolster her argument, hoping that what Milla had said was true.

Her father frowned slightly. He clearly hadn't considered this inconvenience. It wasn't his custom to consider anything but his own will.

"I would like Milla to stay," she said. "She is well trained and willing."

"She has a bastard child."

"She will fall even further if we abandon her. I would like Milla to stay," she said again. She was perfectly aware of what she *wasn't* saying—that she understood now how such things could happen.

"*You* would like," he said after a moment.

"Yes. I attended the delivery of her baby. I feel responsible for it—and her."

"That is something you will have to remedy. One cannot indulge in personal attachments."

Jane looked at him, wondering if he meant only when it came to patients or if the emotional distance had to be extended to friends and family, as well.

Yes, she thought. It did. *He* did not welcome closeness with anyone or anything.

"Nevertheless, the attachment is there, Father," she said. "There was no question of my needing to guard against such things then. It would trouble me very much to have Mother's comfort disrupted in order to accommodate me. I think she wouldn't be, if Milla were to stay on hand."

"It is up to us to set some kind of example for these people," he said.

"Yes," she said. "Precisely. An example is easier to set if they are in proximity."

She waited, knowing that her idea of an "example" and his were complete opposites. His had to do with retribution; hers with forgiveness. But she had presented the facts as best she could—as he had taught her.

"This matter aside, it is your intention, then, to set yourself to the task I've proposed?"

"I...hope to do so," she said, the subtle tentativeness of the remark in no way meant to dilute its true meaning.

Quid pro quo.

She didn't think she had ever truly understood the term until this very minute.

"I have one more question, Father."

"Go on."

"What if I am not capable of this...endeavor?"

"There is no question of your not being capable," he said. "I would not have suggested it if I thought otherwise."

She stood there, once again surprised by the unexpected compliment and trying to subdue a sudden and ridiculous urge to cry.

"Milla Dunwiddie will stay—so long as she does her chores satisfactorily and behaves in a moral manner."

"Thank you, Father."

"And what is your decision?"

Jane took a quiet breath, but she still didn't answer him. The baby began to fret, its initial whimpering expanding to lusty crying almost immediately. She went to the crib and lifted the baby out, placing it carefully on her shoulder, feeling the downy soft hair against her cheek. She swayed gently, and the baby stopped. She looked at her father, wondering if his self-imposed lack of grandchildren would trouble him any at all.

"Jane," her father said, impatiently. "Have you decided or have you not?"

"I have, Father," she said. "I am ready to begin whenever you are."

She saw by the expression on his face that she hadn't surprised him. The baby began to fret again, and she moved her to her other shoulder.

"Very well," he said.

He turned to leave then stopped. "There is one other thing. Milla's staying will depend on your behavior, as well."

"Mine? I don't understand."

"You will have no more society with miners—sick or well—especially the man Tregear."

She looked at him, startled by the unexpected condition.

"Milla's child thrives here, does she not?" he said. "It would be a shame to see that undone."

Jane glanced past him. Milla stood poised in the doorway. Jane had thought herself so clever for making Milla's being allowed to stay a point necessary for her agreement. But he had turned the tables, using the same condition for his own end.

Quid pro quo.

"I'm waiting," he said.

She stared into her father's eyes, but she was the one to look away. "Very well," she said.

"What did you say? I did not hear you."

"I said very well, Father."

He gave her a curt nod and walked away, passing by Milla as if she did not exist.

"I thought I heard Charia," Milla said, glancing furtively in the direction the doctor had gone.

"You did," Jane said, handing the baby over. "Father says you can stay," she added. "If you do your work well and don't..." She stopped, not knowing quite how to word it.

"I'm going to be a good girl, Miss Jane."

So must we both, Jane thought.

Milla took the baby and sat down in the nearest chair to suckle her.

Jane walked out of the surgery, but she didn't return to the house. She stood in the yard for a moment looking at the now empty wagon and wondering briefly how Miss Chappell had managed to get down from the high seat unaided *and* take herself inside.

She began to walk aimlessly through the trees in the direction of the narrow wagon road, and when she reached it, she didn't stop. She kept walking, her mind in turmoil, in spite of the fact that she had done the best she could. The same question repeated itself over and over.

Now what? Now what?

Her father was going to pass his skill on to her. It was what she wanted. She understood her own motives well enough, even without the incentive of helping Milla and her child. She had had a small taste of what it was like to be a participant in the world, to have adventures, as Eugenie put it, and she hadn't wanted to let it go.

But the price was too high. Her father never intended that she should marry, so her capitulation regarding that was token at best. She had thought to have at least the prospect of Tregear's company from time to time—at church, perhaps, if he ever deigned to attend, or at the Mannion house.

Tregear.

"I want him more," she said aloud. She wanted him—and there was no hope for it.

She looked around suddenly at a noise behind her, a horse galloping along the road in her direction. She moved to the side, but the rider reined in sharply before he reached her. She watched for a moment, then gave a soft cry.

"Sion—Sion!"

He dismounted, leaving the horse standing, and walked in her direction.

"Sion!" she called again as he covered the distance between them.

"At your service, my dear lovely sister," he said, half smiling in that way he had. He hugged her hard, swinging her off the ground.

"Let me look at you," Jane said, stepping back to see his face. "Are you all right?"

"Am I sober, do you mean? I am. Sober and hardworking. Here," he said, holding out his hands. "Look at these."

His hands were heavily callused and in some places still raw from the blisters.

"What have you been doing!"

"Digging graves, actually. And don't look like that. Somebody had to. The line of volunteers was very short, believe me. At the moment, however, I am about some important business."

"What kind of business?"

"I'm not sure it has a name."

"Well, try to find one," she said. He seemed so much his old self that she couldn't help smiling.

"It seems that I'm acting as a kind of lackey and messenger."

"Too bad," Jane said to tease—as she might have done when he was still at home. "I don't believe you are suited for either one."

"Right you are, sister dear. But it's all part of the bargain I struck."

"This seems a day for bargains," she said. "What kind is yours?"

He smiled and ignored the question. "How is the family?"

"Mother and Eugenie are in Salisbury. Father sent them there until the epidemic was over. They'll be home day after tomorrow."

"Do me a favor? Don't tell them I came."

"But why?"

"It's better for them if they don't have reason to ever expect to see me."

"Sion—"

"Sometimes you have to be cruel to be kind, Jane."

Jane looked at him, then gave a quiet sigh. He meant it.

"Is *he* here?" Sion asked after a moment.

"Yes," Jane said, watching his cheerfulness fade at that bit of news. "Father's in the house. Sion, can you and he not—?"

"Never," he interrupted, and looking at him as he said it, Jane believed him.

"Tell me about the bargain you struck. Who is it with?" she said both to change the subject and to keep him as long as she could.

"Tregear."

She looked at him in surprise. "What kind of bargain have you made with Tregear?"

"He thought it important that I come and let you see for yourself that I am still among the living."

"And?"

"And I want to be his apprentice in the mine. He is a very persuasive man."

Jane looked at him, realizing that he wouldn't have come

here if Tregear hadn't been. He would have been "cruel to be kind" to her, as well.

"Is Tregear all right?" Jane asked in spite of all she could do.

Sion looked at her for a moment before he answered. "He's...I've seen him better. And worse," he quickly added, perhaps because of the look on her face.

"He shouldn't have left."

"If I understand Coley correctly, I don't think he had much choice."

"No," Jane said after a moment. "Is he really going to take you on as an apprentice?"

"If he doesn't die first. Or so I think. I have done his bidding. I've come to see you. I believe he is a man of his word."

"Sion, why on earth would you want to be a miner?"

"I don't want to be a miner. I want to learn what Tregear does. It's fascinating work. And it doesn't hurt that the pay is better than anything else I might try. I need the money."

"I have a little money put aside—"

"Which you must guard with your life and not waste on worthless brothers."

"You are not worthless."

"Oh, but I am—at the moment. I shall endeavor to remedy that with all possible speed, however." He suddenly rested his hands on her shoulder. "I must go before Father sees me."

"Will you come again? Like this? Father doesn't have to know—"

"No," he said. He kissed her forehead and began to walk away.

"Sion," she said when he'd gone a few steps. He looked back at her.

"Tell Tregear I—"

Sion stopped and waited when she faltered.

"Nothing," she said.

Chapter Eleven

"Eugenie, what are you doing?"

"Looking," Eugenie said, the muffled answer underscoring the fact that she was lying halfway under Jane's bed.

"What are you looking for?"

"Nothing," she said again, sliding back and getting to her feet. "A button," she added clearly as an afterthought.

"Did you find it?" Jane asked anyway.

"Oh, no. It's lost and gone forever, I think." Eugenie smiled her lovely smile and looked at Jane's bed.

"I can't believe he was actually here—right here."

Jane made no comment. Eugenie made the same observation regularly, and she wished Milla had never told her that Tregear had been brought to the house to recover.

"You have a letter," Jane said, handing her the mail their father had just brought back from Smith's store. The fact that it had been opened and probably read surprised neither of them.

Eugenie turned the letter over in her hands. "Mr. Thomas Hunter," she said. "Of Salisbury. He asked Mother's permission and he said he might write to me." She tossed the letter aside, her interest in the arrival of the mail a sharp contrast to that of Miss Chappell, who had been waiting anxiously on the porch for the doctor to return with something—anything—for her.

"Aren't you going to read it?"

"Later," Eugenie said. "I'd much rather you told me about when Tregear was here."

"I've told you," Jane said, hoping Eugenie had given up trying to pry out of her whether or not Tregear had a tattoo.

"Tell me again."

"He nearly died," Jane said to be as succinct as possible.

"I know," Eugenie said reverently. "It is so... so...*tragic*," she decided.

"Well, hardly. He is quite recovered now—or so I'm told."

"Oh, I know. And he's moved out of the hotel to a cabin at the edge of the village, Milla said. Milla said he was wild sometimes—when he was so ill. She said he didn't even know who he was—and he thought you were somebody else. Were you scared?"

"No," Jane said truthfully. Even during Tregear's worst moments, she had not been afraid of him, only that he might die.

"It's changed him, they say—being at death's door."

Jane made no reply, crossing the room to sit in the chair by the window and pore over the pages of medicinal formulas her father had given her to commit to memory.

Eugenie was undaunted. "He's coming to church now."

"Is he?" Jane said, trying to focus her attention on the Latin terms where it belonged instead of on Tregear where she wanted it so desperately to be.

"Mrs. Oliver says he even sings in the choir. I can't wait to hear him—Father says we are going to church today. Perhaps Tregear and I will sing a duet sometime. 'Farewell,

My Friend' would be a good choice. I *love* that hymn.''
She began to hum it and picked up Mr. Thomas Hunter's
letter to read, chuckling to herself just often enough to
break Jane's concentration.

"He is a witty boy, I take it," Jane said after a time.

"Very," Eugenie said. "Only he's not a boy. He's a
man. He's at least Sion's age. Maybe older. And he's very
clever."

"Is he?" Jane said absently.

"It's a secret letter," Eugenie whispered, apparently in
case Miss Chappell felt compelled to enjoy her letter vi-
cariously and had her ear to the keyhole.

"It doesn't look very secret to me. I'm sure Father has
read it."

"It's a code letter," Eugenie said, still whispering.
"When you read it as is, it seems very innocent. If you
read every other line—well, it's an entirely different matter."

"Eugenie, where in this world did you learn about such
things."

"In Salisbury, of course. The girls there get them all the
time, and their mothers and fathers don't suspect a thing."

"I'm beginning to think you shouldn't be receiving any
letter—coded or otherwise."

"That's what Bobby Reid said—he was listening when
Mr. Hunter asked if he might write to me. And I told Mr.
Hunter that Bobby heard, but he said not to worry—he
would send a coded one. And so he has. They must be very
hard to write." Eugenie went back to reading—briefly.

"He's very sad, Jane."

"Perhaps Mr. Thomas Hunter should just write the reg-
ular kind of letter—or give up correspondence altogether."

"No, not him—Tregear. I really do think being sick had
done something to him. Mrs. Oliver does, too."

"It was a bad time here, Eugenie. Everyone is different now—whether they were sick or not."

"Especially you," Eugenie said, looking on the backside of her letter.

"What do you mean? Especially me?"

"Well, you're still going with Father on his rounds and everything, but you don't argue with him anymore—about anything. Not like you used to. You have become very...docile. Father must be ever so pleased." Eugenie sighed. "Oh, I hope Tregear is at church today. I shall ask him how he fares—that would be quite proper, I think. He was here in this very room all that time, so it's not like he's a stranger."

Jane frowned and tried to endure Eugenie's relentless chatter. Eugenie had no idea how much she had changed. Jane stared at the page of the *Materia Medica,* trying again to commit to memory which herb or which chemical compound did what. But the memories of Tregear kept getting between her and the printed words. She still remembered his mouth on hers, his arms around her. Sometimes the memory caught her completely unaware and was so acute it left her knees weak—as if it were happening all over again. And yet sometimes she could barely remember it at all. She hadn't known he was living in a cabin—Milla's cabin? She hadn't known he was going to church. The only thing she knew was that she was staying well away from any possible encounter with him. She was doing what he said—letting whatever might be between them die—because she had no other choice.

"Jane!" Eugenie said, making her jump.

"What!"

"I asked if you are coming to church."

"No."

"Then may I carry your fan?"

"Take it," Jane said, more sharply than she intended. "I'm sorry," she said immediately, because of the hurt look on Eugenie's face. "It's just—Father expects me to know this and I don't."

"You will," Eugenie said. "You are always able to do whatever it is you're supposed to do."

Whatever I'm supposed to do.

Not always. She tried to study for a time after her father and Miss Chappell and Eugenie had left for church, but it was hopeless, and she ultimately gave in to her restlessness.

She went in search of her mother, but found her entertaining Charia in a patch of sunlight by the window while Milla tidied the room and made the bed. She watched for a moment from the doorway, pleased about this aspect of her bargain with her father, at least. Milla and Charia were here and safe. And her mother was clearly enjoying the baby.

"Jane," her mother said without looking up. "Are you not tired of studying so hard? I do wonder that your father expects it on the Sabbath."

"I thought I might go walk a bit, Mother. Do you need anything first?"

"No, my love. I am in good hands here," she said, caressing Charia's chubby fist, her attention taken with smiling at the child.

"There's some cheese wrapped in a vinegar rag on the cupboard shelf, Miss Jane," Milla said as she unfurled a sheet over the bed. "In case you get hungry as you go."

Jane stood for a moment longer, then went downstairs. She put on her straw hat and took the flat basket she used for gathering the plants necessary for her father's practice, knowing if she encountered something needed, she would pick it, Sabbath or no.

She walked quickly from the house and down a path that

led into the wood and ultimately to a grassy meadow. When she reached it, she put the basket down and stood looking around her, aware of the buzz of insects and the birds singing. It was a restful and private place, and she loved it here.

She watched two pale lavender-blue butterflies circling each other above a wild carrot bloom, spiraling together, higher and higher into the air far above her head, until, suddenly, they joined together and plummeted back to earth.

Tregear watched Dr. Ennis leave the church and walk toward the Mannion house. Miss Chappell followed in an almost exact execution of the doctor's haughtiness. Eugenie was taking her time, lingering along the path from the church door, stopping to speak to people she knew as she went.

Tregear began walking toward the road, intending to go to the mining office. He had no business there, he merely wanted to be occupied with something other than his convalescence and the whereabouts of Jane Ennis.

She didn't attend church—again, and there was no point in his trying to pretend that his sitting through yet another of the reverend Oliver's long sermons had nothing to do with her. It had everything to do with her. He wanted to see her. He wanted to talk to her.

He wanted to take her to the nearest bed and stay there.

Thus far, since he'd left the Ennis house, he hadn't been able to even catch a glimpse of her. People who might know where and how she was weren't saying and wouldn't unless he asked—perhaps not even then, if the doctor didn't want it.

He realized suddenly that someone was walking behind him.

"Good morning, sir," Eugenie Ennis said when he looked over his shoulder.

"Miss Eugenie," he answered, and she smiled shyly, falling into step with him.

"How is your health, sir?" she asked politely.

"Improving daily—and yours?"

"I am quite fine." She took a breath. "We've been invited to the Mannion house for Sunday dinner. Will you be there?" she asked.

"No," he said.

"Oh," she said. "I—"

She stopped midsentence, but she didn't try to catch up with her father and Miss Chappell. She continued to walk with him, unmindful of the eyebrows that would be raised.

He was aware that there was no one within earshot, and it was for that reason that he asked.

"How is your sister?"

"She's well," Eugenie said.

"I'm glad to hear it. I thought she might not be. I have not seen her about. I haven't voiced my thanks to her—for her care during my illness. I had intended to do that."

"Oh, but you can't," Eugenie said.

"Why not?"

"Well, because *she* can't—" The girl broke off, obviously flustered.

"Can't what?" he persisted.

She didn't answer him. She gave him the bewildered smile of one who had misjudged a situation and now wanted only to make an escape. She stepped by him, intending to go on ahead.

"Miss Eugenie, please speak plainly. If there is something I need to know—something that might save me embarrassment, I would appreciate your telling me."

He could see her struggling to decide. She owed him

protection from an embarrassing situation. They both knew that.

"Please," he said to help her along.

"Father says she can't have anything to do with you."

"I see," he said.

"Or any miner," Eugenie hastily added.

"Your sister told you this?"

"Oh, no. She doesn't know I know about it. Milla told me. She heard what my father said—I must go. Truly." She took a few steps, then turned back to him. "May I ask a question—about the mine?"

"Ask," he said. He was not surprised that the doctor had forbidden Jane to have anything to do with him. But if he admitted it, he was surprised that she would comply so earnestly. He didn't expect her to disappear from Gold Hill society. She was a dutiful daughter, yes. But she wasn't *that* dutiful.

He suddenly remembered Eugenie.

"The question?" he said.

"I wanted to know if visitors can go down in the mine."

"Visitors?"

"Yes," she said. "People who are…interested in what it's like to be where the gold is."

"No. Miners are a very superstitious sort. Women are never allowed below ground."

"Oh, but I'm not a woman—" She suddenly stopped and smiled, clearly pleased that he had just labeled her as such. "Still, it would be fascinating to see."

"A mine is far too dangerous to visit. I think it better if you remain above ground where you are safe."

"Is it true there are ghosts?"

"I have yet to meet one."

"But I heard there is a young woman's ghost—she was murdered by the man she wouldn't have."

"I think not," he said. "And I believe your father is looking for you."

"Oh! I must go!" She turned and fled in the direction of the Mannion house, giving him a little wave behind her back and out of her father's line of vision as she went.

So, Tregear thought, watching her go. Jane had been forbidden to see him. He began walking toward the mine office again, certain that he was relieved that the doctor had intervened. But his conviction only lasted a few yards. He looked over his shoulder to see if Coley was there. He was, and Tregear waited until he was closer.

"Bring me a saddled horse," he said. "And try not to steal it."

"You wanting to go someplace bad like?"

"Yes."

"Soon?"

Tregear looked at him. "Just don't tell me where it comes from."

Tregear rested under the walnut trees near the office porch while Coley was about his business. It didn't take the man long to return—riding a saddled bay Tregear recognized as belonging to Mannion. It was a safe enough source—unless Mannion found out where he was going.

"You want Coley?" the man asked as he got down.

"No," he said, accepting the reins and summoning what strength he had these days to mount. He managed—but not well.

Coley said nothing.

"I want you and Bobby to mind your own business for a change," Tregear said.

Coley said nothing to that, either, and Tregear turned the horse and rode away. He took the shortcut through the woods to the Ennis house, riding into the yard as if he would be welcome. Mrs. Ennis was sitting on the porch holding a baby, and if she was surprised to see him, it didn't show.

He was winded from the ride, and he dismounted slowly.

"Sit down, Mr. Tregear," she said ahead of his greeting. "I fear you may have overextended yourself."

"Thank you, ma'am," he said. "I will."

He sat down heavily on the porch steps.

"Have you come to see my husband?" she asked.

"I have come to see Jane," he said candidly.

She looked at him steadily.

"I have been remiss in extending my thanks to her," he said.

"Milla tells me you were very ill."

"Yes," he said. "Though I remember little of it."

"I doubt she expects any thanks for whatever she may have done," Mrs. Ennis said.

"Nevertheless, I would like her to hear it—from me," he added.

"I see," she said. The baby began to fret. "Well, Jane has gone walking. I expect her return very soon—she will likely come from that direction." She nodded toward the edge of the woods where a large cedar tree grew. "You may wait here if you would like." She stood, the baby cradled in her arms.

"Thank you, ma'am."

"Thank you, Mr. Tregear."

"For what, ma'am?"

"For keeping your word. I'm sure you understand what I mean."

He did understand. She meant his never mentioning that he and Jane together had delivered the child she held in her arms.

She gave a slight inclination of the head to end the conversation and left him alone on the porch. He watched for some sign of Jane near the cedar tree for a time, then decided he was recovered enough to walk in that direction. If he went slowly.

He was out of sight of the house when he saw a basket sitting on the ground. And then he saw her. She was standing up ahead of him in a small field of broom straw, her back to him, and she was doing nothing as far as he could tell.

He stopped and waited, not wishing to startle her, but she heard him immediately and turned around. There was a brief instant, before she recovered her composure, when he realized that she was glad to see him.

Very glad.

She stood looking at him, and after a moment, began to walk in his direction. And how beautiful she looked with her hair tied back with a scarlet ribbon and her straw hat dangling on her arm.

"Are you ill, Tregear?" she asked when she was close enough, perhaps thinking he'd had some kind of relapse and needed her father's services.

"No more so than usual," he said, and she smiled.

Almost.

"Why are you here?"

"I think you know the answer to that," he said, and she looked at him, her eyes searching his, as if to see past the words to his true intent.

"It would be better if you just spoke plainly," she said.

"I always do," he answered.

"Yes. Except now."

He looked away from her and drew a quiet breath. The wind rustled the treetops and a bird took sudden flight from the undergrowth on his left. He had come here with at least some idea of what he wanted to say, but the memory of what had passed between them the last time he saw her filled his mind and his heart. He was so…lonely suddenly. Not for his homeland or his other life. For her.

For *her.*

"Tregear?" she said, and he looked at her, looked into her eyes as she had done, trying to see if she was going to pretend that they had never been in each other's arms, had never kissed.

Yes, he decided. Her father had won—and so easily.

It's what I wanted.

It was too bad Reverend Branwell was not here. He would be able to identify the moral to this sad and fleeting story in an instant.

"I…find myself in the uncomfortable position of needing to express my gratitude—to someone who likely doesn't want to hear it," he said. "I think you understand how that particular situation feels."

"Only too well," she said. "It's especially awkward when the person extending the gratitude sees more in an offhand gesture than was intended."

His attending to her drunken brother lying facedown in the dirt was no more "offhand" than her keeping a vigil at his bedside night and day when he was so ill, and he thought she knew it. But he said nothing.

"I owe you my life," he said after a moment.

"No, I—"

"I owe you my life," he said again. "I am in your debt. I hope someday to repay it."

"There is no need."

"Not for you, perhaps. But there is for me. I'm not accustomed to feeling…beholden. I will repay it—"

"It isn't necessary," she interrupted, stepping past him.

"Do you know how hard it was for me to come here?"

"No harder than it is for me to walk away," she said.

"Jane."

She stopped, but she didn't look at him. He could see the rise and fall of her shoulders, feel her struggle to either bolt or stay.

"You were right, Tregear," she said, looking at him finally. He thought she was about to cry. "We have to let it die."

But she didn't leave him standing there. She seemed to be waiting for him, and he stepped forward and picked up the basket from the ground, then joined her on the narrow path back to the house. Neither of them spoke. There was nothing for either of them to say.

When they reached the yard, he handed the basket to her. For a brief moment, as she took it, her fingers brushed against his.

"Jane—"

"Tregear!" someone yelled. "Tregear—!"

He turned to see a horse coming at full gallop among the trees.

"Mr. Mannion needs you!" Bobby Reid yelled, trying to rein the animal in and causing it to rear and prance. "Miss Eugenie's lost—"

"What do you mean 'lost'?" Tregear said. "I just saw her."

"She went down in the mine—Lolly saw her go. And she ain't come out. They been calling and calling down the shaft. They heard her for a time but she don't answer. Won't nobody go down to look for her. The men say it's bad luck. Mr. Mannion, he wouldn't let me go down. He said—come—and get—you—"

Tregear swore. "I told her plainly she could not go there! Did you have something to do with this, Bobby Reid?"

"Me! No! I never would of let her go in that place! Never!" Bobby said, still trying to manage the horse.

"Tregear, I'm coming with you—" Jane said, grabbing his arm.

"No," Tregear said. "Stay here. I'll get her."

"You're not well enough—"

"I'll get her," he said, making her look at him.

"How can you? If she's hurt—if the others won't help—"

He had no time to argue. He left her standing and untied his horse.

"I have to go with you!" Jane cried.

"You need to see to your mother," he said as he mounted. "She won't thank you if you keep this from her. Tell her what's happened—tell her I will need her prayers—then come."

Jane hesitated, then nodded. "Eugenie—she wanted an adventure—" she said, her mouth trembling. "Tregear—"

He could offer her no reassurances. The mine was full of ways to die. He reached down to touch her cheek, then rode away.

Chapter Twelve

"There is two like," Coley said.

Tregear looked at him sharply. "Two? What two?"

"Sion, he went for to find her," Coley said. "He don't stop no matter who say to. Even Mr. Mannion can't make Sion not to go."

"Goddamn it!" Tregear said, stuffing spare candles into his pocket. "He knows no more about getting around in the mine than Eugenie does—what do you think you're doing?" he said to Bobby, who had one foot on the rim of the ore bucket.

"I'm going along—"

"No, you're not. I'm not going to end up looking for you, too. I want you and Coley up here. I have to have somebody I can trust to pull the kibble up again. You hear me? You and Coley stay here."

"You don't worry none," Coley said. "*She* will be safe like."

Tregear thought at first that Coley meant Eugenie, but when he looked at the man, he realized that was not the case. It was Jane whom Coley was talking about. The man saw everything, no matter how hard Tregear worked to hide it.

"She'll be coming here," Tregear said, thinking of the way she had looked at him as he rode away. There was only one thing he could do to spare her. "If it's bad, you and Bobby stay close to her."

"The doctor is here now," Coley said.

"I see him."

Dr. Ennis was standing apart from the crowd that had gathered at the adit and at the vertical shaft. Tregear realized immediately that he was invisible to the man in spite of the fact that he had lain only half alive in one of his daughters' bed for weeks or that he was about to go in search of the other one—and perhaps his son, as well.

But he didn't waste his time taking offense.

Tregear looked at the rest of the men. None would meet his gaze. He took no offense at that, either. Their ranks had been thinned by the fever, and few of the ones who had survived were born to go underground. It was all too easy to be deterred by superstition when the fear of suffocating in the dark was so strong.

But any one of them might have been able to rise above the fear if it hadn't meant risking their lives for someone like Dr. Ennis. It didn't matter to them that he was a major investor. What mattered was that doctor considered them all lesser men—Tregear included—and they knew it. They wouldn't help him now, even for young Eugenie's sake.

Beware a sharp tongue, Reverend Branwell always said, *lest you cut your own throat.* The same was true of disdain. The doctor had burned his bridge while he was still in the middle of it.

Even so, he had the arrogance to stand and see it through. Tregear would give him that much.

"Does Ennis know his son is down in the mine?" he asked Coley.

"He knows—but he pretends not to. The man, he don't forgive, never."

"Damn fool," Tregear said, meaning the son—but the father was no better. "Was Sion sober?"

"Sober like, Cap'n."

"Well, there's that at least."

"They been fed good, Cap'n," Coley said as Tregear draped a coil of rope over his shoulder and climbed into the ore bucket.

Tregear understood the second abrupt shift in the conversation as well. Coley wanted him to remember that the Knockers had been tended faithfully by them both—every day that they had gone down in the mine. It was a reassuring reminder. He would likely need all the help he could get.

"Bobby," he said to the boy. "If Eugenie's hurt, I won't get her up without a good man at the top."

The boy stared at him, then nodded. "Take my rope, too," he said, handing Tregear the heavy coil he had at his side.

Tregear took it.

"You'll tell her I meant to come," Bobby said. "You'll tell her that."

"I'll tell her. All right then. Let me down."

He waited until he had reached the bottom of the shaft to light the candle on the brim of his hat, using the small and unfashionable tinderbox his father had given him when he was a boy—the only thing his sire had ever given him, save a bruised face or a split lip. The rasp of flint and steel echoed in the quiet darkness of the mine. When the candle was lit, he stood for a moment, letting his eyes and his senses adjust, waiting for the initial heavy, closed-in feeling to pass. The mine was always damp, but a rivulet of run-

ning water glistened at his feet—not alarming in itself but
not particularly reassuring, either.

He debated tying one end of the rope to the kibble, then
decided against it. If Eugenie had fallen down an abandoned shaft, then he would likely need it. He bent low,
trying to see a female footprint, anything that might tell
him which way Eugenie and her brother had gone.

"Eugenie?" he called. "Sion?"

He listened intently, then called again. And again.

Nothing.

He took a deep breath, wishing he'd brought a staff to
lean on. His knees were unsteady from the unaccustomed
exertion. He was beginning to perspire heavily, in spite of
the coolness of the mine.

"See anything, Tregear?" he heard Bobby call.

"No," he shouted back. "I'm going on."

He moved slowly—calling and listening. He was well
away from the vertical shaft before he heard anything—but
where it came from, he wasn't sure.

He called again. "Sion! Eugenie!"

This time he was certain he heard a response. The tunnel
was level here, but it became more and more crooked. He
couldn't tell if the shout came from the shaft he was in or
one of the many offshoots.

"Keep calling!" he shouted. "But stay where you are!
I'll find you!"

He could hear the next shout quite plainly now; he had
to be getting closer. He forced himself to keep moving,
resisting the urge to stop and rest. But, at one point, a
sudden wave of weakness made him have to hold on to the
rock wall.

After a moment, he pushed himself away and started
walking again. The tunnel began to slope downward, and

there were places where he could no longer stand completely upright.

"Sion!"

"Here!" he heard faintly in response.

"Where!"

"Here!" Sion called again. "I can see the light from your candle!"

Tregear moved as quickly as he could in the direction of Sion Ennis's voice.

"Did you find her!" Sion asked before Tregear actually saw him.

"No—it seems my time is taken with trying to find you."

"I had enough sense to stay put, you'll have to give me that," Sion said. "What do we do now?"

"*We* don't do anything. Where is your candle?"

"I didn't duck soon enough. It got knocked off and went out. I couldn't find it again. I thought I heard her this way— but then I got all turned around and I couldn't hear her anymore—"

"Quiet," Tregear said, listening hard.

"What is it?"

"Quiet! I hear her—"

He began to move past Sion, deeper into the mine. He didn't offer him one of the candles in his pocket because he wanted to keep him from impulsively going off in a direction of his own. Sion scrambled to follow him.

Tregear abruptly stopped. He was certain of what he was hearing now—Eugenie Ennis.

Crying.

"Walk where I walk," Tregear said to Sion. There was more water in the tunnel, making the way slippery with mud. "Eugenie!"

The crying suddenly stopped.

"Stay where you are!" Tregear called. "We're coming."

But there was nothing but silence now.

"Eugenie! I need to hear you!"

He listened again and after a few moments he could hear…a song. Eugenie was singing. He moved forward into an intersecting shaft, but the sound seemed to fade. He changed directions, stopping often to get his bearings.

"Wait," Sion said, catching his arm. "I think it's that way."

Another wave of weakness made Tregear reach out blindly for the rock wall again. He clung to it to keep from falling, struggling hard to stay upright.

"Give me the hat," Sion said. "I'll go on ahead."

Tregear's legs were beginning to shake. "No. There's a candle in my pocket. Take that."

Sion found the candle and lit it. "Are you staying here?" he asked unnecessarily.

Tregear nodded, because he had no choice but to wait until the weakness passed. "Don't step anyplace you can't see," he said. "And keep Eugenie close to you."

"All right," Sion said. He started to say something more, then didn't. He turned and began to walk in the direction of Eugenie's singing, leaving Tregear his dignity and the remote possibility of overcoming the sudden exhaustion that threatened to topple him.

Tregear stood as long as he could. Then, when Sion was out of sight, he slid to the wet ground and sat with his back against the rock wall, his eyes closed.

He could hear Sion's progress along the shaft, hear Eugenie singing, but in among all that there was something else. He suddenly sat forward, straining to hear. And, just when he was certain that he had been mistaken, it came again.

Tapping.

Tapping.

"Sion!" he yelled.

"I found her!" Sion yelled. "She's all right!"

"Sion! Get Eugenie back here! Now!"

He pulled himself to his feet, his heart pounding. The tapping was growing louder, more insistent.

"Sion!"

He could hear running footsteps, see the flickering of the candle, and then Sion with Eugenie in tow.

"What—?" Sion began, but Tregear took no time to answer him. He grabbed Eugenie by the other hand.

"Let's go! Run! Run as fast as you can!"

Tregear led the way, all but dragging Eugenie behind him. She kept stumbling and when the shaft widened, it took Sion and him both to keep her on her feet.

"Hurry!" Tregear shouted, leading the way back toward the vertical shaft and the kibble.

"What—is that—noise?" Eugenie asked, still struggling not to fall down. "What is it?"

But the sudden collapse of the mine wall somewhere behind them and the roar of water breaking through rock drowned out any answer he might have made. There was no escape, no outrunning it. Eugenie screamed as the rush of water overtook them, sweeping them all forward. Tregear clung to her for dear life—he couldn't tell what had happened to Sion. They were being washed along in total darkness, bouncing off the sides of the shaft until Tregear suddenly collided with hard metal—the ore bucket dangling in the vertical shaft. He grabbed onto the rim, then locked his arm around the bucket handle to keep from being swept away in the current.

"Hold on!" he yelled as the water roared through. He could feel the ore handle cutting into the bend of his elbow from the strain of keeping Eugenie from going under, and he realized that she must still have Sion by the hand.

Eugenie was slipping from his grasp suddenly.

"Hold on!" he yelled again, trying with all his might to keep from losing his grip on her.

"Sion!" Eugenie screamed.

"Turn me loose, Eugenie!" Sion shouted at her. "He can't—hold us—both—"

"No!" she screamed. "Sion! Sion—!"

The heavy pull on Tregear's arms suddenly lifted. He still had Eugenie, but even in the dark he knew that Sion was no longer there. He dragged Eugenie closer.

"Grab hold of the bucket!" he said, but he couldn't get her attention.

"Eugenie! He's gone! Grab hold!"

She was crying inconsolably, and she reached out blindly, hitting him in the face.

"The bucket! Hold on to it!"

She finally managed to find the rim and cling to it with her free hand. Tregear didn't let go of her. The kibble was half full of water. When it filled and sank, so would they. He wanted to reach to see if the rope Bobby had given him was still there, but he didn't dare chance it.

Eugenie was still crying. "I can't—hold on—"

"Yes, you can! Do you hear me?"

She was crying harder.

"Do you hear me, Eugenie!"

"Yes," she said after a moment.

"Hold on—the water will run into the lower levels. Hold on until then. Understand?"

"Yes," she said, her voice wavering. "Sion—he made me—let go of him—he pulled his hand loose—Tregear—"

"I know, lass. Hold on. Don't make it for naught."

He rested his forehead against the kibble, trying to think and trying not to. He had no hope for Sion Ennis. None. There was nowhere for the water to take him but down.

Oh, Jane!

The water was growing quieter now, but it was still high. Tregear looked upward, aware of a flickering light suddenly. Someone was being let down in a basket.

"Here!" he called.

"Rope coming down," a voice said.

After a moment, it plopped into the water, but Tregear couldn't see or reach it.

"You got it?" the voice said.

"No—"

"I'm going to swing it by."

He could hear it hit the water again, then felt it against his face.

"I've got it!"

The loop had already been made in it, and he pulled it over Eugenie's head and under her arms.

"Pull her up!" he yelled, and Eugenie gave a whimper as the rope went taut and she began to rise out of the water.

He waited in the dark for what seemed a long time before the rope dropped into the water again. The muscles in his arms felt strained and quivery. It was all he could do to get the rope over his head.

"Ready?" the voice said.

"Not unless you want to hang me."

"Not today, Cap'n," the voice said, and Tregear realized it was Bobby who dangled above him.

"Miss Eugenie says her brother's dead. Is he?"

"Yes," Tregear said, struggling with the rope. He finally managed to get the rope under his arms. "Haul away," he said, closing his eyes in exhaustion as Bobby relayed the command to the top and he began to move. He didn't realize until he reached the surface that his arm was bleeding. Hands pulled him to the side, got him out of the rope, wrapped him in a blanket. He was shaking uncontrollably now. Someone ripped his shirt sleeve and bound the cut tightly with a piece of muslin. Someone else gave him brandy.

No one spoke to him, and all the while he keep looking and looking through the crowd.

Jane!

Chapter Thirteen

*R*ain.

Jane sat in the dark staring out the window. There was just enough daylight left for her to see the raindrops running like tears down the windowpane, first one and then another and another, sometimes joining, sometimes finding their own paths. She watched intently, as if it mattered, trying desperately not to let her mind concern itself with anything else.

In the two days since Sion's death she had done nothing but listen to Eugenie sob into her pillow. Now she was finally asleep, and Jane struggled to find some emotion of her own besides the profound numbness that weighed upon her chest like a massive stone.

Sion's dead.

She longed to say the words out loud; surely there would be some release in that.

Sion's dead.

Her body ached for comfort, and there was none. Her mother had shut herself away in her room down the hall, trying to find whatever relief she could in her perpetual solitude. Miss Chappell had disappeared behind a closed door, as well, leaving everything to Milla. Jane was thankful for that, at least. She didn't think she could bear any lectures on how proper mourning was conducted in London. She was certain that it must be acknowledged, at least. She had no idea where her father might be. She hadn't been informed of his plans. The only thing she knew with any certainty was that he would not mourn Sion's death—and he expected all of them to follow his example, even Eugenie. He had wanted her given laudanum, and he had charged Jane to do it. Jane hadn't, knowing somehow that Eugenie had to weep for them all.

The house was so profoundly silent. It should have been full of people come to help ease the Ennis family's sorrow, but there was no one here, not even the Olivers. Mourners did not come to a house where the deceased had been disowned. How forlorn she and her mother and Eugenie were, all of them trapped behind the invisible wall of the doctor's relentless refusal to forgive. And no one knew how to breach it—or even dared—least of all Jane.

She looked over her shoulder at Eugenie's sleeping form. She wondered where Tregear was. Milla had told her he had to be carried away after he and Eugenie had been pulled from the mine. She longed to see him.

Eugenie gave a shuttering sigh in her sleep, and Jane quietly echoed it. But her eyes remained dry. Not because her father wished it, but because the pain of Sion's loss was somehow beyond tears.

Jane started at the sound of someone suddenly knocking on the front door, then stood, debating whether or not she wanted to go answer it. After a moment, the knocking came again—and then again. She walked quietly into the hallway and stood at the head of the stairs. She could hear the door open and her father's voice, but not what he said.

After a moment, Milla came up the stairs, her sleeping baby over her shoulder.

"Is someone ill?" Jane asked.

"No, Miss Jane," Milla said, her voice husky and tired-sounding.

"Who's at the door?"

Milla hesitated. "He's...gone now."

Jane moved quickly to the nearest window to look out. There was just enough light for her to see a man disappearing into the trees along the road.

"Who is that?" she asked, but Milla still didn't answer her.

"It's Tregear, isn't it?" Jane said, and this time Milla nodded.

"What did he want?"

"He wanted to speak to the doctor," Milla whispered. "He wanted to pay his respects—to answer any questions the doctor or Mrs. Ennis wanted answered—about what happened to Sion."

"What did my father say?"

"He said Tregear was getting above himself. He said he had no son—and to get away from here and not come back."

"But Tregear saved Eugenie's life," Jane said.

"Well, the doctor didn't thank him for it. Tregear wouldn't expect it, I know—not from him."

"Is Tregear...all right?"

"He's getting around all right, I reckon. But I think it's weighing heavy on him that he couldn't pull Sion out. Oh, Miss Jane, you could just see how it was with him. He was terrible sad."

Jane stood there trying not to wring her hands.

Tregear.

"Where—" She stopped and took a breath, her mind already made up. "Is Tregear staying in the same cabin where you were living?"

"Yes, Miss Jane. The very same."

She could feel Milla looking at her.

"You'll listen out for Eugenie?" she asked quietly, letting Milla think whatever she would.

"I will, Miss Jane. Your mam just said she wanted me and Charia to sit in there by the bed with her—so I can hear Eugenie easy enough if she wants anything. You don't have to worry none about either one of them."

Jane thought Milla was going to say something else. When she didn't, Jane turned to go.

"Miss Jane?" Milla said, and Jane looked at her. "Me and Charia—we'll be all right."

She knows, Jane thought suddenly. Milla had heard the bargain Jane had struck with her father.

Jane heard the front door open and close, and then the sound of her father's horse galloping away from the barn and down the road toward the village.

"The doctor's going to Smith's store—I mean to Albemarle," Milla said. "I can't never get used to the new name."

"Did he say why?"

"No, Miss Jane. He ain't one for explaining."

"Thank you, Milla," Jane said. "For everything."

"Jane!" Eugenie suddenly called, and Jane went quickly to see about her sister.

"Is Mother awake?" Eugenie asked as Jane lit a candle.

"I don't know."

"I want to go in there with her—even if she isn't," Eugenie said.

"Father said you could have something to make you sleep."

"I don't want to sleep. I want Mother. I have to know if—if she hates me—"

"She doesn't, Eugenie."

"Do you hate me, Jane? Do you?" Eugenie said, on the verge of weeping again. "I only wanted to feed the Knockers. That's all. I had this wonderful white bread—from Mrs. Mannion's table. I wanted to feed them—for Sion's sake. He needed protection if he was going to go underground with Tregear. I wasn't going inside very far—but then I heard them, Jane! I heard them! The Knockers—I wanted to keep Sion safe—I didn't want—him to—"

"Shh," Jane said, putting her arms around her. "I don't hate you, Eugenie. I could never hate you."

"I want to go in with Mother—please, Jane. I'll be quiet. Truly I will."

"All right," Jane said. "Milla and the baby will be in there, too."

Eugenie nodded and got out of bed. "Good."

"Take the candle," Jane said. "And try to rest."

"I will. I'm not going to let Sion die for nothing. Tregear said I shouldn't—and I won't."

Eugenie took the candle, but her hand was so shaky that Jane retrieved it and lit the way to their mother's room for her, her arm around Eugenie's shoulders. Eugenie had had her adventure at last—but at what price?

Jane quietly opened her mother's door. Milla was sitting in the rocking chair near the window and the baby slept at her side in the cradle. Jane waited in the doorway, watching Eugenie lie down across the foot of their mother's bed the way they both used to do when they were small children. She abruptly crossed the room and set the candle carefully on the windowsill, fighting down a sudden urge to cry.

She covered Eugenie with a quilt, then left quickly before she added to Eugenie's distress, but she didn't return to her bedchamber. She went straight downstairs and out of the house, and she didn't look back. She moved as fast as she could in the waning light, running down the road and then onto the path into the woods, completely unmindful of the rain.

She didn't think about what she was doing or why. It didn't matter. Nothing mattered except Tregear.

She encountered no one on the way, and she kept thinking about the last time she had trailed after Tregear like this. She had had a young woman's fascination for an untamed and dangerous man then—perhaps it was no more than that now.

But she kept going.

She was soaking wet by the time she reached Milla's cabin. She could see a candle burning inside, and she stopped short, as if some part of her hadn't expected that Tregear wouldn't actually be there.

But she didn't change her mind. She walked forward, and she didn't knock on the door. She opened it as if she had every right to do so, as if she belonged wherever he was. She didn't even consider whether or not he might not be alone.

She stood for a moment on the threshold, then stepped inside. Tregear was sitting in a chair with his back to her. The rain beat heavily on the roof. She couldn't tell if he'd heard her or not.

The place looked nothing as it had the last time she was there. Then it had been a hovel, an abandoned and unhappy place where Milla had gone to hide her shame. Now it was more a neat and sparsely furnished retreat. There was a different bed in the corner, and a polished table with a straight chair on the other side of the room. And a chair with arms where he was sitting.

A small fire burned on the hearth—made apparently to dry the wet clothes hanging from the mantel. She saw no personal belongings save the satchel that had rested under her bed the entire time he was ill.

The wind shifted, driving the rain against the door behind her, and she was cold suddenly. She walked closer to the fire. Tregear glanced at her, but he didn't say anything, and neither did she. It was just as well. She had no explanation for her arrival, not for herself or for him.

"I couldn't save him," he said after a moment, as if he were answering a question, one she hadn't asked.

She stood with her arms folded over her breasts, trying not to shiver. "Eugenie told me…what happened."

"Then why are you here?"

She didn't say anything, and he gave a quiet sigh, passing his hand briefly on his eyes.

"How is Eugenie?" he asked.

"She's…trying to do what you said."

"What I said?"

"You told her not to let Sion's death be for nothing. She's trying to do that."

"Does your father know you're…out?"

"No," she said, wondering if he would say that he had just been to the house.

"What will you tell him when he does?"

"I don't know," she answered truthfully. "I'm…" She looked away and didn't go on.

"You're going to have to say why you've come here," he said. "I want—need—to know."

"I thought I—it would—" She stopped again, completely at a loss as to what to say. She took a quiet breath and looked at him. He was staring at her intently now. She couldn't tell if he wanted her to go or stay. She could feel the tears beginning to roll down her cheeks. She didn't try to stop them, and she didn't wipe them away. She hadn't thought that she would cry, but she couldn't help it. And it wasn't just for herself that the tears came. It was for him. Milla had been right. He was suffering, as well.

"I couldn't save him," Tregear said again.

She moved closer to the chair.

"Do you think I don't know you would have if you could—even without Eugenie telling me?"

He didn't say anything, and because he didn't, she lost her nerve. She didn't know what she had expected, but she had clearly made a mistake in coming here. There was nothing to be done—for herself or him.

She stood for a moment longer, then abruptly turned to go. His hand shot out to keep her, catching her by the wrist even as he rose from the chair. When he was on his feet, he let go of her, and she waited, awkward and ill at ease, not knowing what to do.

"Are we to play it out then?" he asked. "Are we to pretend there's hope for the likes of you and me?"

She looked directly into his eyes.

"Yes," she said. "Yes!"

He reached for her then, as she had wanted him to do since she came through the door. His arms went around her and he held her tightly. She could feel the anger in him— and the despair.

"Stay with me," he said. "As long as you can."

She bit down on her lower lip to keep from sobbing out loud.

Forever, she thought. *And gladly.*

But there would be no "forever" and she knew it. She would never have the luxury of "forever" with any man. She didn't concern herself with the right or wrong of her being here. There was simply no other place for her to be.

She pressed her face into his neck and inhaled deeply, leaning into him, savoring the scent of his skin. She loved the way he smelled, loved the way he tasted. It occurred to her that she knew far more about his body than he did hers.

She had looked at him—more than once—and found him a beautiful man.

She lifted her head so that she could see into his eyes again. He wanted her the way a man wanted a woman; she understood that. And she also understood how unhappy the wanting made him.

She didn't look away. She could feel his body trembling, and his hand abruptly slid into her hair. His mouth covered hers, and there was nothing gentle in the kiss. It was filled with all the hunger and the hopelessness she herself felt.

She clung to him. It seemed that she had been lonely all her life, but here with him and in spite of the circumstances, the loneliness had disappeared. He was everything to her, more than family, more than life.

But, for all her inexperience, she knew better than to tell him so, just as she knew she would never keep him. He was the wild Cornishman no one here could understand. All they would ever have was this, now.

"Take me to bed," she said.

He started to say something, but she pressed her fingertips against his lips.

"I'm not a child. I want nothing beyond this, now, Tregear. No promises. No lies."

He looked into her eyes for a moment, then took her by the hand and led the way to the narrow bed in the corner. It was little more than a cot, but she didn't care. She felt a wildness and a willingness in herself that she couldn't explain—and she felt afraid and shy—all at the same time. So much so that when she shivered again, it was from a delicious kind of anticipation, not from the chill of her wet clothes.

She let go of his hand, intent upon unbuttoning the buttons on the front of her dress. But she fumbled so much he began to help her, his warm hands brushing her cold ones aside. She studied his face as he worked, thinking how grateful she was to the Saracen's youngest daughter. She loved his dark hair, his dark eyes. When he realized she was staring at him, he gave her one of his rare smiles.

But then, the smile faded, and he kissed her mouth again. There was still no tenderness in it. She neither wanted or needed it. His hand moved to her breast, and the pleasure of his touch took her breath away.

He was impatient now, dragging her wet clothes away from her body piece by piece and leaving them in a pile on the floor. She stepped out of them and into his arms. He lifted her off the floor and half carried her to the narrow bed, laying her down, one knee resting on the edge of the straw mattress. She sat up again and helped him bring his shirt over his head and undo the fastenings on his breeches, wondering if he knew that she had done it before.

When he was naked, he stretched out beside her and brought her close to him; they lay face to face, skin to skin. His body was so different from hers, strong and hard and muscular. She felt small and fragile in his embrace.

And safe. Nothing and no one could hurt her here.

She shivered again, and he pulled her closer.

His left arm was bandaged, but he gave her no time to ask about it. He began to kiss her, his mouth finding hers, tasting her with a hunger and a need that mirrored her own. His callused hands moved boldly over her breasts, her belly, the inside of her thighs, as if he had every right to do such things. He did have the right. She had given it to him. She closed her eyes at the pure joy of being with him like this, and when she opened them, he was waiting for her to do just that.

"Are you afraid of this?" he asked.

"Yes."

"So am I," he said.

His hands still caressed her. There was no part of her that he did not touch. She wanted to touch him as well, and she began to do so, tentatively at first, then with growing boldness, pleased that she could make him respond with a caught breath, with a moan, with a wavering sigh.

He began to kiss her breasts, to gently suckle, and an urgent need in her blossomed and grew until she couldn't lie still. She wanted to be closer to him, *had* to be closer to him.

In spite of his earlier impatience, he took his time. Slowly, deliberately, he made her whimper with desire for something she couldn't begin to name, and finally, when his body sought to enter hers, she welcomed it.

Such pleasure—and then a sharp pain—and then the pleasure again as he thrust deeply into her.

She heard him say her name, and she clung to him. At that moment, nothing existed for her but Tregear.

Nothing.

She would always love him, even if she never told him so. And she would never forget.

Her body rose to meet his every thrust. The pleasure suddenly peaking, rushing through her being in a torrent of sensation that was so exquisite, so incredible that she cried out, her senses soaring and soaring until, completely spent, she tumbled back to earth again.

"Will they find him?"

Jane had lain in Tregear's embrace a long time without speaking, their bodies spooned together, his warm breath against her neck, his hand resting on her breast.

She felt him take a deep breath in the darkness.

"No," he said, and she closed her eyes against the tears that threatened to spill down her cheeks again at his simple and candid response. She had known without a doubt that he would tell her the truth.

"Did he say anything?"

"There wasn't time. He saw what had to be done to save Eugenie and he did it."

"Will they close the mine?"

"No," he said again.

She turned to him. She wanted to see his face, to look into his eyes. But for him, Eugenie would be dead as well. Perhaps they were even now, and they owed each other nothing.

She reached up to touch his face, and he covered her hand with his.

"Your brother was a brave man. There isn't a miner here who won't respect what he did."

A miner.

But not Sion's own father.

"I don't want to think about anything," she said suddenly, because it was the truth. Time was already running out for them. She could feel it.

"There are things you need to know, Jane. About me—"

"No," she said. "There's no need. You and I have no past and no future. There's just this…now…."

She lifted her mouth to his, and he began to kiss her, softly at first and then with increasing urgency. The hunger they had for each other had not been sated after all. He took her quickly, deeply. It was better this time, the abandon, the pleasure—and no thought of consequences.

Afterward she slept a dreamless sleep, and when she awoke, she was alone.

She abruptly sat up. The cabin was empty—but then she heard voices. Tregear was talking to someone—a woman.

Jane took the blanket from the cot and wrapped herself

into it. Her clothes had been hung over the back of the straight chair, and she grabbed them up and quickly dressed, then crept quietly to the door. It was slightly ajar.

"I'll wait," she heard Miss Chappell say.

"You are wasting your time," Tregear said.

"Never," she said. "If you don't call her out here, I will."

Jane pushed the door back and stepped into view. "What is it?" she asked. And, for all her certainty that Jane was inside, Miss Chappell looked taken aback, as if she didn't really expect her worst fears to be borne out.

"You father is asking for you," Miss Chappell said when she recovered.

"I'm sure you told him where you thought I was," Jane said.

"No. I did not. I came to get you—before Eugenie and your mother find out what you've done. The doctor doesn't I know I left. I brought the saddlebag with the medical supplies. We can tell him you went out on a call and I accompanied you—for propriety's sake."

"No," Jane said.

"What is wrong with you?" Miss Chappell cried. "Have you no—"

Jane thought she was going to say "decency" but she didn't. It was all too obvious that Jane had passed the night in Tregear's bed.

Miss Chappell looked at Tregear.

"Will you let her ruin her life for you?" she asked him. "Will you let her ruin Eugenie—ruin all of us? For *you?* Tell her! Or I will!"

But she gave Tregear no chance to say anything.

"No matter what he's promised, he can't deliver it. He's married, Jane," Miss Chappell said. "Did he bother mentioning that? No, I can see he didn't."

Jane said nothing, her eyes on Tregear. It was true. She could see it on his face.

Catryn.

He was married to Catryn.

"He has a wife in England," Miss Chappell said. "He married well, our Tregear. A squire's daughter. He seduced her, talked her into going to Gretna Green for one of the 'anvil' marriages. Then he took her money and left her to come here. I wonder if she sits by the window waiting?"

"Jane—" Tregear said, reaching out to touch her arm. She stepped away.

"Do you hear him denying it, Jane?" Miss Chappell said. "One word of it?"

"I told you there were things you needed to know, Jane," he said, stepping around Miss Chappell, who deliberately put herself in his way.

"It doesn't matter," Jane said.

"It matters to me. *You* matter to me. There is nothing I would not do for you. Nothing! I have not had much tenderness in my life. What little there is has come from Reverend Branwell and his wife—and you. I want to tell you the truth as I know it—with Miss Chappell standing here as witness. Yes, I married Catryn Angwin. It was an elopement to Gretna Green. But her father interfered. I have not seen her since that day—"

"Please!" Jane cried. It took everything she had to look into his sad eyes. She had heard him call Catryn's name over and over when he was so ill, and now she understood the reason for his sadness. He still loved the woman he'd married, regardless of the circumstances.

"It doesn't matter," she said again. "I have always known how it was with you and Catryn. I meant what I said. I want nothing."

She took a few steps, then looked back at him. "I thank you for…everything. We are even at last, you and I. The debt you said you owed me has been paid."

Chapter Fourteen

I have always known how it was with you and Catryn.

Because he had asked for Catryn when he had the fever and didn't even remember it.

But Jane couldn't know his true feelings regarding Catryn Angwin when he himself did not. All he knew with certainty was that it was Jane who filled his every waking minute and haunted his dreams. He wanted to see her so badly he ached with it. He didn't care about her father's wishes. He didn't care about Mannion's edict to the miners. He would risk anything to see her, to talk to her.

Even so, he didn't go looking for her—for her sake, not his. Instead, he once again spent his time hoping from some glimpse of her in the village or at the church. He knew she was going with her father when he made his calls to the sick and injured of the area, but thus far, he hadn't been able to catch even a glimpse of her.

It had been nearly three weeks since Sion Ennis died. Three weeks since they had lain in each other's arms. He still couldn't believe she had come to him—as if she had known how much he needed her. He couldn't stop thinking about her, no matter how busy he kept himself or what accommodating woman called out to him as he passed by or how many brawls he had.

He gave a heavy sigh, making the dead blacksmith's replacement look up from the forge in his direction. It was likely the man thought Tregear's overt exasperation was meant for him. Tregear had been waiting a long while to see if the new smithy could repair the kibble damaged when the shaft flooded well enough to be paid for it. The sun beat down on them both, and after a time Tregear moved a short distance away to the spotty shade of a black walnut tree. He toyed with the idea of going to the tavern, but then his attention was taken suddenly by the sight of Dr. Ennis, passing through the village on horseback.

The doctor looked at him as he rode by—then through him—and it was all Tregear could do not to step up to him and drag him off his fine steed. The man was keeping Jane close to him and out of Tregear's way, he was certain of that. Perhaps it was merely because Tregear had the effrontery come to the house and offer his condolences. Perhaps because he had saved Eugenie's life. Or perhaps Miss Chappell had told the doctor everything, after all.

He had no way of knowing if the woman had actually given Jane the necessary alibi. He thought she must have, or he would have been called in by now. And if she had, he couldn't imagine what price she would exact for it. All in all, it must be a difficult strait for Miss Chappell to be in, having to choose between her revenge and her nebulous social position.

Tregear no longer concerned himself with how she had found out about the scandal he hoped he had left behind him in Cornwall. A few well-directed letters to people who could make inquiries, he supposed. It didn't really matter. Nothing mattered but the look on Jane's face the last time he saw her.

He had told Jane the truth when he said that he hadn't abandoned his wife, but he hadn't been able to make himself say that Catryn had, in fact, abandoned him—and only hours after the ceremony, when her irate father had finally caught up with them. The squire had given her a choice— return to Cornwall with him as an unwed daughter in good standing or stay with her essentially penniless husband and lose everything.

She had chosen her father, in spite of the fact that the marriage had been consummated. Tregear had stood in disbelief and watched her ride away from him and never once look back. He had truly believed that she loved him, but she had tossed him aside as if he were nothing.

He'd had no alternative but to return to Cornwall, as well. His pride wouldn't let him do otherwise, no matter how humiliating it might be. He refused to just disappear. His self-respect was far more important to him than whatever embarrassment she might suffer if their paths should cross. He came back, and he went about the business of hiding his suffering from the Branwells, pretending that nothing bad had happened to him and never once mentioning her name.

But the squire was a man of influence. Word of his daughter's elopement had gotten out, and someone had to suffer for it. That someone was Tregear. He suddenly found himself unemployable, no matter how skilled he was at mining or how educated he had become at the hands of the Reverend Branwell and his wife. All the talents he had were suddenly useless—until the Methodist reverends put their heads together and arranged for him to come to Gold Hill.

From the very beginning, he had seen in Jane Ennis the potential for another debacle like the one with Catryn happening all over again. And no matter how determined he'd been to prevent it, he'd still gone to her like an already singed moth to yet another flame.

Except that it was different with Jane.

He had been admittedly flattered by Catryn Angwin's determined and inexplicable infatuation with the Reverend Branwell's orphan. Perhaps he had garnered her notice because it was her father's mine that had orphaned him. Or perhaps it was the pure novelty of it all, because it had never occurred to her that the son of a rough and ignorant miner could be taught music and poetry and Greek—not to mention the proper use of a knife a fork. He had never dwelled on her motives; it was simply too painful. She had swept into his life and right back out again. He didn't know if he'd loved her. All he knew was that whatever he'd felt was not the same emotion he associated with Jane Ennis.

Jane was the kind of woman Reverend Branwell had once warned him about. The kind whose heart and soul were worthy of a man's admiration and protection. The kind whose welfare meant more to him than his own. The kind who had the power to hurt him at every turn, yet would not do it. *That* kind, the reverend said, rendered a man helpless—and was the only kind ever worth having.

More precious than rubies—or gold.

Tregear had always assumed that the squire, with his important connections, would have somehow made all record of a Greta Green ceremony disappear. He had worried a long time about the possibility of there being a child, knowing that the squire would likely make it disappear as well. It had been Tregear's plan all along to return to Cornwall—with money in his pockets—to settle the matter of his ill-fated marriage once and for all.

But there was nothing he could have said to Jane—except that he loved her and would stand by her if she needed him. It was she who had wanted no promises. He had nothing to offer her but his presence. Still wedded or not, he had nothing.

He looked around sharply at the sound of wagons coming down the muddy street—three of them loaded down with a shipment of gold from the mine and headed for the mint in Charlotte. The wagons continued past where he stood, all of them heavily guarded. He expected to see Bobby Reid among the drivers. The boy was notorious for protecting Mannion's property at any cost.

But Tregear didn't recognize any of them. As he was about to turn away, a wagonette came into view, and Bobby was suddenly accounted for. It appeared that he was now in the doctor's employ. Jane and Eugenie sat on the bench seat behind him.

Eugenie saw Tregear immediately, and he thought for a brief moment she was going to call out to him. Instead, she abruptly looked away and bowed her head.

But Jane didn't turn away. Her steady gaze met his and held. For as long as she could, she stared directly into his eyes. It was like the first time he ever saw her, all those months ago. He had thought that she wanted to despise him then—just as she wanted to despise him now. But she didn't. He knew she didn't. He could feel it. The sudden memory of her lying in his arms filled his mind again, the touch of her small hands and her taste. The feel of her body around his.

He stepped blindly out into the street.

Jane!

"Tregear!" someone yelled from the opposite direction. Mr. Mannion, out for his afternoon ride.

"I want to see you at the mining office," he said as he approached.

Tregear stood looking in the direction Jane had gone without acknowledging the man or his command.

"Now," Mannion said over his shoulder as he passed.

Tregear stood a moment longer, then followed the mine owner on foot to the office. A scrawny stray pup took an interest in the trip and scampered happily along with him as if it had an invitation.

Mannion was already waiting inside the office when Tregear arrived. A bevy of young boys, ever hopeful for some task that would earn them a penny, waited under the trees as usual. Some of them had tops and were playing a lively game of peg-in-the-ring, the childishness of the game belied by the fact that some of them had already been bloodied in the competition and most of them were smoking clay pipes.

Tregear had no expectations as to what the summons from Mannion was about. He didn't really care. Mr. Mannion looked up when Tregear opened the door and motioned for him to come in and sit down. As Tregear did so, the mine owner pulled a leather pouch from his pocket and dropped in on the desk.

"I should have gotten this to you last week, but I had business at the county seat. Take it," he said.

Tregear looked at it and left it lying where it fell. "What is it?"

"I would say it's your reward. From Dr. Ennis."

"For the one I saved or the one I let drown?" Tregear asked bluntly.

Mannion looked at him, but didn't respond to the question.

"I don't want the man's money," Tregear said. "I didn't go down for him."

"Nevertheless, he intends for you to have it."

"I don't much care what he intends."

"A thousand dollars," Mannion said, and Tregear gave a short incredulous laugh.

A thousand dollars. An absurd amount of money. Tregear could sail home easily with that much coin—which was probably the motive behind this unexpected generosity. He could return to Cornwall and find out once and for all whether or not the Gretna Green marriage continued.

But even as the notion came to him, he knew he wouldn't do it. He wouldn't leave Jane. Her father would put her out of the house if it happened that she was with child. She would find herself in the same situation as Milla had been, with no hope but prostitution with the shame of an illegitimate baby on her. He would not abandon her to that.

"Surely you can find some use for a thousand dollars, Tregear."

"None the doctor would approve of."

Surprisingly, Mannion smiled. "That is so," he said.

Tregear looked at the leather pouch, then reached across the desk and picked it up, savoring the heavy feel of it in his hand for a moment, weighing yet another possibility before he abruptly made up his mind.

"There is something I would like to buy," he said. "But I would need you to broker it."

"What is that?"

"I want Coley's ownership papers."

"You don't need me for that."

"I don't think Warren would sell them to me—at least not without a lot of posturing about how I could have come by the coin and jacking up the price. I read the newspapers. A man as old as Coley would bring less than six hundred at the Fayetteville Market House."

"Only if Warren wants to part with him."

"He'll want to—if the offer comes from you."

Mannion reached into his pocket for a cigar and lit it, taking a few puffs on it before he replied.

"You're a strange man, Tregear. I never know what to

expect. I thought you would be heading back to Cornwall. This much money could have the home folks looking at you in a different light.''

Tregear made no comment. He had never been sure how much Mannion knew about his past—and he wasn't about to chance giving him any information he didn't already have.

"All right,'' Mannion said after a moment. "I'll see what I can do. In the meantime, am I to tell the doctor how grateful you are?''

"You do that,'' Tregear said.

"And if he asks what you've done with his reward?''

"Tell him that, as well,'' Tregear answered, and he waited, because he didn't think the meeting was over. He had the distinct impression that Mannion had something else on his mind.

"The water is receding,'' Mannion said. It wasn't quite a question.

"Yes.''

"But I understand the men don't want to work.''

"Not with Sion Ennis unaccounted for.''

"What can we do about that?''

"I have been looking for him in the places I can get into—but I don't expect to find him.''

"Does his family know that?''

"Jane does. I can't say about the rest.''

"And?''

"It would be better to close the lower shaft where he likely ended up. It's not a proper burial, but it will satisfy the men.''

"Do it,'' Mannion said, reaching to take the doctor's bribe and put it in his pocket.

Tregear stood and turned to go.

"I'll get the best price for Coley I can,'' Mannion said,

but he waited until Tregear was about to open the door to broach what was really on his mind. "I told you how it was with the Ennis daughters the day you came here."

"Yes," Tregear said.

"Dr. Ennis will never stand for any undue…interest in Jane, Tregear. The girl is beyond your reach, you know that, don't you? He'll see you dead first."

Tregear looked at him. Mannion was making a bold assumption about the seriousness of his involvement with Jane, and Tregear wasn't about to enlighten him about that, either.

"I know the doctor better than you do," Mannion said.

"You know *him* better, but not his kind," Tregear said. "The man is nothing new to me."

"I'm telling you for your own good. Stay away from her."

"Only she has the power to direct that—not her father. And not you."

"I don't intend to see my interests compromised, Tregear."

"I will do my job."

"Indeed you will. Now see to this business of getting the men back working, and then come find me. I will tell you then what that job will be."

Jane was standing in the empty church when flooring under her feet began to shake.

"Is that him?" Eugenie asked, grabbing Jane by the hand. "Is that Tregear?"

Jane could hear the blast now, and the rumbling seemed to go on and on, longer than Jane had ever heard come from the mine. She looked at Eugenie and nodded.

"Oh, Jane," Eugenie whispered. "I kept hoping and hoping…."

Eugenie stopped and put her face into her hands, but Jane knew exactly what her sister meant. Eugenie had been holding fast to the impossible belief that Sion could still come walking out of the mine somehow, a little thinner perhaps, but smiling and telling one of his outlandish stories about how he'd gotten washed into a safe place and had only just made his way back out again.

But all hope was gone now. Sion was buried forever. They would never see him again, at least not in this world. Jane wondered what her father was doing right now and if he even knew what was happening in the mine.

No, she thought. Who would tell him? She certainly hadn't dared do it. Thanks to Milla, she had known that Tregear would close the shaft today, and she had chosen to forgo her father's permission and come to the church, bringing Eugenie along with her, knowing it would be deserted and she and Eugenie could say their prayers for their brother in peace.

Jane sat down on the nearest bench, and Eugenie sat next to her, sobbing quietly, still holding on to her hand. She was so tired suddenly, tired enough to wonder if she would not come down with the fever after all.

She looked around at a small noise. Reverend and Mrs. Oliver came quietly into the church. Then Milla carrying Charia on her hip. And Lolly and three of the Midges. And Bobby Reid. And Mrs. Mannion.

More and more people were arriving. Miners. The boot maker. The man who owned the tavern. The fallen women who would not have dared come into the church on any other occasion. They were all here for Sion.

After a moment, Reverend Oliver moved to stand in the middle of the church rather than at the pulpit, so that he was among them.

"The souls of the righteous are in the hand of God, and

there no torment shall touch them," he began. "In the sight of the unwise they seem to die and their departure is taken for misery…but they are in peace.

"As gold in the furnace hath He tried them…and…they shall shine…."

Jane wiped hard at her eyes. Mrs. Oliver had come to sit beside her and reached to put her arm around her and Eugenie both.

"Let us pray," Reverend Oliver said.

The rest of the service passed in a blur. People came and spoke to Jane as they left. She tried to say something to them all, to thank them for coming.

"I'm going to take Eugenie to the house with me," Mrs. Oliver said at one point. "I think you would like a little time alone."

Jane looked at her gratefully. "Yes," she said as Mrs. Oliver led Eugenie away.

She sat for a long time, telling herself that she just needed to rest for a little while before she fetched Eugenie and they went back home. But she had no intention of hiding where they had been from their father. If he asked, she would tell him. Some part of her wanted him to ask, so that she could let him know that no matter what he thought of Sion, the rest of the village didn't agree with him. He was wrong about Sion—and perhaps he was wrong about Tregear.

Jane had been trying so hard not to think about Tregear, but how could she not when every night she lay in the same bed he had lain? She hadn't seen him since that day he'd been standing beside the blacksmith shop. She had thought for one instant that he was actually going to step out into the street and speak to her, that he might even try to stop the wagonette.

And if he had, what would she have done? That was the

question that scared her so. Free or not, if he wanted her to go with him, would she? She feared it would be better if she were never put to that test. Perhaps her father understood more than she gave him credit for. Perhaps her weakness for Tregear was obvious to him and always had been—and that was why he kept her so busy at the surgery of late. He had even gotten to the point of leaving her on her own to see to whatever patients came while he made his rounds among the better families of the area. She was glad of it. The family had been shattered by Sion's death, whether her father admitted it or not. All of them were affected, especially Eugenie. Eugenie would carry the guilt for Sion's death as long as she lived. It was only Tregear's admonishment that she not let Sion have died for nothing that gave her any kind of peace.

Oh, Tregear—

Jane stood and walked down the aisle to the back of the church. She looked back over her shoulder at the altar.

"God bless you, Sion," she whispered.

She waited for a moment before she went outside, because she was feeling unwell again, so unwell and so overcome with a sudden nausea that she barely made it to the corner of the church before she had to stop. She hid there among the shrubbery, holding on to the building for support, willing the nausea to pass.

She realized suddenly that she was not alone. Eugenie stood on the path, watching. But she said nothing, and she didn't come forward. She merely waited for Jane to come so that they might begin the walk back to the Olivers.

After a moment, Jane forced herself to join her. Eugenie kept looking at her, but she asked no questions—which was not like her at all.

"Mrs. Oliver said Tregear brought up the slate," she said as they walked along.

Jane looked at her, not understanding.

"It's from the part of the mine—from the place where Tregear thinks Sion is. It's for us to put in the cemetery— to use as a memorial stone so we'll have a place marked for him."

Jane didn't say anything. She kept walking.

"He's very kind to us, isn't he?" Eugenie said. "Tregear. And he didn't have to do that—especially since Father paid him and he ought not offend him. But I think he must not care if Father won't like it if Sion is to be remembered—"

"What do you mean, paid him?" Jane interrupted.

"Milla says Father gave Tregear a big reward. For saving me, I guess. Lolly heard Mr. and Mrs. Mannion talking about it. Mr. Mannion was all cross because he thinks Tregear will take the money and go back to England and he'll have a devil of a time—that's what he said—'devil of a time'—finding somebody half as good to replace him. Do you think Tregear will really go? Here comes Bobby with the wagonette," she said before Jane could answer, stepping out into the street to flag him down.

"Don't Eugenie," Jane said. "Father must have him doing something this afternoon."

But it was too late. Bobby stopped the wagonette, and if he had an errand for the doctor he couldn't abandon just to transport Eugenie and Jane home, he didn't say so. He stopped immediately and hopped down, wiping his rough hand on his breeches before he offered it to Eugenie to help her climb in.

"I'm going to have to take the shortcut," he said to Jane as helped her into the wagonette. "It's a rough ride, but I have to, if I'm going to get you back ahead of the doctor."

More conspiracy, Jane thought. She wondered if her

father realized that it was his own personality that inspired it.

They rode along in silence, the sadness of the day weighing heavy on all of them. Jane didn't feel any better as the
trip progressed, but thankfully, she didn't feel any worse.

"Jane?" Eugenie whispered.

Jane didn't answer her.

"Jane," she whispered again and Jane looked at her.

"Does Tregear want you?" Eugenie asked bluntly, her
voice hopefully low enough for Bobby not to be able to
hear over the noise of the horses' hooves and the creaking
and bumping of the wagon and the scraping of saplings
that dragged against the sides as they passed.

Jane glanced at Bobby's back then at her sister. "What
on earth are you talking about?"

"I'm talking about you and Tregear. I heard Miss Chappell tell Father again that he did—but I've always thought
it, because of the way he looks at you. It's the same way
Reverend Oliver looks at Mrs. Oliver and Sion looked at
Milla."

Jane stared at her. *Sion looked at Milla?*

"Does Tregear love you?"

"No, he does not," Jane said.

"Do you love him then?"

"Eugenie—" Jane said in exasperation. She did not feel
up to this conversation.

"Tell me. Please. If you love him, say so."

Jane looked at her. Eugenie was close to tears again.
"Why would you need to know such a thing?"

"Because I do. So I can—" Eugenie stopped suddenly
and gave a heavy sigh. "You're so sad, Jane. I need to
know if it's that or if I'm to blame—because of Sion—"

"Eugenie, let's not talk about this."

"Why not? No one ever tells me anything—because I'm

supposed to be a child. But I'm not a child. I understand things. I understand a lot more than you think. Would you marry Tregear if he asked for you?''

''He can't ask for me, Eugenie. He is already married.''

''Are you sure? He thinks he's married?''

''He doesn't 'think' it Eugenie. He *is* married.''

''But how do you know?''

''He himself told me.''

''When? When did he tell you?''

''Right after Sion died.''

''Then he must not—''

''Must not what?'' Jane asked when Eugenie didn't continue.

''Nothing. Are you feeling better now? You're very pale still.''

''Yes,'' Jane said, lying.

''You must stay well, Jane. I don't know what any of us would do if you didn't—Mother and me, Milla—even Father. I don't know what the people here would do, either. It's you they want to see now when they're sick—''

Eugenie suddenly stopped and looked past her into the woods as they rode along, her eyes filling with tears. ''I'm going to cry again, I think,'' she said, no longer whispering. ''I'm sorry. I know Father doesn't want us grieving but I—oh, Jane, I can't believe Sion is gone!''

Jane reached to put her arm around Eugenie's shoulders. Bobby stopped the wagonette under the nearest tree.

''Horses need resting,'' he said without looking back.

And his beloved Eugenie needed a safe place to weep.

Chapter Fifteen

Jane realized the moment they rode into the yard that Tregear was not the one leaving Gold Hill. It was she—and the entire family. Three wagons stood in the yard already loaded with the furniture from the house, and several men milled about trying to make room for more.

She didn't wait for Bobby to help her down from the wagonette. She forgot her earlier indisposition and climbed over the side to step on the wheel and jump down. And she realized as she did so that Bobby Reid had not showed up to take them home by accident, nor was it likely that she and Eugenie had actually slipped away to go to the church today. Once again, her father had wanted them out of the house.

But Jane doubted that she and Eugenie could have given him as much trouble as Miss Chappell was clearly doing now. The woman was more agitated than even Jane could have imagined. Her hair was coming undone and her cheeks were flushed.

And she turned on Jane the moment she saw her.

"This is *your* fault," she snapped, clearly no longer caring now about protecting Jane and ultimately the family reputation.

"What's wrong? What's happening?" Eugenie said, hastily wiping her eyes before her father saw that she'd been crying.

"We're leaving here—that's what's happened!" Miss Chappell cried. "And all because you and your sister can't leave that vulgar miner alone!"

Eugenie looked at Jane, clearly baffled by the accusation. "What does she mean?"

Miss Chappell ignored her and the question. Jane sidestepped the woman and went into the house. Everything had already been cleared out on the ground floor. She went upstairs. She could hear raised voices coming from her mother's room.

"I will not go unless Milla and the baby come with us," Jane heard her mother say.

"That is out of the question," her father answered.

"It is not out of the question! Are you not listening to me! I will not leave here without them!"

"Of course, you will leave. Your place is with me—"

"What will you do if I don't? Have me packed up and carried off like the rest of the furniture!"

"Be quiet! People will hear you!"

"Ah! It matters to you that these people—the ones you hold in such contempt—overhear? Perhaps there is hope for you after all!"

"You know what people think—"

"About you or me?" Jane's mother asked, her voice still rising.

Jane had never heard her mother speak in anger before. Never. And she realized suddenly that the French accent her mother had supposedly lost years ago was somehow very much in evidence—as if she couldn't be irate and obliterate her heritage all at the same time. Jane understood, too, her mother's sudden fire. It was easy for an observer to mistake indifference for dutiful obedience. Jane's mother was no more compliant than Jane herself was—when the thing in contention mattered.

"Or perhaps you will simply have me committed to a lunatic asylum or locked away in an attic," her mother said. "You have the authority as my husband—and even if you did not, who would not believe that I am mad with grief? My son is dead. Do you hear how I have said it? *My* son. He may have already been dead to you for months, but not to me. Milla and the child give me comfort—and at no inconvenience whatsoever to you. How could you tell Milla she has the day free and just leave her to return here and find us gone with no explanation and no word of farewell? It is a terrible unkindness—one I will not be a party to."

"There will be other servants—"

"Then there will be other wives as well! I cannot believe there was a time when I was flattered by your jealousy. Little did I know it would extend to your children as well— that you would try to keep them for yourself forever."

Jane heard the door to her mother's room rattle, and she bolted into her own bedchamber. The beds and chests, the dresser and Jane's small desk were gone. There was nothing left but her and Eugenie's trunks and their clothes.

She heard her father coming down the hallway.

"You and Eugenie will pack your things as quickly as possible," he said from the doorway. "There will be no dallying."

He left immediately without even looking at her. She didn't say anything to try to keep him. She didn't ask where it was they were going, knowing she would find out soon enough. She didn't really care where they were going or that they were leaving in such haste. There was no one here she needed to say goodbye to but Tregear, and that was not possible, no matter how much she wanted it.

Tregear.

If her father had paid him money, then there must be a desired result from his doing so—or he wouldn't have done it.

Of course, Jane thought suddenly.

He would have wanted—expected—Tregear to leave these parts once he had the funds to do so. But in the event that he didn't, her father would still make sure that the Cornishman was not a part of their lives—her life—even in the most casual of ways.

Jane moved to look out the window. Her father stood in the yard, speaking to one of the men, while Miss Chappell hovered on the sidelines. Jane couldn't hear the conversation, couldn't tell anything about what he was saying by the man's response. She could only tell that Miss Chappell's distress had not lessened. She wondered if her father had decided to let Milla accompany them or if he was making arrangements to have his wife carried out bodily.

After a moment, her father walked toward the surgery. As far as Jane could see from her vantage point, it had been stripped as well. Even the plants in the greenhouse had been taken up and placed in tubs of dirt on one of the wagons. It wasn't merely a whim, then. They were going and the move was permanent.

Jane gave a tired sigh. She was exhausted from the day's events and didn't feel up to facing anything else. She stood for a moment longer, then walked quietly down the hall to her mother's room, listening for a moment before she knocked on the door.

"Mother?" she called when there was no immediate response. She pushed against it. It had been latched from the inside. "Mother, please let me in."

There was a long pause, and then the door finally opened. Jane stepped inside, and her mother immediately latched the door again behind her, a gesture that would hardly keep anyone out who was even mildly determined to get in. It had apparently sufficed, however. Hers seemed to be the only room in the house untouched.

"Did you hear the blasting?" Jane asked gently, and her mother looked at her for a moment as if she didn't understand the question, then shook her head no. Jane could sense the effort it was taking for her to seem calm and normal.

Her mother moved away and sat down in the rocking chair by the window.

"Tregear...closed the part of the mine where Sion was lost," Jane said. "So that he would have at least a semblance of a decent burial—"

Her mother gave a sharp intake of breath, and Jane stopped and waited. When her mother looked at her, she continued.

"Eugenie says Tregear brought up slate from the place— so that we would have a memorial stone."

"Does your father know?" her mother asked.

"I don't know—I think that he likely does."

"We're leaving, Jane. Do you understand that? He is taking us to some mountaintop—"

"Mountaintop?" Jane said blankly. There were mountains—part of an ancient range—not far away, but no one lived there.

No one.

"Somewhere along the Pee Dee River. I can't say what the place is called—but he is taking us into the mountains," her mother said, gesturing in the air with one hand. "He has bought the land. He has had the house built there already—and what are we to do but go? He means to leave immediately—now. We must go like thieves in the night even if it means we will be forced to sleep in the wagon somewhere along the way.''

''Mother—''

''There will be no one there but the four of us, Jane. No one. I don't think I can bear it.'' She gave a heavy sigh, shivering slightly as she did so.

She suddenly stood and forced a smile that was far from reassuring. ''Forgive me, my darling. It is wrong of me to burden you with this. My poor Sion. He has his resting place at last?''

''Yes,'' Jane said.

''We must thank Tregear when we see him. Perhaps he will visit—or I shall invite him to make sure he does. That would be better, wouldn't it?''

''Yes,'' Jane said, wondering if her mother had forgotten that they would not be here and that Tregear had been turned away when last he came.

''Will you find Milla for me, darling? I wish to speak to her about the baking.''

''The baking?''

''Yes. I was not much pleased with the job the miller did grinding the cornmeal this time. I think she must speak to him on our behalf. I'm certain she will be able to handle it. It will save your father the aggravation. He is not overly tactful about such things.''

Jane stood there, trying to understand. ''Milla...isn't here, Mother.''

Her mother looked at her, then suddenly put her face in her hands. Jane went to her, but she immediately put her hands down and refused to be comforted.

''I will do what I must,'' she said, more to herself than to Jane. ''Go along now, darling. Help Eugenie get her things together. You do not wish to vex your father.''

Jane hesitated, still worried about her mother's state of mind.

"Go on," her mother said kindly. "Now please."

Jane went. She expected to hear her mother lock the door behind her, but she didn't. Jane waited a moment longer, then continued to her all but vacant bedchamber. From the doorway, she saw Eugenie lifting a floorboard where Jane's bed had stood.

"What are you doing?" she asked, making Eugenie jump.

"Looking," Eugenie said. "It's loose."

"Well, put it back. Father says we are to pack," Jane said. She made a halfhearted attempt to do so, then sat down on the floor instead. She could feel Eugenie staring at her. And worrying.

"Mother says we are moving to a mountaintop," Jane said, looking at her sister. "Somewhere along the Pee Dee. Father has had a house built there."

"It must be the place Mrs. Mannion asked about," Eugenie said. She sat down on the floor beside her and touched her on the arm. "Jane, are you all right?"

"Yes, of course. I'm just…tired. I think I could sleep right here."

"You rest. I'll put your things in the trunk for you. Where we are going—is it far away, do you think?"

"Well, it must be twenty miles or so to the river. It depends on where the place is."

"Will we come back here ever?"

"No," Jane said with conviction. She could not see her father allowing her the opportunity of encountering Tregear again, however unlikely it might be. The realization that she might never see him again suddenly swept over her.

"What?" she said absently in response to whatever Eugenie just asked.

"I said is Mother all right?"

"No," Jane said. "She's very...distressed."

"I don't think I ever want to marry," Eugenie said after a moment. "Never ever."

"Eugenie, you are too young to know such—"

"Look at Mother," Eugenie interrupted. "What has marriage done for her? Father got all her dowry money and she got nothing—except us, I guess. But she had to give up her family and her friends and her country to go to England and then to come here just because Father wanted it. I never want to have to do something like that. She had no one to speak French with but Sion—"

"She and Sion spoke French?" Jane asked in surprise, because her mother had always declined when Jane had wanted to practice the language, pleading a headache or some pressing matter she couldn't ignore. Jane had accepted the excuses at the time, but now she wondered. Was it simply that Sion was her mother's favorite and the one with whom she had the most in common, or was it that she only dared converse with one of her children for fear of discovery? If the latter was so, she had chosen well. Sion would never have given her away.

"I used to hear them sometimes when you and Father went to Smith's store to get the medical supplies. They would talk for a long time after I went to bed. It must be very lonely—not having parties and things like Mrs. Mannion talked about especially when you're used to it. You and I—we don't know the difference—not really—because we've never had them. But poor Mother knows. She doesn't have anyone else like herself around, Jane. Even Tregear and the rest of the Cornwall men have each other to talk to. But Mother—all she had was Sion. I must make it up to her somehow—for taking Sion away."

Jane put her arms around her to comfort her, to comfort

herself, and they sat there like lost children. But she didn't want to think about her mother's sadness or Eugenie's remorse. She didn't want to think about anything. After a moment, she got up from the floor and stood for a moment looking around the room. Regardless of her resolve, she couldn't keep from remembering.

Tregear.

She was trying so hard not to love him, not to need him. It was best that she go away from here.

"Why can't things just stay the same?" Eugenie asked. "It's so—" She stopped because a strange man came as far as the doorway.

"The doctor, he says I'm to be taking the trunks, miss," he said, shuffling his feet awkwardly.

"Take mine," Eugenie said, pointing it out. "It's ready."

The man returned for the other trunk before they had finished putting all of Jane's clothes into it. He stood and waited in the hallway—until Bobby came halfway up the steps and called him away. Bobby came to get the trunk himself, both his ears flushed red. Jane supposed it was more because he was actually in Eugenie's presence and in her bedchamber than from the exertion of climbing the stairs.

"Bobby," Jane said as she closed and locked the trunk lid. "Do you know where exactly we're going?"

"I know," he said. "But I ain't to say. To nobody," he added, dragging the trunk out of the room and into the hallway.

"What do you mean you're not to say? Surely Eugenie and I can be told," Jane said, following after him.

Bobby didn't answer her. As he dragged the trunk to the head of the stairs, her mother's door opened. Surprisingly, she was dressed for traveling, and she held out her hand for Jane and Eugenie to join her. Together they followed Bobby's bumping progress down the stairs.

"Mother—" Jane began when they reached the first floor, but her mother shook her head.

"No use," she said. "No use at all."

Jane followed her outside. Her mother walked purposefully to the wagonette and waited for Bobby to notice and give her a hand up. She made no pretense at looking for her husband anywhere on the premises. She merely took a seat and, like a condemned criminal, waited to be hauled away.

Eugenie climbed in behind her, but when Jane was about to step up, her father called from the surgery.

"Jane! Come here! Bobby Reid, you know what to do."

"Yes, sir, Dr. Ennis," the boy said. He waited for two of the wagons loaded down with furniture to start out, then coaxed the team pulling the wagonette to follow.

"Isn't Jane coming?" Eugenie called to their father.

"Jane will follow with me and Miss Chappell in the other wagon," he said, waving them on. "You are to take care of your mother."

Jane could see the perplexed expression on Eugenie's face, one that belied the brave little wave she gave and the wagonette rolled out of the yard.

Jane watched them as long as she could—until her father called her again. She heard him perfectly—but the weakness she'd experienced at the church had returned. She simply couldn't make her body obey, and she could barely see him when she looked in that direction. The swirling blackness at the edge of her field of vision grew until it obliterated most of him and Miss Chappell, who stood at his elbow.

Jane reached out blindly for something to hold on to, but there was nothing handy. She could feel herself falling, hear Miss Chappell's cry of alarm, remember Tregear's sad eyes.

Tregear!

"I got her," someone said.

Tregear...

"Father, it is not *my* fault—you can't blame me for this," she thought an annoyed Eugenie said.

No. Eugenie had gone.

Jane tried to lift her head, but she couldn't, and the blackness closed over her.

When she opened her eyes again, the sun was nearly gone. She immediately tried to sit up.

"Lie still," Miss Chappell said. "You've had a bad faint."

"Have I?" Jane murmured. Her head hurt. She looked around her. She was lying on the cot in the small side room in the surgery. The surgery hadn't been completely stripped after all. Even so, there was little evidence that Milla and Charia had been living in it.

"You said *his* name, you know," Miss Chappell said. "Tregear's. The doctor heard you. I hope you're pleased with yourself."

No, Jane thought. She wasn't pleased with herself. She wasn't pleased with anything.

She tried to sit up again.

"No," Miss Chappell said, pushing her back. "The doctor says you must lie still. He's mixing something up for you."

"I thought everything was packed away," Jane said.

"Well, if it was, it had to be unpacked—thanks to you."

"I want to reassure my mother—"

"Your mother and Eugenie have long gone, don't you remember? The doctor sent them on without us. And now we've had to delay even longer because of you."

Jane's first inclination was to say she was sorry, but she didn't. She wasn't sorry. She wasn't anything.

"You realize it's your fault we have to leave here," Miss Chappell said.

"So you keep telling me," Jane answered. She remembered *that* well enough.

"And so I shall again. You are a stupid, stupid girl—" Miss Chappell stopped at the sound of footsteps.

Jane tried to sit up again, and this time Miss Chappell let her. Her father entered the room carrying a tin cup.

"Drink this," he said, handing it to her.

She took the cup, but she didn't immediately drink it. She held it with both hands, looking at her father.

"Drink it," he said.

The aroma of the brew wafted upward, and she knew what it was—immediately. She had prepared too many infusions for him in the last year not to, and even if she hadn't, she'd collected enough medicinal plants, committed enough of the *Materia Medica* to memory. She knew the smell of this particular plant and she knew its effect on the female body in the proper doses—and if the concoction was made too strong.

She had no doubt as to purpose of this one, and the shock of her father's plan left her silent. Her mind raced to understand how it had all come to this. Had he known about Tregear or had he guessed? Had Miss Chappell told him she had spent the night with Tregear after all or was her father merely not taking any chances?

But none of that mattered. Not now.

"Drink it," her father said for the third time.

Chapter Sixteen

"Woman waiting for you up top," one of the men making his way into in the new shaft said.

Tregear peered at him in the candlelight, trying to see his face so that he could tell if he was telling the truth or if it was another crude miner's joke.

Closing the place where Sion Ennis lay had opened a new bed of slate and quartz that promised a substantial vein of gold. The men had gone back to work immediately, those who were well enough since the fever epidemic—but there were some aspects of normalcy Tregear would just as soon do without.

"I hear she's crying," the man said, and the others within earshot laughed.

"Whose skirt you had your hand up now, Tregear?" another one asked.

"Tregear's women don't wear skirts—they get shed of them at the first sight of him," the first one opined, and the laugher multiplied.

Tregear ignored their sport and moved quickly through the darkness to the kibble in the vertical shaft, knowing Coley would follow without having to be told. When they reached the top, he saw Milla standing a few yards away from the opening. He had hoped against hope that it might somehow be Jane, and he could feel Coley looking at him and likely noting just that.

"Tregear!" Milla called as soon as she saw him.

He handed Coley his satchel and walked to her. The baby—Charia—rested contentedly in the crook of her arm in spite of her mother's obvious distress.

"What's wrong?" he asked. He reached out to touch the little girl's soft hair for good luck. What little bit of luck he might have once had must be depleted by now.

"They're gone. Jane and all of them. The furniture— everything—"

He looked at her, not quite understanding what she was telling him.

She gave a sharp sigh. "I was to have all of yesterday free to visit Lolly—the doctor said I could stay till noon. But when I come back a while ago, they was gone."

"Gone where?"

"Well, you'd know that better than me!" she said, wiping her eyes.

"No, I don't know, Milla."

He looked at Coley, who was standing not far away. "Do you?" he asked the man pointedly.

"Did Miss Jane give in to you or not?" Milla asked before Coley could answer.

Tregear didn't say anything.

"You're not going to just walk off from it, are you?" she asked as if he'd admitted it.

"Milla, I don't—"

"All right, then," she interrupted again, shifting Charia to her other arm. "If it's plain speaking you want, I can do that. I'm thinking there is a chance that she's with child and I'm thinking you're the reason—and if you are, then damn you for it, Tregear, if you're going to leave her to face it by herself—are you listening to me!''

Tregear walked a few steps away before he turned and looked at her.

''Has she said—?''

''No, she hasn't *said!* She's a babe herself when it comes to this kind of thing. I doubt she would even know if she was getting a baby, for all her studying doctoring—at least not this early. If she did know, there's a good chance she wouldn't tell you—not if she thought it would cause *you* trouble. If there's a chance she's got your babe, you've got to do something while it's early, Tregear—make an honest woman of her so people won't know—''

''I can't marry her, Milla.''

Milla stared at him, and it was all he could do not to look away from the disappointment he saw in her eyes.

''But you could still keep her, marriage or no, so everybody would know she belongs to you and not take advantage of her. You could see she's not alone and she's got food to eat. If the doctor finds out she's been with you, carrying or not, there's no telling what he might do. It's for sure he'll throw her out, Tregear. Look at what he did to Sion. She ain't got her own money like Sion did. She'll end up whoring or worse. You care about her, don't you?''

''I care, Milla.''

''Enough not to let anything bad happen to her? You'll do for her, won't you?''

''I'll do as much as I can—as much as she'll let me.''

''All right then,'' Milla said. ''That's all I wanted to know. I always thought you had a good heart—I wasn't looking to have to change my mind about it.''

She turned and began walking away, then stopped and looked back at him.

''You mind how you go, Tregear. The doctor, he's a

devious man. He always gets what he wants and he's got no mercy in him. You don't know.''

"He's not the first I've run into. What are you going to do?''

"I'm going back home. I reckon they'll have me now that Charia's here and all. But I'm going to Lolly's place first. Maybe her or one of the others heard something today—about where Miss Jane is.''

"You'll tell me if you find out anything—''

"I will, Tregear.'' She gave him a little half smile. "If I have to hunt you down like a dog.''

Tregear stood for a moment after she'd gone, staring at the ground.

Jane, Jane—

Where would the doctor have taken all of them? To Salisbury? To Raleigh? Even if Tregear found her, what could he say to her that she would believe? He loved her. With all his heart. And he should have told her so—long before they passed the night together—when she might have believed it. It was too late now. Whether she was pregnant with his child or not, the words would be meaningless to her. He knew her well enough to know that. She would not accept a profession of love she thought belonged rightly to his wife.

But first he was going to have to find her. He would worry about the rest of it later.

Coley had come closer and stood watching him. Tregear recognized the look.

"Did you hear any of that?'' Tregear said, and for once Coley didn't prolong it.

"I heard like.''

"What do you know about it?''

"They say the doctor is going,'' Coley said. "Maybe done gone already.''

Tregear looked at him. "Well, you're late with that news. Why didn't you tell me sooner?"

"Didn't know sooner. Knew this morning. You can't leave the new shaft then—without big trouble. Mr. Mannion, he don't know what to do with you as it is. Maybe you'd be gone already if blasting for Mister Sion didn't find more gold for him."

"Where do you think Dr. Ennis went?"

"Old mountain by the Uharie—before it gets to be the Pee Dee."

"I don't know what that means, Coley."

Coley didn't enlighten him.

"You know which mountain?"

"That he don't say out loud for folks to hear. He got to keep *her* away from you. It don't matter if *you* want her. It's *she* wanting you, he hates. Maybe he don't want you finding her soon if he needs the time to change her mind. He don't hide her on a big mountain—just a little one. You got to be careful like anyways. Or somebody die."

Tregear didn't need to ask who the "somebody" might be, and he didn't take the time to worry about it. "Then you'd better stay clear of me," he said.

"Death Angel used to seeing us two, Cap'n. Might get too bold if two is just one."

"No," Tregear said. "My troubles are mine—"

"Tregear!"

He looked around. One of the errand boys was coming at a run.

"Mr. Mannion—he wants you—now—" the boy said. He was completely out of breath, but he somehow managed to find enough air to blow his hair out of his eyes in an effort to see.

"What does he want?" Tregear asked, looking in his pockets for a coin.

"Didn't say," the boy answered. "But he's—in a—hurry."

He's not the only one, Tregear thought. He found the coin and tossed it to Coley. "Get me a horse—from the blacksmith. Don't you go 'borrowing' one, you hear?"

Coley didn't say whether he did or didn't.

"When I get done here, I want the horse and I want your best guess about where this mountain is."

He took his satchel from Coley and walked off with the boy. They followed the narrow path that ran behind the row of miners' cabins, dodging small children and alarmed chickens as they went. He could smell the boiled cabbage suppers cooking as he passed, women waiting for their men to come home from the mine. He tried to imagine bringing Jane to a place like this to live and couldn't. He would "do" for her gladly—but she deserved far better than this.

The boy stayed ahead of him, but not too far. He was taking no chances that one of the other runners might try to step in and take credit for Tregear's retrieval.

But, regardless of the haste with which Tregear was supposedly required, the mining office was empty. He locked his satchel away in the office storage room, and then he paced back and forth on the porch as he waited, feeling the interest of the boys hanging around outside as they tried to decide what his agitation meant and whether or not it would translate into a coin or two.

"Any of you boys know where Dr. Ennis went?" he asked suddenly. No one answered him, but all of them looked at him—except the one who had fetched him here.

Tregear considered that a very promising sign.

He suddenly caught a glimpse of Coley coming through the trees leading a saddled horse, and he stepped off the porch.

"Wait! You can't go, Tregear," the boy cried. "I'm needing that penny!"

"You're not going to get one from Mannion—or me," Tregear said, walking on. "Unless I find out where Ennis went."

The boy dogged his heels toward where Coley stood waiting. "I...ain't sure," he said.

"I'm not paying for a guess, boy," Tregear answered.

"Mr. Mannion ain't going to like it if you ain't here when he gets back," the boy said, clearly hoping to put the fear of God in him.

"No, I don't believe he will."

"Tregear, this ain't fair—you got to wait. Mr. Mannion, he's the boss and you can't just go when he's wanting to see you—"

Tregear kept walking.

"I'll tell you!" the boy suddenly cried.

"First, you say how you know—then we'll see."

The boy stared at him. Tregear could feel him trying to make up his mind.

"I got a cousin what lives way on the other side of Smith's store. He's a carpenter—he helped build the doctor his new house," he said finally. "He said where it was. It ain't that hard to find, if you know. I reckon everybody's going to know there's a doctor on the mountain before long. Doctors can't hide from sick folks needing them."

"Then you better be selling the information while there's a market for it. Tell me the way."

"Three pennies," the boy said.

"Two and I'll box your ears for you."

"Two, then," the boy said.

Tregear spit into his palm and held out his hand for the boy to shake. The boy did likewise to seal the bargain.

"Come with me," Tregear said.

He took the boy inside the mining office and found a small piece of brown paper from the stack one of the shift foremen was saving and a pointed charcoal stick from the fireplace. He drew an ''x'' in the lower left corner and handed it to the boy.

''That's where we are now. Show me what roads to take.''

''It's a trading path that goes over the mountain. Don't know where it starts—but my cousin says it will end you up at Cross Creek and Fayetteville.''

The boy took the charcoal and began to draw. Tregear got the bottle of ink and a quill from Mannion's desk, stopping the boy from time to time to label the lines he made in ink. They had a passable map by the time they were finished.

The boy held out his hand for his fee.

''When I'm sure this map is true,'' Tregear said.

''Who's going to pay me if the doctor has you shot for following him? He don't like our kind much.''

The boy had a point.

''Half then,'' Tregear said. He took a penny from his pocket and dropped it into the boy's still outstretched hand.

''Are you sick, Tregear? How come you want to find the doctor?'' the boy asked, looking at him closely for some sign of illness.

''To get what's mine,'' Tregear said.

He opened the office door, scattering curious boys as he did so, because they were so intent on trying to hear what was said they hadn't expected him to leave yet.

Coley walked forward with the horse.

''You got a pistol, Cap'n?'' he asked, and Tregear shook his head.

''Might be you be needing one.''

Tregear agreed, but he was no hand with firearms. He'd

been too poor to even lay eyes on a pistol before he went to live with the Branwells, and afterward, he'd had too much respect for the pacifist minister to take up the affectation of carrying a fancy sidearm about.

Tregear handed him the map. "See what you make of it."

Coley looked at it, and Tregear read the names of the streams and roads to him. There were very few houses along the way.

"This one," Coley said, putting his finger on the trading path line. "Don't go looking for a road like. Trading paths, they look like a dry creek bed or sometimes a gully. A gully big enough for a wagon to pass. Ground is soft now. Maybe you see wagon tracks from the doctor in it."

"How long do you think it will take me?"

"Good part of a day like—if the mountain not too steep and you don't get lost."

"The map maker better hope I don't. I thought you said it was a little mountain."

"Little to look at. Big to walk. Better you wait until morning."

"I'll be stopping at Smith's store for the night. I'll be that far at least when the sun comes up."

He took the reins and mounted the horse. "If Mannion asks where I am, tell him."

Coley looked at him doubtfully.

"Tell him," Tregear said again. If this quest went badly, he wanted someone to know what happened to him.

"Find your woman, Tregear," Coley said. "She can shine happier with you."

Tregear nodded, then kicked the horse sharply in the sides and rode west from the village. He could find his way to Smith's store well enough. After that, he'd just have to see. It didn't occur to him until he was well on his way that Coley had finally dared to call him by his name.

It was dark by the time he reached the store. The proprietor was still up, and Tregear stepped over the men sleeping on the porch and went inside. He bought hay and water for the horse and a hunk of stale bread and two boiled eggs for himself—and paid the fee for the privilege of stretching out with the rest of the travelers under the porch roof. He didn't ask any questions about the doctor's relocation, in spite of how badly he wanted to. He would rely on Coley's judgment of the map and take no chances that the doctor might have bribed people to influence anyone looking for him to go the wrong way.

He stabled the horse, and then found himself a space at the far edge of the porch just under the eaves to eat the bread and eggs. The night was clear, the stars bright. He stared up at them, knowing that when he lay down, sleep would not come.

Jane.

His mind filled with images of her. She had been afraid of him the rainy night he'd come knocking on her father's door. She had been afraid, but she'd still gone with him for Milla's sake. How brave she was. Brave enough to come to him on another rainy night and lie in his arms. He loved her, and he must make her believe it. Whatever else happened he wanted her to know that. If he was a praying man, he would pray now that she was brave enough to come with him again.

He tossed the last bit of his bread to a hound dog that sat and watched him hopefully with its tail thumping in the dirt. Then, he lay down and closed his eyes.

The sleep he thought wouldn't come turned out to be deep and dreamless. He awoke dew-covered and aching, the last one on the porch—except for the dog he'd made the mistake of feeding. It lay sprawled on his side near his head, and he had awakened to better smells in his time.

He got up slowly. Every muscle hurt as he walked to the stable and readied his mount. He took the time to buy a half dozen corn dodgers wrapped up in greasy brown paper. He took two out and rewrapped the rest and put them into his shirt. He would eat on the way. He looked at the map one more time before he rode out.

As it happened, it was Coley's information that was the most helpful. What Tregear thought was likely the trading path was indeed more gully and dry creek bed than road. He took the chance and rode a short distance down it, seeing evidence of wagons having passed that way almost immediately. He was able to make much better time now. The trading path supposedly went right past the doctor's new house. All he had to do now was ride.

After a time, the terrain began to slope upward. Here and there he could see the deep ruts of a wagon carrying a heavy load. He kept going—until the horse was in a lather. Then he dismounted and led it off the trail to a small branch of the stream to let it water and feed on the violets growing on the bank. He ate the last of the corn dodgers and washed his face and hands in the branch. The water was icy cold. He sat watching it tumble over the rocks, trying to formulate some kind of plan.

But when all was said and done, he still had none, except to try to see Jane. When the horse had rested enough, he set out again. The sky clouded over and he could no longer see the location of the sun. He lost all track of time, but he kept going.

He came upon the house without expecting it. It was in what must be a natural meadow. Very few trees grew in it, and there was no evidence that the land had been cleared. He had not realized that he had reached the crest of the mountain until he suddenly breached the clearing and saw the house—several houses actually. A main house, and what he supposed must be another surgery. And then three small cabins at the lower end of the clearing. Servants' quarters?

No, he decided immediately. Slave quarters. The doctor would likely be moving toward the kind of help he could control—the kind he could make sure would stay in this lonely place.

Tregear rode boldly into the yard. He could see no point in doing otherwise. He could see another mountaintop beyond this one. Coley was right. The mountain wasn't big to look at—but walking it was something else again.

It was eerily quiet. Birds—insects—and the occasional shuffling and blowing of a horse in the stable. But no one was about as far as he could tell. He dismounted and walked up onto the porch of what he thought would be the family residence and knocked, looking around him as he waited. He could smell the new wood. It surprised him that this house was so much smaller than the one the Ennis family had vacated.

He could hear movement inside, but no one came to the door. He continued to stand. He had no intention of going until he had at least spoken to someone.

Just as he was about to knock again, someone called through the closed door.

"What do you want, Tregear?"

Miss Chappell.

"I want to see Jane," he said.

"No."

"No? I believe you are overstepping your authority again, Chappell. I said I want to see her. Tell her I am here."

"You have no right to be here—"

"I have every right—as you well know. Now, tell her!"

There was a scuffling on the other side of the door.

"She is not to see him!" he heard Miss Chappell say, but the door opened anyway.

Mrs. Ennis stood looking at him, saying nothing. She was very pale and haggard-looking, as if she had not slept.

"I'm here to see Jane, ma'am," he said.

"That is not possible, Mr. Tregear," she said. "My daughter cannot receive visitors—"

He reached out and caught the door before it closed again. He could see Eugenie standing on the stairs behind Mrs. Ennis.

"You must go, Mr. Tregear," Mrs. Ennis said. "My husband will not abide you here."

"Is something wrong with Jane?" he asked, still holding on to the door. "I want to know."

"Jane is not your concern—"

"I love your daughter, ma'am. It is very much my concern. There are things I should have said to her and didn't. Let me tell her now—"

"I cannot—" she began. He thought for a moment she was going to weep. "You must go!"

"Tell her I am here at least—"

"No. Go now," she said more kindly. "For *her* sake, Mr. Tregear. Do you love her enough to do what is best for her? If you do, you will take yourself away before my husband returns. Please," she whispered, as if she didn't want Miss Chappell to hear her pleading. "*She* is the one who will suffer if you do not. Please!"

He stood looking into her anguished eyes, then abruptly let go of the door. It closed immediately. He stepped off the porch and mounted his horse. But he didn't leave. He rode in a slow circle around the house, looking from window to window for some glimpse of Jane.

He saw nothing. No one.

For her sake.

He would do anything for her. Anything. Even this.

He reined the horse in and sat staring at a tiny upstairs window a moment longer. Then, he wheeled the animal and began to ride away. He was nearly out of the yard when he heard the rattle of the front door opening again.

He looked over his shoulder. Jane was standing in the doorway, her hair tumbling down her back, her feet bare. He immediately turned around. As he neared, she stepped forward. He rode right to the edge of the porch, as far as he could go, and reached for her, lifting her onto the saddle in front of him. She clung to him to keep from falling. He couldn't see her face.

"Are you all right?" he asked, making her look at him. "Tell me—"

She was trying hard not to cry. "You have to go," she said. "Father will be back soon—"

"Answer me! Are you all right?"

"Yes," she said, but he didn't believe her.

Mrs. Ennis came out onto the porch, and she grabbed Miss Chappell by the arm to keep her back when she would have rushed past her.

"You cannot let this happen!" Miss Chappell cried.

Tregear urged the horse away from the house, and he didn't stop until they had reached the very edge of the clearing.

The horse pranced nervously, and he set Jane down on the ground and dismounted, tying the reins to the nearest tree.

"Why have you come?" she asked, looking into his eyes, searching for the truth no matter what he said.

"To see you. To tell you—" He stopped.

"Tell me what?"

"All the things I have no right to say. That I love you with all my heart. That I'd rather be dead than never see you again—"

"Don't!"

"Are we to have a child, Jane?" he asked, and she turned away from him.

He came closer and put his hand on her shoulder. "Tell me."

She looked at the ground and didn't answer him.

"Jane?"

"I think yes, Tregear."

"Your father knows? Your mother?"

She gave a wavering sigh instead of answering.

"He wanted me to drink the infusion," she said, her voice barely above a whisper.

"What infusion?"

"It…would cause a woman to lose—" She stopped. He could feel her struggling for control. "I wouldn't drink it. I think he'll…try again, Tregear."

He moved so that he could see her face. Tears ran down her cheeks.

"No, he won't try again. I'm taking you with me."

"You can't."

"I can. And I will."

She looked at him. He thought that she didn't believe him. But he also thought that she desperately wanted to.

"I love you, Jane. I can't offer you anything—except myself. But there is nothing I wouldn't do for you—and the child. Nothing. Come with me. Now—"

"Mr. Tregear," Mrs. Ennis said behind him. "Did you speak the truth? Do you love my Jane?"

"I do, ma'am."

"But according to Miss Chappell, you will not marry her."

"I cannot marry her, ma'am." Not without knowing if he was free.

"There is a scandal surrounding that, I take it."

"Yes."

"Yet you dare come for her anyway."

"I dare," he said, looking into Jane's eyes again. "She is safer with me. I want her—and the babe."

Mrs. Ennis stood looking at them both. "What do you say to this audacity, Jane?"

"I love him," Jane said simply and without hesitation. The candor of her reply took him completely by surprise.

"The price of love is high, Jane," her mother said. "Especially this kind—as I expect you are already learning. If you go with him, you will be ostracized from decent society. You will lose everything you have. Your family. Your good name. Everything."

She looked at him. "I love him, Mother," she said again. "And no matter what happens, I'm the better for it. Even if we are never together, even if I must go on with my life alone."

"She honors you, Tregear," Mrs. Ennis said. "Are you worthy of such honor?"

"No," he said. "But I will do everything in my power to keep her from ever thinking I am not."

"Give me your word, Mr. Tregear. As you did once before."

"You have it, ma'am."

"Swear!"

"I swear it."

"You must go quickly then," she said.

"Mother, how can I go and leave you here—"

"I don't want you to sacrifice your happiness for me! How could I bear that?" She embraced her daughter, then looked at Tregear. "I am French, Mr. Tregear. We French are not so...disconcerted by what happens between a man and woman. I want my daughter to have whatever happiness she can. There will be none for her here." She took a deep breath and rested her hand against Jane's cheek. "When my young man came for me, I would not go, Jane. For the sake of propriety, I turned him away, knowing he loved me better than life itself. Propriety here is your father's will—otherwise I would not condone your going. I can only tell you what I have learned the hard way. Such a love as you and Tregear have for each other will not come again."

Jane looked at her, uncertain still. Tregear held out his hand, and she came to him. He put his arms around her, holding her close. He could feel her trembling.

"Are you sure you want us?" she asked.

"Yes!" he said fiercely.

"Quickly!" her mother said.

Eugenie came running toward them, carrying a pair of shoes and stockings.

"You can't go in bare feet, Jane," she said, thrusting them out to her sister. "Hurry—hurry."

Tregear gave Jane no time to take them. He lifted her up and sat her on the horse, then gave her the shoes to hold. He had to get her away from here.

"Goodbye, little sister," he said to Eugenie.

She tried to smile and stepped back to give him room to mount. "Goodbye, Tregear. I think now you've saved Jane, too."

Jane reached to clasp Eugenie's hand for a moment before Tregear made the horse walk on.

"You have my word, ma'am," Tregear said again to Mrs. Ennis, and he urged the horse forward.

They rode past Miss Chappell, who stood with her chin

up and her mouth trembling. "A miner's whore," she said. "That's all you'll be!"

"And what are you, Miss Chappell?" Jane asked without looking at her.

"What do you mean?" she cried. When Jane didn't answer her, she began trotting along beside the horse. "I asked you a question! What do you mean!"

"I heard you, Miss Chappell," Jane said. "People oftentimes hear a great deal when they seem insensible."

"You heard nothing—"

"My father will be needing a legitimate daughter. I heard you call him 'Father.' I can guess now why he brought you here. I think my mother has always known. Make him claim you, Miss Chappell. It's what you deserve. It's what *he* deserves."

Miss Chappell followed along with the horse a few more steps. "My name is Jane," she called after them, trying not to cry. "Did you know that? *My* name is Jane. He wouldn't let me use it—because of you!"

"You can use it now," Jane said.

Tregear caught a glimpse of movement at the corner of the house and reined the horse sharply.

"Get down, Jane," he said, trying to put her on the ground. "Stay out of the way."

"What is it?"

"Stand, Tregear!" Bobby Reid yelled. He stepped into view and raised the pistol he held at his chest and took careful aim.

Tregear tried to set Jane on the ground out of the way, but she clung to him.

"No! No—" she cried. The horse began to prance and sidle as Tregear struggled to keep the animal from rearing and Jane from being in the line of fire.

"I've been hired, Tregear!" Bobby yelled. "I got a job to do here! You ain't taking Miss Jane no place."

"You'll have to kill me to keep me from it, Bobby. You know that," Tregear said.

"I'll do it if I have to!" the boy said. "And you know *that!*"

"We all have to make choices, Bobby. Mine is already made. Yours is whether or not you want Eugenie to see you kill me."

The boy had always done whatever he'd needed to do to survive—even if it meant taking a man's life. But he was still a boy and he still had at least one spot of tenderness left in him. He clearly hadn't realized that Eugenie was near, and the pain of that realization was obvious on his face.

"I never got the chance to tell her, Bobby. I never said what you wanted me to say the day she was lost in the mine. I had better do it now, I think. It's better she knows you were willing to risk your life for her before she sees you do murder."

"Bobby, you aren't going to shoot him, are you?" Eugenie asked, coming closer. "Please, Bobby. Don't hurt Tregear."

"You can't ask that of me, Miss Eugenie. Your daddy wants me to see he stays away from here—"

"I do ask it. Tregear is going—if you'll let him. Please—"

"The doctor says he's not to have anything to do with Miss Jane."

"My mother has given them her blessing, Bobby. Let them go."

Eugenie continued to walk forward.

"Stay back!" Bobby cried. "You're going to get yourself hurt, Miss Eugenie."

"That's in your hands, Bobby Reid. Not mine."

"Eugenie—" Tregear said, trying to get the horse under control so that he could intercept her.

"Eugenie!" her mother called, but she ignored them both.

"I trust you, Bobby," Eugenie said, still advancing. "I trust you not to hurt me—or my sister."

But she had the good sense not to force his hand. She stopped a short distance away from him and waited. She said something to him, and he shook his head.

"He saved my life," she said. "I would be lost in the mine like Sion but for him. Let me repay him. Let me give him his life in return."

Bobby stood there, his arm still outstretched in a deadly aim, his hand trembling.

"Please," Eugenie said. "Bobby—"

"All right!" the boy cried, lowering his weapon. "Go on, Tregear! Now! Before I think better of it!"

"Go on, Jane!" Eugenie cried. "You and Tregear go!"

"Eugenie—"

"Go on!"

Eugenie stepped closer to Bobby, putting herself between him and a clear aim in the event he did change his mind. He looked at her for a moment, knowing what she was doing, then turned away. Tregear took the chance and urged the horse on, looking back over his shoulder once. Bobby was still standing in the same place with Eugenie by his side.

"Are you all right?" he asked Jane, and she sagged against him.

"Yes," she said.

"Don't be afraid—"

"I'm not," she said quickly. "Eugenie—"

"Bobby won't hurt her," he said. He could feel her misery, and there was nothing he could do to comfort her.

"There's no going back now."

"I know," she said. "I love you, Tregear."

"So I've heard," he said, because she had told her mother of it, not precisely him.

"Now you've heard it directly from me."

"Yes. I love you, Jane. Do you believe that?"

"I believe everything you say—it's been most annoying."

He laughed out loud. In spite of the gloom of the woods around them. In spite of their precarious and unsanctified situation.

"I wish I—"

"No," she said, turning as much as she could to see him. "No regrets. We will take whatever we can get and be happy for it."

He kissed her cheek and tightened his arms around her. His free hand slid to her belly.

A child. His child. And damn her father for what he would have done to it.

"We're going to have to rest the horse," he said. "There's a stream not far ahead."

"Good," she said. "I think I'd best put on my shoes."

When they reached the place where he had left the path earlier, he got down and led the animal into the woods, listening all the while for the sounds of someone following. He didn't think Bobby would come after him—but he had no idea what the doctor would do when he returned and found Jane gone.

"Where will we go?" Jane asked.

"Go?"

"Will we leave Gold Hill?"

"Everyone there will know we can't wed, Jane."

"I don't care if people know."

He looked at her. She meant it.

"You may lose your work in the mine because of this," she said.

"I doubt it." He had just uncovered a new vein. That would carry far more weight with the investors than Dr. Ennis's pique.

"Your father gave me money—for bringing Eugenie up from the mine."

"He may have called it that," she said.

"I...gave it to Mannion."

"To Mannion? Why?"

"For Coley. To buy his ownership papers. If Mannion can do it, I'm going to give them over to Coley. He knows enough about mining now to make his own living and go his own way. There may be some money left. I need to know if the Gretna Green marriage still stands. I was thinking to use whatever remains to find out. Would that trouble you? If your father's money was used for that?"

"No," she said. "Tregear, you don't..."

"Don't what?" he asked when she didn't continue.

"You don't have to marry me. I don't require it."

"I require it," he said. "I very much require it."

"It doesn't make you happy."

"What doesn't?"

"Loving me."

"Jane, Jane," he said. "Loving you makes me happier than I've ever been in my life. It was the—"

"The what?"

He shook his head, not willing to admit his fear. "It's an awesome thing—to feel this way about another person. I fought it long and hard."

"So did I," she said.

He could see the brook up ahead, and he lifted her to

the ground. She looked up at him, her hands resting on his forearms.

"You're safe with me," she said, and the mischievousness with which she said it reassured him as nothing else could. He felt such an overwhelming love for her suddenly, this woman who had defied her father on his behalf and on behalf of their unborn child. He brought her to him and held her tightly. They had come such a long way since the first time he saw her and likely still had far to go before they found any peace.

"Will Bobby say which way we've gone?" she asked.

"I don't know. Miss Chappell will probably be more trouble to us than he will. But I think—" He abruptly stopped.

"What?" she asked leaning back to look into his eyes.

"I think all will be well with us—the three of us."

"You're not sorry then?"

"To have you and our babe? Never. I'm only sorry I can't make it better for you."

She was still clutching the shoes and stockings Eugenie had given her.

"Put your shoes on, love," he said, and he led the horse the short distance to the water.

"I didn't plan this well," he said when he returned. "I brought no food with me. For all my dark past and my Saracen blood, I'm not that accomplished at stealing away daughters."

She smiled. "I don't mind—as long as I'm the last one you steal."

She sat down on a large boulder to put on her shoes. The stockings were pushed down inside them, and when she pulled one out, a small packet of letters fell to the ground.

"Whatever is this?" she said, reaching to pick them up.

"They're yours," she said in surprise and handed them to him.

"Mine?" He looked at them. They were the letters from Branwell he'd never opened. "I don't understand. These were in my satchel."

There was a note tucked under the string that bound the packet. He pulled it out and unfolded it. The note had obviously been written in great haste. It was filled with splotches of ink and marked out letters and words.

"'Dear Tregear, please forgive me,'" he read aloud. "'I found these at our other house and I kept them. They must have fallen out of your belongings when you were sick and stayed there. I should have given them to you a long time ago, but I just wanted to have something of yours. A keepsake I think it would be called. All the girls in Salisbury had tokens to remember people by, and it seemed such a nice...custom,'" he decided after studying the smeared word for a moment. "'I didn't read them for the longest time. Then I did. I broke the seals, and I am very sorry for doing that. You must read them, too. For my sister's sake. I can only—'"

He turned the sheet of paper over. "There is no more."

He looked down at the letters and undid the string around them. All the wax seals had been broken. He moved to sit near Jane and began to read.

The first three were exactly what he expected—carefully executed cheerfulness from old Branwell, elaborate descriptions of the Cornwall weather and Mrs. Branwell's garden and not much else. The reverend had made certain that they were meticulously devoid of anything that might have made Tregear feel worse. Even so, they surely would have done so if he'd read them when they arrived.

The fourth and last letter contained two additional sheets folded up inside. The first from a lawyer in Truro to Reverend Branwell—a few terse lines to explain that the second one had been sent to Branwell in the hope that he would be able to forward it to "the party for whom it is intended."

Tregear unfolded the second sheet. It was longer, and he recognized the handwriting immediately. The recognition was like a physical blow. He looked at the date at the bottom of the page. It was written before he left to come to America.

This one he didn't read aloud.

My dearest Ban, it began. He took a deep breath. Jane got up from the boulder and walked away a few steps.

"I'll see to the horse," she said—to leave him alone with the letter, not because the horse needed tending.

He looked down at the page again.

…If you are reading this, then Mr. Davy will have done his job well and found the means to deliver my letter to you. I shall be direct, as I know your Cornish heart admires such things.

First, I ask you to forgive me for hurting you. I see now how unkind it was of me to encourage you. I should never have done it, but please believe this one thing if you can. I loved you as best I could, and I am thankful for what we had. I'm sure, however, that you realize now, as I do, how ill-advised the liaison was, even from the very beginning. I want you to know that, thanks to Mr. Davy, the union was quickly and successfully annulled. We are lucky, you and I, to have escaped our impetuousness with so little damage done.

I wish only the best for you, dear Ban. I am to be married soon to a man who actually prizes me for my wild streak. My father has forgiven me completely and has provided a splendid dowry to seal the upcoming nuptials. I earnestly hope someday you will find as much happiness I have. I trust that you will wish me well and I hope that in time you will be able to think of me kindly.

Sincerely, Catryn Angwin

He sat looking at the handwritten page, but seeing nothing.

So. The marriage had been made to disappear after all. He took a deep breath and looked up at the sky, surprised at how lighthearted he felt and that he could indeed think of Catryn, if not kindly, then with a decided indifference.

Because of Jane.

He suddenly looked around. She was standing with her back to him at the edge of the stream, her arms folded over her breasts. He stuck the letters into his pocket and walked to her. She immediately turned to him, and he couldn't keep from smiling.

"We have to go to Albemarle," he said, lifting her off her feet. "Right away."

"Why?" she asked, startled by his exuberance.

"Because I love you. Because my heart is bound to you," he said, looking into her eyes. "And because there is going to be a wedding."

Epilogue

W hat Tregear didn't say was that there was going to be *two* weddings.

Jane had never expected to have even one marriage ceremony, much less a spare.

The first had been done as hastily as possible. As soon as Tregear found a bondsman to guarantee the two-hundred-dollar pledge he had to make in order to satisfy the state that he was free to lawfully wed, an eager magistrate performed the marriage in what passed for the Albemarle courthouse, signing the back of the marriage certificate to indicate that the wedding had taken place as promised even before the ink on the declaration of intent on the front had dried. She had no idea how such expediency had come about, but the speed with which it had all taken place left her stunned.

And happy.

She had expected to return to Gold Hill and stay in the cabin Milla had once occupied, but Tregear had taken her to the Olivers instead—leaving her with them until the second, ''real'' wedding—the Cornish one—could take place. If he could not take her to Cornwall and the Branwells to be married, he would bring Cornwall to her, he said.

Mrs. Oliver had been delighted by the idea, and, in spite of her recent illness, she had jumped into the kind of organizational frenzy that was her forte. It was incredible to Jane that she could have put together such an elaborate event in so short a time, but apparently she had, making it a celebration for the entire village—not just to honor the marriage but to give thanks for having survived the epidemic and the disaster at the mine, as well. Somewhere along the way, she had even managed to find Jane a suitable wedding dress.

All was ready now—hopefully—and Jane stood looking at the fit of the dress in Mrs. Oliver's best mirror, wondering if it was sinful to be so enthusiastically anticipating the long-awaited moment when Tregear would take her out of it. She had been able to think of little else since Milla had whispered to her that, thanks to Mr. and Mrs. Mannion, there was a very fine feather bed all ready for the occasion of her wedding night. She had seen so little of Tregear since she rode off with him from her father's house—at least not alone. It was a bit like locking the barn after the horse was gone, to her way of thinking, but she had complied. Mrs. Oliver was nothing if not an accomplished chaperon, as well. There had been hours of supervised conversation, with Tregear staring boldly at her from across the room, and she—just as boldly—staring back.

"It's time, my dear," Mrs. Oliver said at the doorway. "You have the silver coin Tregear gave you in your shoe?"

"Yes," Jane said dutifully.

"And you remember that one of the Cornwall men will hand you a horseshoe for good luck on your way to the altar."

"Yes," Jane said again.

"And you understand the other Cornish thing," Mrs. Oliver said obscurely.

"Yes."

That was the part of the wedding night Jane was perhaps not looking forward to—the chasing of the bride and groom to their very bed and then lashing them with braces or stockings or whatever came to hand so that the couple would be assured good luck, long lives and many children.

Jane looked at herself one last time in the mirror, then took a deep breath and turned around.

"You look lovely, my dear. Our Tregear is a lucky, lucky man."

Jane smiled, hoping it was true and that he would never suffer for loving her. Her smile faded as the memory suddenly surfaced of what her father had tried to do. It was a cruel thing, a dangerous thing, but it hadn't mattered to him in the least. What had mattered was that she was his property, and no one could buy her ownership papers and set her free. All her life she had been groomed entirely for his benefit, and she had dared to upset his plan.

"Are you thinking of your mother?" Mrs. Oliver asked gently.

"Yes," she said—a little white lie to spare Mrs. Oliver's tender heart and her father's reputation. She was still, after all, his daughter. "But I'm not sad," she added, more in keeping with the truth this time. "I wish she could be here. I wish Eugenie could sing for us. But I have their blessing."

"Yes," Mrs. Oliver said brightly. "Well! Let us go and show that groom of yours how very fortunate he is."

Jane took a deep breath and braced herself before she followed Mrs. Oliver out. She would be a curiosity to the people who came today. She knew that. She had been cast out of a prominent family. It was obvious as to why, but there would still be a great deal of speculation regarding the details.

She stepped outside, smiling at Milla and Lolly and the rest of the women who waited to escort her to where the ceremony would take place. Mrs. Oliver had determined early on that the church would be far too small for such an event, and she had decided that the nuptials could only be held in a brush arbor outside. She had also determined that, on at least one point, she and Cornish tradition would have to part ways. The weather was simply too hot to hold a wedding and the subsequent celebration at midday. She had moved the time to late afternoon instead, and she was right to have done it—especially given the bride's condition. It wouldn't do for Jane to swoon midceremony from the heat.

Jane was amazed by the number of people who had come, some she recognized as patients she had tended when they were ill with the fever. Clearly, Mrs. Oliver had spread the word of the marriage far and wide—but Jane had no idea whether her mother and Eugenie knew.

She had received a letter from Eugenie only a few days ago—one scathing in its attack on Jane's character and morals—until she read every other line. It still made her smile to think of it. Sweet, clever Eugenie, to whom she owed this day.

But Jane understood only too well that she and Sion were no longer in their sire's heart or mind—if they ever had been. It would be as if they had never existed. Perhaps there would be some footnote in history about the eccentric doctor who had gone to live alone on a mountaintop with his wife and two daughters. If Miss Chappell stayed, it would be the truth.

But in time, people would forget the rest of it, and there would be no hint of the daughter who had run off with the wild Cornishman or of the disinherited son who died in the mine.

She had been thinking of Sion a lot in recent days, wondering if he was her father's son after all—or if he was the son of the young man her mother had turned away. Perhaps the latter would account for the very large dowry her father received and the fact that Sion was the only one with whom her mother spoke French. Jane had been thinking, too, of Eugenie's remark about the way Sion had looked at Milla Dunwiddie. Jane's mother adored little Charia. Perhaps there was something of Sion left behind, after all.

Jane gave a quiet sigh. She herself did not mind being disowned so much as she minded the utter waste of it. It was far more her father's loss than hers, and he didn't even know it. She had been a good daughter and she had married a good man. She had a child on the way, and she had no regrets. She would be with Tregear, to help him, to have children with him, and, God willing, to grow old with him. He would be her family from now on, and she, his. She would not look back. And if sick people came to her for help, she would do that, too.

The bevy of fiddlers Mrs. Oliver had somehow recruited for the occasion caught sight of Jane walking in their direction and began to play—nothing she recognized, but beautiful just the same. One of the miners approached her and handed her a horseshoe tied up with blue ribbons and decorated with bachelor's buttons.

"Bedheugh why lowenak. Bennatew genough," he said. Cornish words Tregear had already explained to her.

Happiness to you. God bless.

She smiled and took the horseshoe. She could see Tregear waiting for her at the beginning of the grassy aisle. She looked into his eyes every step of the way and saw herself there.

I love you, Tregear, she thought, and he smiled suddenly, as if he'd heard her.

When she was close enough, he offered her his arm. As

they walked together to the place where Reverend Oliver stood, she noticed the sunset for the first time.

The Borders of Heaven, she thought.

It was a wonderful place to be.

Author Note

Not many people have ever heard of the North Carolina gold rush, but it was a significant part of state and national history prior to the discovery of gold in California in 1849. It was also a significant part of my own family history. Two great-great grandfathers managed to turn up in what few records of the period exist—Peter Earnhardt, who dug the first gold nugget out of the Randolph shaft in Gold Hill in February, 1843, and, years later, Henry Davis Plyler, who discovered a gold nugget in the Barringer Mine which was supposedly large enough when sold to enable him to buy each of his six sons a farm.

But, as a writer of historical fiction, I must confess that these incidents were not the source of inspiration for this novel. In fact, I had all but forgotten about the gold miners in the family until my interest was piqued by some obscure sketches done for *Harper's Magazine* in the 1850s. The sketches were of Gold Hill, North Carolina, and of miners with names like ''Moyle'' and ''Trevethan,'' men who came here from Cornwall, England, where mining was a way of life.

I looked at the sketches, and I began to remember remnants of a story my grandfather had told me when I was a little girl, one about the men who had worked in the mines long, long ago—"Englishmen" who lived in the same big wooden house together, because they spoke a strange language no one else could understand.

I hadn't been to Gold Hill since I was a child, but I started going again, just to look at the mine entrances and the stone wheels and to walk around the grounds where the mine owner's mansion once stood. The village itself is in the process of being restored as a historical site. The graveyard is still there. It's a quietly eerie place. A number of old slate headstones from the gold rush days are in the far end, some inscribed, some not. The branches of the big trees growing nearby have become entwined, and when the wind blows, they make a strange and lonely sound.

I listened. And I began to write a love story....

* * * * *

SAVOR THE BREATHTAKING ROMANCES AND THRILLING ADVENTURES OF THE OLD WEST WITH HARLEQUIN HISTORICALS

On sale March 2003

TEMPTING A TEXAN by Carolyn Davidson

A wealthy Texas businessman is ambitious, demanding and in no rush to get to the altar. But when a beautiful woman arrives with a child she claims is his niece, he must decide between wealth and love....

THE ANGEL OF DEVIL'S CAMP by Lynna Banning

When a Southern belle goes to Oregon to start a new life, the last thing she expects is to have her heart captured by a stubborn Yankee!

On sale April 2003

McKINNON'S BRIDE by Sharon Harlow

While traveling with her children, a young widow falls in love with the kind rancher who opens his home and his heart to her family....

ADAM'S PROMISE by Julianne MacLean

A ruggedly handsome Canadian finds unexpected love when his fiancée arrives and he discovers she's not the woman he thought he was marrying!

Don't miss the breathtaking conclusion of
New York Times bestselling author

HEATHER GRAHAM'S

popular Civil War trilogy
featuring the indomitable Slater brothers....

If you *savored* DARK STRANGER
and *reveled* in RIDES A HERO,
you'll *treasure* the final installment
of this intoxicating series!

In January 2003 look for

APACHE SUMMER

*Born and raised in frontier Texas, beautiful Tess Stuart needed
a hired gun to avenge her uncle's murder. But the only one willing to
help was the infuriating, smolderingly sexy Lieutenant Jamie Slater—
the man whose passion set her soul on fire.*

You won't want to miss the opportunity to revisit these classic tales
about the three dashing brothers who discover the importance of
family ties, loyalty…and love!

DARK STRANGER	RIDES A HERO	APACHE SUMMER
On sale August 2002	On sale November 2002	On sale January 2003

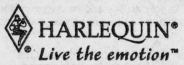

HARLEQUIN®
Live the emotion™

Visit us at www.eHarlequin.com

From Regency Ballrooms to Medieval Castles, fall in love with these stirring tales from Harlequin Historicals

On sale March 2003

THE SILVER LORD by Miranda Jarrett

Don't miss the first of **The Lordly Claremonts** trilogy!
Despite being on the opposite side of the law,
a spinster with a secret smuggling habit can't resist
a handsome navy captain!

BRIDE OF THE TOWER by Sharon Schulze
(England, 1217)

Will a fallen knight become bewitched with the
mysterious noblewoman who nurses him back to health?

On sale April 2003

LADY ALLERTON'S WAGER by Nicola Cornick

A woman masquerading as a cyprian challenges a
dashing earl to a wager—with the stake being an island
he owns against her favors!

HIGHLAND SWORD by Ruth Langan

Be sure to read this first installment in the
Mystical Highlands series about three sisters
and the handsome Highlanders they bewitch!

  Harlequin Historicals®
Historical Romantic Adventure!

HHMED29R

COMING NEXT MONTH FROM
HARLEQUIN HISTORICALS®

- **THE SCOT**
  by **Lyn Stone,** author of MARRYING MISCHIEF
  After overhearing two men plotting to kill an earl and his daughter,
  James Garrow, Baron of Galioch, goes to warn the earl. Instead,
  he meets the earl's daughter, freethinking, unruly Susanna Eastonby.
  Despite the sparks flying between them, James and Susanna enter
  into a marriage of convenience. Will this hardheaded couple realize
  they're perfect for each other—before it's too late?
  HH #643 ISBN# 29243-0 $5.25 U.S./$6.25 CAN.

- **THE MIDWIFE'S SECRET**
  by **Kate Bridges,** author of LUKE'S RUNAWAY BRIDE
  Amanda Ryan is escaping her painful past and trying to start a new
  life as a midwife when she meets Tom Murdock. As Tom teaches
  Amanda to overcome the past, they start a budding relationship. But
  will Amanda's secrets stand in the path of true love?
  HH #644 ISBN# 29244-9 $5.25 U.S./$6.25 CAN.

- **FALCON'S DESIRE**
  by **Denise Lynn,** Harlequin Historical debut
  Wrongly accused of murder, Count Rhys Faucon is given one month
  to prove his innocence. In order to stop him, the victim's vengeance-
  seeking fiancée, Lady Lyonesse, holds him captive in her keep and
  unwittingly discovers a love beyond her wildest dreams!
  HH #645 ISBN# 29245-7 $5.25 U.S./$6.25 CAN.

- **THE LAW AND KATE MALONE**
  by **Charlene Sands,** author of CHASE WHEELER'S WOMAN
  Determined to grant her mother's last wish, Kate Malone returns
  to her hometown to rebuild the Silver Saddle Saloon and reclaim
  her family legacy. But the only man she's ever loved, Sheriff
  Cole Bradshaw, is determined to stop the saloon from being built
  and determined to steal Kate's heart....
  HH #646 ISBN# 29246-5 $5.25 U.S./$6.25 CAN.

KEEP AN EYE OUT FOR ALL FOUR
OF THESE TERRIFIC NEW TITLES

HHCNM0103